BLITZ: (V) \'BLITS\ AN INTENSE CAMPAIGN OR
ATTACK: A SUDDEN OVERWHELMING BOMBARDMENT

BLITZ

EBONEE MONIQUE

*From the Breakout Author of Suicide Diaires
and Walk a Mile...*

Giving Your Soul a Rise...One Page at a Time

ISBN-13: 978-0-9829672-7-0
Library of Congress Control Number: 2011905559
BLITZ © 2011 by Ebonee Monique

PEACE IN THE STORM PUBLISHING, LLC.
P.O. Box 1152
Pocono Summit, PA 18346

Visit our Web site at www.PeaceInTheStormPublishing.com

BLITZ

A NOVEL BY
EBONEE MONIQUE

PEACE IN THE STORM PUBLISHING, LLC

THANK YOU...

Writing a book is the easy part. Compiling a list of people to thank...now that's tricky! ☺

First, I have to give honor & gratitude to my Heavenly Father, Jesus Christ. Without His grace & mercy...I would be N-O-W-H-E-R-E. Saying "Thank You" a million times over still wouldn't be enough. Regardless of what I'm NOT, it only matters what God is! To my partner in crime, husband and best friend, Marvin.: Thank you for dreaming with me and allowing me to think creatively and out-of-the box. Your support is priceless. Thank you for loving me in spite of me. To my rock...my foundation...the reason I am as humble as I am: my parents Mr. & Mrs. Council (Anne) Rudolph, Jr....I love you beyond what words can express. Thank you for your sacrifices and constant uplifting words & actions. While it might not be spoken every day, you are the reason I am determined to dream beyond anyone's expectations. I love you both dearly. To my brother, Mr. Higher Hustle, Council Rudolph, III you have no idea how much I love you. You have always had my back & pushed me towards greatness. You are the epitome of a great friend. Thank YOU for loving me!! Your dreams are so inspiring: Higher Hustle Clothing! Let's go! I'm Jay & you Dame ('cept there's no breakup! LOL!) Or Michael & Dwight! DINKIN FLICKA! To my mother & father-in-love (Mr. & Mrs. Marvin and Valencia Thompson, Sr.) and brothers (Emmanuel, Martavius and Javaris) thank you SO much for always being so excited about my books. You have no idea how much it means to me! To my god-son Octavious, I'm so proud of the little man you're becoming. I'm only a drive away...remember that! ☺ To my god-daughter, M.J. I loved you before you were born and can't wait to see you grow up! To the reason I'm sane despite my insanity...my friends: I love you all! Tasha, thank you for your honesty & loyalty; you've remained a constant in my life since high school and I know I can always count on you for anything. I'm so blessed to see you in your next phase: a mother! I Love you! Jason- I love you for always being enthused about anything I'm doing ("Oh you're changing your socks? I'm so proud of you, Eb!" LOL) Those little things matter! Lynette- My personal assistant/support system/Vice President/Forty-K President/#1 Fan/One-woman Focus group...yes, you're everything to me! I love you so much & am thankful to God for placing you in my life, 'Black Butterfly'! Sean- when I'm feeling down you always give me that much needed push. Thank you for being there for me as a best-friend and Brother/Brova all rolled into one. Kelli- I know I'd never verbalize this to you but...you're kind of cool. Thank you for being as honest & real with me as you are. It's almost like we were born with the same thoughts...I love you for all the laughs when I want to strangle someone! ☺ Dr. Deshawndre- You have no idea how thankful I am to #1 have been placed in a cramped dorm room with such a hustler like yourself & #2 to have been blessed to have remained friends with you all these years. To say you inspire me would be an understatement. I love you & am so proud of your growth & progress! Thanks for your support & motivation! To all my friends/supporters: JaNay, Faith, Nichole, Ebony Dukes, Ashley Bilon, Angela Krietz, Edris "Dreese", Torrey "Racer", Ryan "Bo Weezy" Jackson, Mr. Booberry, Sean Nevils, Mr. Keith Miles, Christi McCray, Felicia Plummer, my CCC's (Becks, G-$ & K-Rob), Sydney, Stess the Emcee, DJ Leezy , Brinton "One Champ", Jai Jai, Shanelle "Coco", Melissa Mitchell (thanks for always being uplifting!), Vernis Johnson, Danielle Ardister, Candace Smith, Elliott Griffin and JacQ Griffin. To my hairstylist Gloria, for always keeping my 'do did! To my Twitter supporters/followers, thank you for always keeping me laughing & updated! To my blog buds, Frehsalina (Crunk 'N Disorderly) and Brook & The City (Absolute Brook) for keeping me in stitches. To Zawcain, thank you for your talent & for being so humble. Thanks to K. Michelle for always dreaming large and inspiring me with her talent!

To my family: The Rudolphs, The Thompsons, The Curles & The Smiths...thank you for your continued support. It goes without saying that it's because of your love that I am where I am. Jamie...I'm still "putting it down for big cuz." I love you. Thomas, thank you for constantly reminding me of your presence.

To everyone at 90.5FM, Florida A&M University & the School of Journalism & Graphic Communications- Keep striving for excellence and proving why we're the #1 HBCU!

To my village: Greater Bethel Baptist Church in Tampa, Florida, Community of Faith in Tallahassee, FL Tony Gaskins and Joel Osteen for their continued words of wisdom & spiritual guidance. My former teachers that have remained in my spirit: Ms.Olga Barnes, Ms. Gipson, Mr. Adams (R.I.P.), Mrs. Frisco, Mr. E.L. Williams and any other teacher who believed in me when I couldn't see my own strength.

To my writing family: Elissa Gabrielle-Thank you for ALWAYS believing in me...for accepting me and my thoughts and helping me grow to be the author I'm destined to be. It's so very rare to have a publisher who not only believes in you but ALSO pushes you beyond what you think you can do. I love you beyond words! Jessica A. Robinson, we are kindred spirits and I love you for always being an ear for me and for reading things & giving me your opinion. Yes! I promise I'll finish that story...someday! ☺ To all my Peace in The Storm Publishing family: Being supported is vital and our family is exactly what the doctor ordered! I love you all. To all book reviewers, book clubs, book stores who have every picked up one of my books: THANK YOU!!

To my publicist, Dawn Hardy (Dream Relations): Thank you for believing in me and helping me see a new way of looking at things! Here's to new heights & new accomplishments! ☺

To everyone who's helped in putting any element of the book together (the book itself, the trailer, etc.) thank you! To Eddie De La Rosa & Graphik Films for all of your hard work & to all of the actors/actresses who've put in time! To Shakida Harvey for being ready, willing & able to help!

Lastly, thank you to you for reading this creation of mine. It's appreciated more than I can tell you! When you dream a dream, you never (in a million years) believe that people will actually take to your dream. This ride as an author has been inspiring and I'll continue to write stories that reflect my growth as a woman, a friend and everything in between! Stay tuned!

If I forgot to list your name, charge it to my bad mind & not my heart. Love is love and is not calculated by what's listed here.

Be sure to be on the lookout for my 4th book and remember to continue to **"Dream Big & Then Snatch It!"**

Ebonee Monique

Blitz

(**Blitz n:** an intensive campaign or attack: a sudden
overwhelming bombardment)

Chapter 1

Some people say "Money isn't everything."

Yeah right. Those are the same people that already *have* money; the ones who have fifty dollar bills dangling from their perfectly manicured fingers while they walk down their gold paved walkways. The curiosity on a wealthy person's face is apparent when it comes to the things poor people do for money. Nevertheless, I know that money *is* everything; always has been and always will. It buys clothes, food and keeps a roof over your head. And yet they say "money isn't everything". Yeah, right! The people who are born privileged never know about the struggle to obtain, live with or keep money; so, to them, the ability to spend is nothing more than a swipe of a card. But I'm a little different; when I swipe my card I'm automatically calculating how much *more* I'll have to work in order to ensure that money will be back in my account. People will have you believe that there are more important things in life; like friends, family and extracurricular activities. Again, I say, yeah, right.

Money makes the world go 'round and without it our value for the finer things would be non-existent. How would we know the difference between a finger painting and a *van Gogh* masterpiece? Or between a shack and a mansion? What would we have to strive for if there was no monetary value on material things? Would the poor just stay poor while the wealthy bathed in their $100 bills? Our desire to compete and survive would be cut short the moment money was removed from our day-to-day routine. The bottom line is money makes you hustle harder to get the things you want. And while I love my family, I know that without my struggle for money, power and respect, we wouldn't be experiencing the happiness that we currently know as our life.

Money *is* everything.

I knew this to be more than true. I've seen both sides of the coin: being broke and being wealthy and, without a doubt, money *has* made my life much easier.

"Honey, as much as I love you, if you're going to work here you have to tuck your shirt in." I said pointing to the untucked shirt that was hanging out over the perfectly creased pants that my assistant was wearing.

"Sorry, Miss Robinson." The kid said as he nervously tucked the shirt in and looked up to me for approval.

"Perfect." I said winking my eye and returning my glance to the computer screen in front of me.

"I finished the Harrison posting." He said with his hands behind his back.

"Great. Print out a copy for me and bring it here so I can proof it before it goes live on the website." I replied without taking my eyes off the screen.

"Yes ma'am." The boy said as he scurried out of the glass door in my office towards his own desk. I took one glance up and smiled at the progress my assistant, Cecil, was making.

Cecil was a cute kid, a year out of high school and not a clue in the world of what he was going to do with himself. Although he'd been in a little trouble during high school-all meaningless things-he had made a conscious effort to do better with his life.

He had skin the color of cardboard and small slits that served as his eyes. His dimples were as deep as all the lakes and rivers I'd seen in my life. His mother, Glenda, had cleaned my office for many years and asked if, by chance, I was looking for any help around the office. I had just fired my previous assistant and quickly said yes. I knew all about the power that one open door could have on someone's life; especially when all other doors have been shut in your face. I wanted to be Cecil's open door.

He was a good kid with a slightly rough exterior. On his first day, he came in wearing an *Enyce* velour jogging suit and white *Air Force Ones*. Needless to say, I gave him an advance on his first paycheck so that he could purchase some business casual attire. I'm a firm believer that how you dress determines how seriously people will take you in the business world; which is why I only wear the finest suits, pants, shirts and shoes. My hair is always immaculate and my facials, manicures and pedicures are always at the top on my list of priorities. Image comes in second place, right behind money, in my book.

I own one of the largest real estate companies in Tampa, Florida, Robinson Realty, and the last thing I need is someone bypassing my company because of non-professional dress or attitude. If someone isn't going to choose me as their realtor let it be for some reason other than how I look or act, like personal feelings or a clash in personalities; I can deal with that.

"Here it is." Cecil said widening his lips to show a smirk as he returned to my desk with a print out in hand.

I smiled, took the piece of paper and looked it over. There were a few typos, but for the most part Cecil was catching on perfectly.

I took out my red pen; circled the errors and handed it back   to   him. "This is great, Cecil. Just go back in and change these things and we're good to go!"

"Aight, that's w'sup."

"Excuse me?"

"I mean, yes ma'am." He said clearing his throat apologetically.

Not only was professional attire a huge part of the requirements to work in my office, but so was professional verbiage; even if the conversation was only between Cecil and I. If he got used to speaking properly in a small crowd I knew it wouldn't be hard for him to begin speaking like that at all time.

"Perfect." I said chuckling as Cecil wiped his brow of a little bit of sweat.

"You can take an early lunch today; I know your mother told me that you are looking into getting a car of your own, right?" I said crossing my legs and leaning into my mahogany desk.

"Yes, ma'am. I found this Honda Civic that is perfect for me." Cecil said quickly as he spoke with his hands.

I was paying Cecil enough that he was finally able to own a car; I was proud of that.

"I'm proud of you. Take two hours for lunch and find out everything you need to do in order to get that car and make it yours."

"Thanks Ms. Robinson!" The excitement of his smile could be felt in the room as he rushed to his desk outside of my office and grabbed his khaki colored jacket.

In seconds, Cecil was gone and I was left in the office by myself. In all actuality, I loved being in the office alone. I was proud of my elegant surroundings. I'd bought the property in downtown Tampa almost seven years earlier and had invested over one million dollars in renovations. After being the highest-selling female realtor in Tampa for the past six years, money stopped being an issue and started being an ally. The moment I sold my first multi-million dollar home was the moment I knew that what I was doing was what I was *supposed* to be doing.

As I sat at my computer, waiting on my next appointment to arrive, I thought over my journey to the top. I wasn't born with a silver spoon in my mouth, but I worked like hell to make sure no one snatched it out of my mouth now that it was there.

I was born and raised in Houston, Texas, lived a plain, poor life-wishing for the high life-and envied everyone and anyone with money. I saw wealth as the only way to make everything right. My parents, who both worked low-paying factory jobs, barely had money to cover the rent for our two-bedroom house, which was home to my parents, myself and my four other siblings. I used to spend hours staring at magazines, which I would find in a neighbors trash can, praying that I could one day own a fancy car, pretty clothes and a huge house. I remembered when I was no more than thirteen years old and had received a pair of Levi stonewashed jeans for Christmas. I must've washed those jeans a hundred times, to get them to the skin tight consistency that all the girls were wearing, and strutted my stuff like I had no cares and plenty of money; it felt wonderful. But at night, when I'd go home and take the jeans off, I was back to skimming magazines and dreaming about the glamorous life I craved to live.

At eighteen, I got married to the worst mistake in my life, my high school sweetheart, Branson. Branson was just as poor, if not poorer, than me and had no aspirations or goals in life. But what he did have was my heart and, at that time, that was all that mattered. He'd promised me the mansion, the cars and the beautiful clothes, but I knew it would never happen. And just like that, I began to fall into a life of regret and, surprisingly, dead-end wishes.

As a married woman, I was back to skimming magazines and praying at night that God would somehow grant those wishes. But as I stared around my one-bedroom apartment and poverty stricken neighborhood, I wondered if I had any type of escape route.

Branson and I lived paycheck to paycheck and started the cycle that both of our parents had grown accustomed to: barely paying the bills. There were plenty of times when we'd have to decide between eating and staying warm; normally staying warm won. I always knew I wanted more than living in Houston and the broken down neighborhood Branson and I called home; so I started secretly taking real estate classes, thinking Branson would be thrilled when I brought the certificate home. Instead, the night I brought my license to his attention, he slapped me to the ground and cursed me for spending "hard earned money on a stupid dream". From that day on, the abuse continued.

Sometimes he'd hit me for reasons, which he voiced, other times it would be out of the blue and unexpected. My guard was constantly up, even in my own house. A feeling that made me feel less than human. Nevertheless, no matter how hard he beat me or how many times he did it, I still didn't have the backbone or the courage to leave. This was my husband; my mother didn't raise me to divorce. Plus I *loved* that man with everything I had.

So, after Branson convinced me that real estate wasn't a viable or realistic option for income, I put my knowledge and license on the back burner and continued working as a waitress. But the entire time, I wondered whether or not that little piece of paper could serve as my lottery ticket out of the life I was living.

Three years into our marriage, I gave birth to our daughter Brandi and immediately, Branson seemed to be smitten with her. I saw a beacon of light and hoped that the beatings would stop since our beautiful bundle of joy was in our presence. But a week after Brandi was born, he knocked two of my teeth out for "not getting the baby quick enough" after she started crying. I studied my swollen face in the mirror, trying to convince myself that the busted lip and missing teeth weren't *that* bad. I remember staring at myself and replaying the scene over and over in my head. It all happened so quickly and for some reason it was playing in slow motion in my head. I stared off into space as I envisioned the veins popping out of Branson's neck as I tried unsuccessfully to quiet Brandi; seconds later I watched as he began pacing the room like a possessed man and before I knew it I was shielding Brandi with one arm as I watched Branson's oversized hand come towards me with a force that raised the hairs on the back of my neck. Thankfully, I was able to take the bulk of the fall as Brandi and I fell to the floor. I wasn't sure what Branson did immediately after knocking my teeth out, but I remember him cracking open a beer and demanding to have dinner ready as I tasted the bitter blood in my mouth. Later that night, I took our daughter and moved in with my mother and father and struggled to make it living on the couch in a crammed house with a newborn.

After a week of apologizing, though, I moved back in with my husband and made him promise not to hit me again. Of course, the beatings continued for another four years until I couldn't ignore or hide the black eyes, bruises and broken promises. Branson had turned to alcohol more than ever and was drinking two bottles of Whiskey a day. I tried to keep Brandi from seeing things, I tried to shield her eyes from the ugliness that I knew even her tender years could comprehend. But there was no way to hide why I was crying when I stood in the mirror with a swollen eye and blood dripping from my lip.

So I made the decision that I had to leave Branson, not for myself but, for Brandi. I didn't want her thinking that this was behavior she should accept from a man. I had to run away from my past in order to get to the possibilities of a brighter future for her.

I was determined that when I left with my daughter, that Branson wouldn't know where Brandi and I were. I had to be strong enough for both of us. I didn't tell my family or friends that I'd been saving money for months to get from Houston to Tampa, Florida. I'd read about Tampa in one of the magazines I read religiously and I saw that it was a booming place for young, black professionals. And while I only fit two of the three descriptions, I decided the beaches, activities and friendly faces would be a welcome change from the place I'd dreamed about leaving for as long as I could remember.

I packed a small bag, with only the essentials-underwear, pants, shirts, pictures and jackets and some of Brandi's favorite toys-so that Branson wouldn't notice anything missing; one night while he slept I snuck my four-year-old daughter into a waiting cab, took it to the Greyhound station and got on board of a bus headed for the sunshine state. I didn't know what I would do when I got there, but I had five hundred dollars to my name and a real estate license that I knew would come in handy.

Our first year in Tampa was the roughest for me and Brandi. I couldn't find anyone to hire me in real estate so I worked as a waitress while we stayed in the projects in West Tampa. We lived poor, too. *Really* poor; so poor that I thought about doing illegal things, at times, to feed my child. But it never came to that, thank God. I was tired of living in the same conditions I'd left back in Houston, so I prayed for some kind of chance to prove that I had what it took to sell houses. I hoped that when my chance came I would be ready.

One day at work, I was assigned Maestro Jones' table. Maestro was a wealthy retired realtor turned real estate mogul with plenty of ties to the Tampa real estate market. I had read articles, upon articles, about him and knew meeting him was the opportunity I had prayed to God for. So, I spilled my story, every last bit of it; from the poverty, to the abuse, to the fleeing and my current situation. I begged Maestro for a chance and before he paid his bill, I had been offered a job in his office.

"You get one chance, kid; after that we'll see if you stay or go." He told me as he ran his hands through his silky silver hair.

"Yes sir." I eagerly smiled as I gripped my order tablet to my chest.

My chance had come; I wasn't letting it go.

I studied my real estate information the night before I started and vowed to wow Maestro and everyone in the office the next day.

And wow them I did. I sold my first house in two weeks; a record for someone as new as I was.

Blitz

I quit my waitressing gig and started selling homes full-time for Maestro Realty and I loved it.

I'd heard, through the grapevine that Branson- whom I'd divorced six months after leaving him- had been in and out of jail on robbery and petty theft charges. It didn't surprise me at all; although it did make me sad. I had no doubt in my mind that if I'd stayed around I would have been involved in what he was serving time for. Desperation for fast money is so much stronger than the desire to work for it.

I wrote Branson while he was in jail, letting him know Brandi was okay and the general area we were in. It was my duty as her mother to at least try and give her a relationship with her father, even if they were miles and lifestyles apart. I figured if he wanted to reach out to her, he would do just that. After a few years of sitting on edge, thinking Branson would pop back into our lives; I finally eased up and realized he was *finally* gone. When Brandi was six, she asked where her father was and I told her he'd died. End of story.

After selling homes with Maestro, I officially started my own real estate company, Robinson Realty, on Brandi's seventh birthday; my career has been a constant boom ever since then.

I smirked to myself as I thought about how far I'd come. I was worth more money than anyone I'd read about in any magazine while growing up. I hadn't calculated my net worth in years, but the last time I checked I was worth well over $10 million. I only sell to and sell for people in a certain bracket; it's the only way to really ensure that I'll make the money I'm now accustomed to. I had a fourteen-going on fifteen-year-old-daughter who had expensive taste, and since I was the breadwinner, I had to pay for that. Louis Vuitton, Coach and Gucci purses; Seven, True Religion and Antique Levi jeans and any type of sneaker or heel a girl could want; anything Brandi wanted, I wanted to give her. I wanted Brandi to have everything she missed out on growing up and everything I fantasized about as a child.

I stared at a picture of the two of us and traced my fingers over my daughters' chocolate face. She is absolutely stunning and I'm not saying that because she's my child. She *is* beautiful. She has slanted dark eyes that sparkle when she talks, a beautiful, white smile, smooth dark chocolate skin and a well-developed body that even baffles me. She looked more like Branson that I could've ever wished for; despite that flaw, she was unbelievably gorgeous. I'd thought about starting her a career in modeling, after a few clients suggested it, but once scouts saw how short Brandi was, they were a little hesitant about signing her. But it didn't matter, either way; Brandi was well taken care of.

"Hey mama!" Brandi said sticking her head in my office door.

"Hey baby!" I said setting the picture down, a little startled by her being in my office in the middle of the afternoon.

"What are you doing here?" I asked worried.

"Remember I told you today was a half-day?" She said pulling her long hair back into a ponytail.

I could've smacked myself. Normally I was on top of Brandi's school activities and days off, but I'd been so busy with my clients and showings that I had been slipping.

"Right!" I said exhaling as I shook my head. "I'm sorry baby. How did you get here?"

"Andrew brought me." She said grinning widely.

"Didn't school get out like an hour ago? Why are you just getting here?" I asked raising one eyebrow as I checked my watch.

"Well, after you didn't pick me up Andrew took me to get a bite to eat and then we headed over here." She said nonchalantly. "It's no big deal, ma."

I watched as Brandi sat in the chair directly in front of my desk and stared back at me. Her eyes begged me not to start trippin' on her.

"You make sure you call me next time and tell me what you're doing. You're not grown, little girl. Remember that!" I said sternly as I cracked a slight smile.

"But I thought you liked Andrew. You said he's a good kid, didn't you?" Brandi said reminding me of my own words.

"Yeah but..." I stuttered "I also know he's a hormonal eleventh grade boy hanging out with my fourteen-year-old, ninth-grade daughter." I sarcastically responded.

"Fifteen in two months, ma." Brandi joked as she tugged at her school uniform.

Every high school has an "it" guy that all of the girls want to be with or be seen by, and Andrew Whittaker, my daughter's boyfriend, was that "it" guy. He was a good kid, came from a good family and had good values. His father Leonard Whittaker was a powerful judge, while his mother, Teresa, was a homemaker and ran in a similar wealthy circle as me; you know the circle I'm talking about: women who have plenty of money to spend and no shortage of boutiques, cars or vacations to spend it on. Brandi and Andrew were perfect together, if I say so myself. He was a high yellow handsome boy with a bright smile, muscular physique and beautiful big eyes that Brandi loved. He was the captain of the football team, basketball team and the student body president. Yes, Andrew was Mr. "It" and if he treated my daughter right I didn't have a problem with him at all.

"So, where's Cecil?" Brandi asked looking around the office as she giggled. Cecil was four years older than Brandi but that didn't stop my daughters' eyes from staring at the cutie pie that was my new assistant.

"How about you stop worrying about those boys and start worrying about that paper that I know you have due next week?"

"I'll get on it this weekend."

"You'll get on it now, young lady!" I said pointing to the conference room where Brandi spent most of her time when she came to visit me.

"But ma…"

"This isn't up for discussion or negotiation. I want to see what you have in thirty minutes." I said as I heard the beep from the front door of my office-indicating that someone had just walked in.

"Thirty minutes? Ma, I can't do that."

"You can and you will. I have a client, baby, so get your things and get started." I said standing up and walking towards her.

She stared at me for a second and I could feel the irritation as she rolled her eyes at me.

"You keep rolling them and they just might get stuck." I said kissing her forehead and pushing her towards the conference room.

Ebonee Monique

Brandi said something slick under her breath that I disregarded as I scurried out of the office into the waiting area.

"Hello there Ms. Chambers, how are you this afternoon?" I said as I plastered a smile on my face.

And just like that, it was back to business.

****

After I finished my consultation session with Ms. Chambers-who by the way was the wife of the current Tampa Bay Broncos head coach, Bryan Chambers-I stuck my head in the conference room to check in on Brandi.

But to my surprise, Brandi wasn't alone; the loud laughter in the room was evidence of that.

"I hope you have something to show me." I said as I turned the corner and crossed my arms in the doorway.

Brandi looked startled at my presence, but not as much as Cecil. They were sitting across from each other and it was apparent that there was something between the two. Brandi's hair was wound around her finger and her lips were covered in sticky, clear lip gloss. If I didn't know any better I might have thought that my daughter, my fourteen-year-old baby, was trying to come onto Cecil.

But just like a room full of cockroaches that scurry when the lights come on, Brandi and Cecil separated and leaned back in their chairs as soon as they saw the look on my face.

I raised one eyebrow at Cecil and then turned to face my daughter. I wasn't completely crazy; I knew boys-even men- noticed my daughter's near perfect frame, face and smile. As I stared at her, it was the first time I honestly stood back and looked at my daughter as someone other than the little girl who drew all over her face with permanent marker, when she was six; the girl in front of me was a budding woman.

"Mommy, I was just about to bring my paper to you; Cecil was just helping out." Brandi said as she shuffled some papers and found the one she was looking for. In seconds, she was in my face with her paper in hand and a bead of sweat over her lip. I knew, from experience, whenever my child *knew* she was in trouble because she always threw the word "mommy" in a sentence and expected all impending anger to disappear. I'd peeped her game long ago.

"Well, next time if you have questions you come and see me. I don't pay Cecil to be your personal tutor." I said strictly as I stared at both of them.

"I'm sorry Ms. Robinson. I just came by and saw she was here and we just got to talking about music and...I'm sorry." Cecil dropped his head and stuffed his hands in his pockets recognizing that his lame excuse wasn't working.

I nodded my head and motioned for him to head back to his desk.

"What do you think?" Brandi said peering over at the piece of paper that she'd placed in my hands. I wasn't paying attention to her obvious way of changing the subject, nor her paper. I stared back at her until she had no choice but to look at me.

"What, ma?"

I wasn't sure what I was upset or anxious about. I mean, Brandi was beautiful, sociable and a teenager. I promised myself that I would keep a close eye on Brandi while allowing her the chance to have her fun.

"Nothing. You just make sure the two of you keep your distance." I said firmly. "I don't want to have to hurt that little boy." I whispered.

Brandi leaned back and smacked her teeth playfully as she tried to fake a laugh.

"I'm not thinking about Cecil, ma; we're just friends. Besides, I've got the finest man in town anyway." She smiled exposing her pearly white teeth. I'd spent a small fortune making sure Brandi's appearance was always top notch. I wanted her clothes, face, teeth and nails to always be clean-cut and classy; the amount was of no importance. I knew how important appearance was in the world and Brandi was learning early that she had to take pride in how she looked and how others perceived her.

"Speaking of your fine *boy*, is he picking you up tonight for the dance?"

"No, ma. You're taking me. Remember Ms. Regina asked you to chaperone the dance?" Brandi said returning to the desk to gather her backpack and papers.

I remembered, but I was hoping Brandi hadn't. After the day I had I just wanted to lay in my Jacuzzi, sip a glass of Merlot and relax while listening to some old school Boyz II

Men, a little Teddy Pendergrass and a little Tyrese to top things off.

A night in a room full of horny teenagers was not my idea of a fun Friday night; but I had promised Regina and Brandi. I sighed at the thought of having to keep my promise.

"Right." I said under my breath and I hustled Brandi out of the room and into the waiting area of my office.

By the time I arrived to my office I noticed that Cecil was long gone, which was one less battle for the day. I would deal with him, on the topic of his relationship with my daughter, another time.

I exhaled as I threw my Louis Vuitton duffle bag over my shoulder and turned the light off in my office. As much as my body was screaming and crying for a rest, I knew I couldn't wait to see my baby dressed up in her custom dress, which I'd had shipped in from Japan.

I took my time turning off the rest of the lights in the building and Brandi pulled out her cell phone and started talking loudly into it before heading out to the car.

"I'm going to wait by the car, ma." Brandi yelled as the door shut.

Just as I was about to turn the alarm on I saw a file sitting in a place that it didn't belong so I scurried to put it in its proper place. Out of breath, I turned the alarm on and locked the glass doors behind me.

Damn, I thought, I need to get some exercise. It makes no sense for me to be as fabulous as I am and yet be this out of shape. I mean, literally, there is no excuse, right? I've got the money, the time and plenty of motivation. I'm knocking on forty and if *Halle Berry* can look the way she does, at forty, then I should too.

As I rounded the corner, towards my Mercedes Benz ML500 SUV, I stopped dead in my tracks as I saw Brandi's facial expression.

"What is wrong with you?" I said unlocking the door and throwing my bags into the backseat.

"Ma...who is B-Branson?" Brandi said as she looked down at a piece of paper in her hand.

For the first time in her life, my daughter seemed speechless.

Blitz

I was a little caught off guard, myself, and struggled for the right thing to say. The last time Brandi asked about her father I bluntly told her the bastard was dead. Now, as my daughter's beautiful wide eyes stared at me-begging for an answer-I felt bad for lying to her.

"That's...that's your fathers' name." I said slowly as I approached her and tried to take the piece of paper from her hands.

Snatching the paper pack, Brandi looked at me with confusion plastered on her face. I knew where this was going; I needed to try to rectify the situation as soon as possible.

"Why are you asking me about Branson?"

"No, I'm the one who should be asking questions." Brandi spat out as her eyes got glassy; she was getting ready to cry and I was the reason for it.

"Baby, let's talk about this at home." I said placing my hand on Brandi's shoulder and pulling her into me.

Jerking back, Brandi looked up at me and bit her bottom lip before continuing.

"Just tell me if my father is really dead or not."

I took my time in answering the question because, for me, it was a loaded one. Sure, to me Branson *was* dead. In my mind he'd died a horrible, tragic and painful death. I'd buried him in a baby blue suit with a jerry curl and a pacifier. Yeah, it was a little morbid, but, at the time, it made me feel so much better. But I knew the actual answer, that Brandi was looking for, was 'no' her father was not dead. He was very much alive. I knew one day she would find out the truth. I just hoped that when that day came, I would be on my death bed and Brandi wouldn't hate me for lying to her. But the day of truth was in front of me and my deathbed was nowhere within immediate sight.

"No." I said as I swallowed. "He's not dead, baby."

Unconsciously I was using her tactic of adding on "baby" to my sentence to get a little sympathy from her. I'd messed up by lying to her in the first place but, at the time, it was the right decision for us. We were all we had and we didn't need Branson complicating our goals.

"Why'd you lie to me?!" Brandi screamed as she stormed to her side of the car and plopped in the seat and threw her arms across her chest.

Ebonee Monique

I followed suit and jumped in the drivers' seat and cranked the car up.

I thought about how I was going to explain that her father, the one she was all of a sudden longing to know about, had been nothing more than a drunk, abusive, thief. How could I break her heart more than once in a day? I knew it would've taken some of the heat off of me but I also knew I needed to own up to letting my daughter down.

"Brandi, this is something you'll understand when you're a little older…" I started out saying as I put the car in reverse.

Through her sniffles and cries, Brandi stared out of the window as the city of Tampa passed her by. I wanted to know what she was thinking about, what she was feeling and- most of all- why she was asking questions about Branson.

"Baby, how did you…how did you know?" The words came out slowly as we got on to the interstate.

As expected, Brandi ignored me the entire ride home; allowing me to ponder and think about what I could have done differently now that the end results were in my face.

"Are you still going to the dance?" I asked quietly as Brandi wiped her face of a single tear.

"Yeah."

I could rest a little easier, knowing that I hadn't hurt Brandi so much that she would miss out on the biggest night of her freshman year; the winter formal.

As we got off on our exit and headed towards our gated community, I thought about Branson. I wondered just how he'd gotten word to our daughter that he was alive and well. Had he called her? Sent her a letter? Told a family member? I thought about the times when the hands of the man I loved would cause my body to hit the ground, leaving me in excruciating pain. I was never sure if Brandi remembered those times or if she'd unconsciously blocked it all out.

I pulled the SUV into our four-car garage and waited to see if Brandi was going to bolt out of the car and head to her room. Instead, we sat in silence as the garage slowly closed behind us. I didn't know what else I could say, besides the truth, to make Brandi see the rationale in my lie.

"Brandi, I was wrong and I'm sorry." I said moving a piece of my long weave out of my face as I peered at my daughter who was no longer crying.

She took a deep breath and opened her door.

"Its fine, ma." She said sounding tired and exhausted, which I'm sure she was; she had cried the entire way home.

I got out of the car and rushed around the front of the car, where she was walking towards the doorway to the house, and grabbed her by her shoulders.

"I *really* am sorry, Brandi. I was wrong and…"

"I said it was fine ma. We all make mistakes, right?" She asked shrugging her shoulders.

I sensed the sarcasm in her comment as she looked away and then quickly returned her glare towards me.

"The only difference between other people's mistakes and yours is that your *mistake* cost me fourteen years of having a part of myself that I didn't know I had the option of knowing." Brandi blurted out as she moved back from my grip.

"But how…"

"Branson…I mean, dad, was sitting outside the office when I went to the car. He came up to me and told me who he was and asked me to call him. I told him he had to be lying; my dad was dead. But then he told me a bunch of things about me that only a dad would know!" She said in a rushed tone.

I covered my face with my hands and exhaled. Why did this have to be the way that my daughter was introduced to our past?

"So the piece of paper…" I asked looking up.

"--was his phone number." Brandi said matter-of-factly, as if she was getting a kick out of the painful looks on my face.

"Branson moved to Tampa to be closer to me." She said turning her back and flipping her hair towards me.

I stood still and quiet in my garage as I looked around at everything that I'd worked so hard for. I envisioned it all gone and shuddered; as much as I didn't want to think about losing it I knew Branson returning as a fixture in our lives *couldn't* mean anything good.

Ebonee Monique

Chapter 2

It's something about the heat in Tampa that can't compare to any other city that I've lived in. It's a mixture between unbearable, sticky, humid heat and a slight breeze that masks the reality of the weather. Leaving your house, you never know exactly how to dress. It might be sixty five degrees in the morning and by ten in the morning it's damn near a hundred degrees. But I've come to adjust to the ever-changing weather that this city offers. It's unpredictable, much like the majority of my life has been.

I woke up the next morning, after the huge fiasco concerning Branson and having to chaperone Brandi's dance, with the realization that I had a side-splitting headache. I ran my hands through my smooth locks and sighed as I adjusted my eyes to the brutally bright sunlight coming from my colossal bedroom window. From my bed I could see the flowers blooming from the tree just outside of my bedroom. I wasn't a big fan of flowers, but something about waking up to them on a cool spring morning that spoke to me when I first purchased the home. For a few minutes every morning I could close my eyes and pretend that I was in the middle of an elaborate botanical garden. I rose from my bed and walked slowly to the window and opened both sides. I sat on the edge of the window sill and peered out over my property. It was days like this that I didn't believe everything in front of me was actually mine. The lush grounds below me, the sparkling blue pool, the apartment-sized pool-house and the perfectly manicured grass; this was all mine. Almost immediately, the sun started shining brighter than before and my headache began to pound, making me feel like I had been out dancing, drinking and partying the night before, even though I hadn't. My attendance at the winter formal didn't really qualify me as party-girl of the year.

"Damn" I thought to myself as I wrapped my robe around my body.

"I wish I could've at least tasted some alcohol last night." I laughed while I made my way to the tiled bathroom and searched through my medicine cabinet for some aspirin.

Even though Brandi was still upset with me about lying to her, I was glad that I could be present at her first formal dance. There are few moments in life that stick with us as we grow old; first formal dances are one of them.

At the dance, I stood in the back of the room, with Regina, one of Brandi's best friends' mothers, and beamed as I watched everyone gawk at my beautiful daughter.

Her one shoulder dress clung to her and accentuated her body perfectly. It was well worth the money to see her shine the way that she did. The black and gold dress drew plenty of stares and compliments and I felt like the proud parent I knew I was.

"That dress is beautiful, girl." Regina said as she sipped on some punch while we watched the kids dance.

The dance wasn't at all raunchy as I was expecting it to be. It was actually rather tame. I was expecting someone to spike the punch, boys to be grinding on girls and some degrading music and dances; it was the exact opposite.

I remember in my day, dances were a chance for the kids to let loose and show off their skills at the latest dance moves and their fashion skills. The difference, though, was that all of the kids that attended Brandi's school didn't *have* to show anything off; they all knew what each one of their peers' families had. It was par for the course to have the very best in order to walk through the doors of her school.

Brandi and Andrew stayed close to each other, looking like a celebrity couple that should've been on the red carpet, and they each played their parts well as they posed for pictures and worked the room.

"That Brandi is something else." Regina said as Brandi stood in the middle of a circle telling an animated story with her hands that had all of the girls' laughing hysterically. I could only imagine that it had something to do with something funny that Andrew had said. Brandi clung to his every word and couldn't wait to share his "knowledge" and "humor" with everyone.

"Katrina really looks up to her, you know?"

I liked Regina, enough. I wouldn't classify her as a best friend or anything like that, but she was a sweet house wife that looked after Brandi when I had business trips and events around town. Her ex-husband, Troy, was a really successful investment banker and made sure that she and her daughter, Brandi's best friend Katrina, never wanted for anything. She wasn't as well off as Brandi and I were, but they weren't hurting for anything either.

"That's sweet." I said looking over at Regina who kept her eye on me, like she wanted to say something else.

"I know Brandi loves her some Katrina too."

Just as Regina started to say something else, the principal, Mr. Hemmings, spoke into the microphone.

"Hello students! Please gather 'round and let's get ready for the part of the night that you all have been waiting for. We're going to announce the Winter Dance Prince and Princess and the King and Queen. Are you all ready?' He makes his announcement as he steps back to adjust his thick bifocals while moving a little closer to the microphone as the students began to slowly trickle towards the stage.

I couldn't help but watch as Andrew moved from his place at Brandi's side toward his crowd of friends. Brandi stood with her arms folded; her friends at her side, watching Andrew's every move as he laughed about something in general, but nothing in particular as he did what boys do to seem cool. I wanted to listen and watch what was happening on the stage, but I couldn't take my eyes off of the Brandi and Andrew soap opera as it unfolded.

"Let's get this started!" Mr. Hemmings said as someone handed him a gold envelope.

"Your 2008 Winter Formal Prince is Stewart Barber. Stewart, come on up here young man!" Mr. Hemmings said with a smile on his face as he pointed out Stewart who was standing close to Andrew.

The winter formal Prince and Princess were two students in ninth to eleventh grade who had shown a strong interest in going to college after graduation who also had great academic potential and were popular among their peers. In short, the total package for those in the lower grades of high school. The list of students who'd shown interest in the prize and title, had their names narrowed down by guidance counselors and teachers; and the final vote came from the students based on a list of ten finalists. The vote decided who the prince and princess of the year was. The winners had the opportunity to ride on the spring formal float and received assigned parking spots in the student parking lot. They were also given a five hundred dollar scholarship from *Alpha Beta Sigma* sorority which could be rolled over until they graduated from high school.

I loved the thought of Brandi being able to possibly win the title every year of her high school career and being able to have a portion of college paid for when she graduated. It was all that Brandi and Katrina could talk about for the past 2 months; with both of their names in the running for the title, I was excited.

Stewart made his way to the stage and pumped his fist high in the air playfully. The stage hands quickly rushed in, placed a plastic crown on his head and a sash around him and returned to their places beside the stage.

"Now your 2008 Winter Formal Princess is...Miss Brandi Robinson!" The principal screamed as he slightly jumped up and down.

I quickly turned to Brandi and watched as she hugged a group of her friends and covered her face at the same time. I was thrilled, although I tried my best to keep my reaction minimal, I heard myself hooting and clapping louder than anyone else in the room. My heart felt like it was about to jump out of my chest and I could only imagine what Brandi was feeling.

"Come on up Brandi!" Mr. Hemmings said into the microphone.

Brandi slowly made her way past Andrew and leaned in for a hug with him. I watched as Andrew lightly pecked her cheek and nudged her towards the stage.

The stagehands did the same work on my daughter, as they had Stewart, and she stood there with a bouquet of flowers nestled in her arms. She looked around the room like she was looking for someone, and finally we locked eyes.

I wasn't sure whether or not she would be happy to see me, but her thumbs up and big grin were all that I needed to feel content.

Ebonee Monique

"This is an honor voted on by all of your peers. You are the most respected and admired students for the ninth through eleventh graders. So congratulations!" Mr. Hemmings said proudly.

I couldn't stop smiling as my daughter and Stewart walked down the red carpet laid out for them. She was definitely headed in the right direction and I was so proud.

Snapping out of my daydream of the night before, I tossed the aspirin into my mouth and washed it down with some ginger ale that I kept in my bathroom fridge and started a bath in the Jacuzzi; then I heard a banging at my bathroom door.

"Yes, honey." I said hoping that I didn't have to leave the comfort of my steamy bathroom to find out what Brandi needed.

"Telephone." I heard Brandi say through a sleepy yawn.

I smiled to myself, as I clamped my hair into a banana clip in the center of my scalp and hurried to the door to get the phone.

Opening the heavy wooden doors, I smirked at Brandi.

"Thanks baby." I said as I took the phone from her still keeping my eyes on her face, which was blank.

"How are you feeling this morning?" I asked Brandi as I covered the mouth of the phone and leaned against the door frame.

"I'm fine." She said slightly rolling her eyes and sighing heavily with the irritation that only a teenager can express. "Can I go to Trina's house and spend the night?"

Honestly, I didn't feel like fighting with my child, I just wanted to relax, but I knew that we needed to fully discuss the incident from the night before.

Irritated, that my decision was taking me longer than she thought necessary, Brandi crossed her arm and exhaled in aggravation.

"Well, wait a minute; what's going on at Trina's house?" I asked raising an eyebrow.

"Nothing; we're just going to hang out, go to the movies and the mall and probably just chill at her house tonight." Brandi said in a whiny tone which suggested she was tired of me 'playing' momma.

Blitz

Brandi still looked gorgeous as her hair laid flat on her head with a straight part down the middle. Obviously she had been up long enough to have done her hair, which surprised me seeing how she was a not a morning person.

"You know we still need to talk about..." I started.

Brandi held up both of her hands in the air and shut her eyes as she started shaking her head as if she was trying to block out something.

"I don't even want to deal with you about that ma." She said re-opening her eyes.

Looking into her eyes I could see the hurt, the betrayal and the anger. Whatever it was that she wanted to discuss wouldn't be with me but would probably be with Andrew or Katrina. I found myself trying my best to establish myself as the dominant role in our home, but the truth of the matter is that I *did* try to sometimes be Brandi's friend before her mother. This, unfortunately, was one of those times.

"I guess...I mean it should be fine." I said shrugging my shoulders. "But when you get home tomorrow, we are *going* to talk. It's not a choice." I added firmly.

"Fine." Brandi muttered as she rolled her eyes and strutted to her room, down the hall.

I sighed. She was still upset with me and it was as clear as the diamonds on my wrists and fingers.

"Hello." I said exhaling into the phone as I closed my door back and leaned against it for some sort of balance.

"Sounds like you're having a stressful day already. It's only nine in the morning, woman." Charles joked playfully.

"If you only knew." I said returning to the bathroom.

I sat on the edge of the Jacuzzi and stuck my hand under the running water and my skin, pleased at the temperature, got goose bumps.

"Is everything okay?" Charles asked clearing his throat.

"I mean, yes...I guess so." I replied wishing that I could just rewind the clock on the past twenty four hours and un-do how everything had happened.

"I'm on my way over there."

"You don't have to." I said pitifully.

I knew Charles didn't *have* to but I knew him well enough to know he *would*.

Ebonee Monique

"I'll be there in twenty minutes." He said before hanging up.

I smiled to myself as I walked into my bedroom and pulled out my underwear, bra and relaxing clothes and headed back into the bathroom for my bath.

I stepped in the hot water, toe first, and allowed the luxurious suds to drown my body with very little struggle. It felt like no bath I'd ever had. I could feel my muscles tensing up as the water did its job of soothing and relaxing me. I ran my fingers over and through the water and the bubbles and watched as my smooth, naked body reacted positively to the jets that hit every tense part of my being. Laying my head back on the padded tub pillow, I thought about Brandi and everything she was dealing with. For ten years, she had been told that her father, the man she once adored and worshiped, was dead. I knew the realization, which was a lie, *was* something for her to be upset about. I just didn't know when she would finally break the attitudinal phase and allow me to attempt to explain my side of the entire situation.

There were plenty of reasons that I had reservations about *not* telling Brandi about me and her father's stormy relationship; all of those reasons were valid to me.

As I rubbed the soap up and down my body and enjoyed the way the lather made me feel, I thought about Charles.

Charles Griffin, former Tampa Bay Broncos Defensive End and owner of the famous *Mr. C's Southern Fixens*, had been my boyfriend for nearly six years. We'd met about eight years earlier when he hired me as his real estate agent when he began looking for commercial buildings in Tampa for his budding restaurant.

One look at Charles and I knew that everything I'd worked on ignoring, primarily fine black men, was out of the door. He changed all my preconceived notions in that regard.

Charles stood about six foot three and weighed two hundred and fifty five pounds, which was all pure muscle. Numbers on a scale mean nothing when the package looks good. Charles had the complexion of smooth caramel, beautiful dark brown eyes that pierced my body each time he looked at me, he also had strong masculine hands, was really smart and he loved my child. I couldn't have asked for a better man in my life, honestly. As I neared 37, which in my mind was just a step closer to 40, I thought about why I hadn't remarried yet. It wasn't that Charles wasn't interested in walking down the aisle-because he'd let me know he wanted to marry me and have children more times than I could remember-but it was something within me that just wouldn't allow marriage to come to the top of my list of priorities. Hell, as far as I was concerned, I'd done pretty well all by myself, I didn't *need* a husband to complicate things.

"Maybe when Brandi goes off to college." I said to myself as I closed my eyes and relaxed a bit more.

I'd have plenty of time to think about my future once my daughter was secure; with Branson entering the picture again I wondered how secure anything would be.

****

I strolled down the marble, curved staircase and headed into the kitchen for a drink. Standing in front of the refrigerator, contemplating *Fiji* water or Lemonade, I heard the arguing coming from one of our guest bedrooms off of the kitchen.

"But I didn't…yes but…no I swear! Andrew listen to me!" I heard Brandi plead. I could tell, from the stuffiness in her voice, that she was crying. I didn't want to pry but as loud as Brandi was talking, I couldn't help but listen.

"But I love *you*. You said you loved me. Stewart is lying to you, why don't you believe me?" I heard my daughter say through tear-filled sobs.

From what I could gather from the screamin and crying, Stewart told Andrew that Brandi had either made a pass at him or had tried to kiss him; either way I knew it was a lie and I had a feeling Andrew did as well.

Just as I was about to knock on the door, I heard the front door close and walked in to see Charles holding two plastic bags full of food.

"What is this?" I asked taking one of the bags from him as we both made our way into the kitchen.

"I stopped off at the *Waffle House* and got us some food." Charles bent down to kiss me on the lips as he put the bags on the counter.

In that second, nothing in the world mattered to me. I inhaled his smell, which filled my nostrils with a mixture of

Egyptian musk and cocoa butter, and couldn't stop grinning. He was my normalcy and my dose of reality and I loved it.

I set the food down that I was carrying and leaned into his muscular chest and smiled; that's when Charles heard the screaming for himself.

"What the hell is going on in there?" Charles asked stopping mid-motion as he attempted to hug me back.

"Brandi and Andrew." I said nonchalantly. "I think it's some hear-say stuff."

Charles shook his head and gently hugged my body back before beginning to unpack the food.

"I told you I thought she was too young to be getting involved with boys." Charles licked his finger to get some of the syrup off.

"I know, but…Andrew is a good kid. He comes from a good family and if there's anyone I wouldn't mind Brandi dating I thought, you know, he'd be perfect." I sighed. I needed to emphasize on the word *thought*.

This routine, the arguing, the bickering and the sadness in my daughter's eyes had been going on for over two months and it seemed to be ongoing.

"He's still a kid, Mia." Charles was not looking at me as he made his statement.

Charles never claimed to be Brandi's father, but he had been the only father figure she'd had in her life since I'd left Branson. He was the one who took her to father-daughter dances and the person Brandi shopped for on Father's Day. Charles was, for all practical purposes, her father.

And before I had a chance to update Charles on the whole Branson situation, Brandi flung open the guest bedroom door and stopped dead in her tracks when she saw we were right there, possibly listening to her conversation.

Her hair was pushed to one side of her head, her eyes were swollen and bloodshot red-from crying, and she looked exhausted.

"Hey Bran." Charles said slowly and tenderly as he and Brandi locked eyes.

Without speaking, Brandi started wiping her eyes with the back of her hands and walked slowly towards the breakfast on the table and nodded her head in Charles' direction.

Blitz

"I got the bacon; egg and cheese wrap meal for you." Charles said lifting up the black plastic plate that housed Brandi's favorite meal from *Waffle House*.

"Thank you." Brandi wrapped her arms around Charles' waist and hugged him lightly. Grabbing the food, she walked to the fridge and grabbed a bottle of water and turned to face me staring at her.

"What?" She spewed.

"Is everything okay with you and Andrew? I heard your conversation and…"

I could literally see the steam starting to rise from Brandi's head as she pursed her lips together and started breathing heavily.

"It's one thing for you to not tell me that my father was alive and now you're spying on me too?" She said as a group of tears ran down her cheeks.

"Can't I have any privacy around here!!!?" She screamed as she pushed past me and Charles and stormed up towards her room.

I kept my back turned from Charles for a couple of minutes, with my head hung, before turning around to face him. His face was white as a ghost and I couldn't tell if he wanted to grab a seat or gather his things and leave.

Charles knew about my past with Branson but he didn't know that I'd had Brandi thinking her father was dead. We both agreed Branson was out of the picture and that was that; no conversation needed. But with the new information, brought to the forefront, I knew I had some 'splainin to do with Charles.

"Branson is back." I sighed as I leaned against the fridge.

It wasn't the way I'd anticipated telling him about the new turn of events, but the cat was out of the bag and running around rampant.

"He's back and he's already ruining everything." I said burying my head in my hands.

Chapter 3

Branson English is officially back in my...I mean, *our* daughters' life.

As I stood in front of my full-length mirror, studying my appearance, in preparation for dinner with Brandi, Andrew, Charles and Branson, the irony is eerie. How the hell did I get roped into hosting a dinner for a man who, at one point, made every part of my body bruise? One part of me was excited for Branson to see the fighting spirit he had helped create, and the lavish life I was living. The other part of me just wanted him to exit our lives immediately.

I had gone through two or three outfits before I realized I wasn't dressing to impress but rather to flaunt; that's when I chose my gold cowl-neck sweater and black form-fitting slacks. Even my worst enemy would have to admit I looked good in that outfit. I was wearing my hair down with cascading curls and pulled some of the pieces selectively around my face and back to accentuate my features. My body was tight, my face and makeup were on point and I smelled delectable with Notorious by Ralph Lauren sprayed in all the right places. Charles was bringing dinner from his restaurant and I was supplying the bottles of wine. I still hadn't talked to my ex-husband, but Brandi had done all of the planning and negotiation for his presence. I didn't have the heart to tell her no.

She was excited about introducing her some-time boyfriend to her newly-found father; I was supposed to just shut up and play along.

I smoothed out my slacks and stepped into my black boots and examined myself one last time.

Who would have thought that the man I despised more than anything in the world would be having dinner in my home, eating off of my good china, digesting my man's food while guzzling wine I had bought? I don't think anyone in their right mind would have predicted the possibility of that.

As I strolled around the second floor of my house, I picked up a few stray items in the guest bathroom and tidied up as much as possible. Branson was not about to catch me slipping at all.

I picked up a pair of Brandi's Air Force Ones and headed to her room to drop them off. I kept trying to prepare myself for the moment when my past waltzed into my house and sat down at my dinner table. Would he spill the secret about his abusive past or would he be so ashamed that he would have no choice but to basically gravel at my feet? I was hoping for the latter.

I came to Brandi's door and shook my head at the amount of bass that was coming from her state of the art stereo system. I swear the girl is going to end up deaf. If I had known that it would create this much noise, I would have never allowed Charles to buy it for her. I listened for a second outside her door as R&B singer, *T-Pain* crooned about *Studio Love*. Music these days, I tell you, isn't worth anything more than the airwaves that it's played on. In my day, music was about soul, rhythm and social change. Now? Humph, all I could hear blasting from speakers all over town are songs about rims, clothes, hoes and money. I would've choked on my tongue back in the day if I ever heard *Ron Isley* talking about making sure his pimp hand was strong. I laughed at the thought as I turned the door knob to Brandi's room.

The mess of my daughter's room was all I could see as I stepped in the door of her room. I must have startled her because as soon as she walked out of her bathroom naked, she jumped and ran to grab her robe to cover herself up.

"Haven't you ever heard of knocking ma?" Brandi said from behind her bathroom door.

"I pay the bills around here; I don't have to knock on a damn thing!" I yelled back as I tossed her shoes on the ground.

I'd had enough with Brandi's constant attitude and bitchiness towards me; her sympathy boat had sailed and I was no longer a passenger. If she wanted to be mad at me, fine; but she would respect me whether she liked it or not.

Brandi re-appeared shortly with her hands on her hips and walked towards me.

Ebonee Monique

"What are you wearing tonight?" I asked as I stroked one of the long pieces of hair from out of her face.

Even in the moments when I wanted to be mad at her, I couldn't because of how much she looked like Branson. All she had to do was smile, giggle or joke with me and all anger seemed to subside. But I hadn't seen a smile, giggle or joke in over two weeks.

"I don't know, yet." Brandi said plopping on her bed and shrugging her shoulders.

"Well, Branson will be here in twenty minutes. You might want to get dressed. What time is Andrew coming?"

Brandi shrugged her shoulders and let out a huge sigh. It was one of those sighs that let a mother know that there was something wrong with her child.

I moved some of the clutter on Brandi's bed and sat down next to her. I could see her hands shaking and sensed the frustration in her.

"What's the matter, baby?"

"Nothing...I'm fine." Her answer was short, curt and filled with ambiguity.

"Is it Andrew?"

Brandi bit her bottom lip, something she only did when she was contemplating something major.

"I mean, yeah but...no and...I just don't know what to do."

"What happened?"

"Stewart told him that I tried to get at him; but I didn't. I swear to you, ma, I didn't!" Tears started to form in her eyes. "I love Andrew!"

"I know, baby." I said patting her legs as she curled a little closer to me.

I knew things were bad, but if it took Andrew's screw up to bring me closer to my daughter, I wasn't going to fight it.

"So, then Katrina told me she saw him hanging around Lisa Bradley's locker after school. You know, walking her to her car and stuff..."

"Lisa Bradley, the cheerleading captain?" I asked, knowing that Brandi and Lisa had been at each other's throats since Brandi started school there. It seemed as though they had some sort of un-spoken competition between the two of them; I assumed Andrew was taking advantage of that.

"Yeah, her. So I begged Andrew to just talk to me. I just wanted to prove to him that everything Stewart told him was a lie. I didn't try to get at him like that. But now the whole school thinks I'm a slut and Andrew isn't doing anything to stop the rumors." Tears slowly began to trickle down her beautiful face.

My heart ached for her. I wanted, in that moment, to step inside her body and take all of the pain away from her. I knew the games that high school boys played; hell Branson had pulled that very stunt on me.

I was sixteen at the time, and Branson was graduating that year. One of his friends, Al, had apparently told him that I had tried to kiss him at the end of the year mixer. Al looked like the bottom of my shoe after I'd stepped in two piles of shit, and there was absolutely no way I would have tried to kiss his scaly, pinkish-brown spotted lips. Still, Branson told me we needed a "break" so he could think things over. Of course his break consisted of nothing but meaningless one-night stands with about five girls in our school. I chalked it up to him being so distraught over our "break" and let the incidents slide. Years later when I brought the situation up to Branson, he admitted that he'd made it all up, the kiss with Al, being hurt and everything, so he could have his fun and still keep me.

Now that I knew better, I felt it my duty to hip my daughter to the game that boys' played.

"Do you really know that Stewart said something or is Andrew making this all up so he can be with Lisa?" I said crossing my legs as Brandi looked at me like a light bulb went off.

"You really think he'd do something like that?"

"He's a man, Brandi." I smiled hoping it would make her feel better.

"So you think he's making me feel bad all so he could *do* Lisa? I...I...I don't think he would but let me make a call, ma." Brandi walked quickly to the other side of the room where her desk sat and picked up her cell phone.

"Brandi..." I said as I held a hand up to her in an effort to stop her from walking right into a trap; I already knew that Andrew would deny, deny, deny. I think it was in some sort of man's manual or something. *"If presented with an accusation, lie, lie, lie and then deny, deny, deny!"* Before I could stop her,

Brandi was already on the phone with Andrew screaming at the top of her lungs.

"I know what game you've been playing Andrew, and I just want to let you know that we're through! You can go be with Lisa if you want!"

I slowly rose up from the bed and made my way outside of her door and exhaled. This was an unhealthy rollercoaster and I just wanted it to cease so I could get the old Brandi back.

Maybe Charles had been right, I thought to myself as I walked towards the dining room, and Brandi had been too young to start dating.

I must have been in a deep thought as I made my way down the stairs because the housekeeper, Rose, was waving her hands in front of my face to get my attention.

"I'm sorry, Rose, what did you say?" I said trying to get myself out of the daydream I was in.

"I said you look beautiful Miss Mia." Rose said wiping her forehead of sweat as she chuckled.

I looked down at myself and held my head to the side, as a way of saying thank you.

"You think?" I asked, knowing Rose would never lie to me.

"I do." She winked as she walked towards the dining room table.

Rose had been my loyal housekeeper, part-time nanny and overall friend for about three years. She was a short, stumpy Dominican woman with beautiful features. She had lightly sun-kissed skin that was flawless; her hair, which stopped just at her chin, was reminiscent of mine without the fabulous weaves.

Before I hired Rose, I had managed to try to run my house all by myself. I was home after PTA, Jack and Jill and client showcases and was able to keep the house clean, food on the table and help Brandi get her homework done. But as I got busier, my time became more limited, my house messier and my child became more aggravated with her mother. Charles was the one who recommended Rose to me. Apparently her mother cleaned his house, which was a few thousand square feet bigger than mine; so I knew Rose would do wonderfully on my modest mansion and I was never disappointed. Rose has never been late, never broken a dish and has always made sure my house was properly taken care of.

"Wow! This looks great, Rose!" I said as I turned to see the beautifully decorated dining room table.

There were elegantly folded gold napkins lying atop off-white glass Emile Henry plates and Lenox gold utensils laying to the right and left. The matching Lenox clear glasses, with gold trimmed brims, were the ideal settings for that night. In the middle of the table was a bouquet of yellow calla lilies and a few orchids; it was simply beautiful.

"I'm glad you like it!" Rose smiled as she leaned on one of the mahogany chairs.

I fidgeted with one of the flowers and leaned in to smell it.

As a child I never understood why women loved flowers so much; to me they stunk. I could smell a beautiful flower over and over and still never find the aroma that I heard my aunts and friends going crazy over. Now, as I stood smelling the calla lilies and orchids, the scent was one of the most wonderful scents I'd ever inhaled. They were soothing and relaxing. I inhaled once more to calm my spirit.

"Charles should be here with the food in a second. I can help you set up if you would like." I said turning to face Rose who was already waving me off.

"No. I know where everything is Ms. Mia. Besides, I asked my sister to come and help me tonight, if you don't mind." Rose asked.

I'd never met anybody from Roses' family, during the entire three years that she'd been working for me, and the thought of seeing someone from her personal life intrigued me.

"Of course. Is her daily fee the same as yours?" I asked curiously.

"No charge. Carmen is paying me back for a favor I did for her last year with one of her clients." Rose smiled genuinely.

"Are you sure?"

"Positive."

It was things like that, which made me respect and cherish Rose more than anything. I knew that if I looked for anyone else like her they would fall short in all areas where she was damn near perfect.

Ebonee Monique

Rose could tell I was trying to do something, anything to keep myself busy, so she walked over and placed her hand on top of mine and soothingly caressed it. I assumed my nervousness showed all over my face.

"It'll be okay; tonight I mean." Rose said raising both of her eyebrows.

I took a deep breath and tried to tell myself that everything *would* be okay; but what guarantee did I have?

Before I had a chance to ask Rose how she knew I was nervous, about anything, Charles walked through the door juggling four metal pans.

"Dinner is here!" He chuckled as he walked past Rose and I and into the kitchen where he placed the pans down on the marble countertop.

"Hey baby." I said walking towards him and holding my arms out, for a hug.

Out of the corner of my eye, I saw Rose scurry into the kitchen so she could prepare the food for the guests.

"Hey sweetheart; don't you look wonderful?" Charles said hugging me.

He nestled his nose into the heart of my neck and inhaled so deeply that I could feel my skin starting to cover in goose bumps. I loved the way even his slightest touch forced my body to react.

As we separated, I took a chance to look over my boyfriend; I was proud. It's not that I didn't think Charles would show up and show out, because I knew he would, but it was something about staring at that man that made every worry disappear.

"You don't look bad yourself!" I winked playfully as I ran my hands up and down his perfectly creased black slacks. He had a fresh haircut and he smelled of Burberry cologne, which I loved.

"Is Bran any better today?" Charles asked as he gripped my hand and pulled me into the living room.

We both plopped onto the comfortably plush brown leather couch and leaned into each other.

"I guess so. Now she's focusing all her attention on being pissed at Andrew that she doesn't have time to worry about the little white lie her mother told." I said squinting my eyes as Charles shook his head.

Blitz

"Little white lie? More like humongous black lie!" He laughed as he wrapped his arm around my shoulder.

Being with Charles made me feel like I was sixteen all over again.

"Shut up!" I said poking his rib slightly before bursting out laughing myself.

After we composed ourselves, Charles looked towards the front door and then returned his attention back on me.

"So are you nervous about tonight? I mean, you haven't seen Branson in what....?"

"Ten...almost eleven years." I said shortly as I thought about the day I'd left my ex-husband snoring in a bed with no wife or daughter in sight.

"As long as the two of you keep it civil, for Bran, I think everything should be fine. Is he bringing a date, too?"

"I have no idea. Brandi just told me to get dressed, have some food and show up!" I joked as my palms started to get sweaty. Was I really ready to see my monster of an ex-husband again?

"It'll be cool." Charles said with a little confidence in his voice.

"I just keep telling myself that after all this time, maybe this man will have completely changed his life and will be remorseful for what happened; but the reality could be that he is still the same person and I don't want my daughter around that do I?" I asked picking up one of Charles' beautifully manicured fingers and playing with it.

"I don't think *you* have a choice, honey. This is Brandi's decision to make and if she wants Branson in her life all you can do is be supportive. If you aren't, you just might drive her away." Charles said watching my hands play with his.

I sat in that spot contemplating my life with Branson back in it. Would we have Sunday dinners together, like the movie *Soul Food*? Or maybe we'd end up being just like the *Cosby's*, I thought. But I couldn't recall an episode where *Sandra, Denise, Vanessa* or *Rudy* brought home a man who beat on them and yet they tried to make him apart of the family. No way. *Heathcliff* would've had a fit over that.

Damn, I thought, *why couldn't Bill Cosby have scripted my life?* The perfect brownstone, family, job and activities; the *Cosby's* had it all. There was little, to no, drama.

Ebonee Monique

They always resolved their problems in thirty minutes and the family just always seemed happy. I wanted to be on whatever they were on.

I heard the doorbell ring and I headed to the staircase, for Brandi's room. I realized, in that moment, I needed more time to prepare for Branson's arrival.

"Please get the door, Charles." I said as I rushed up the stairs and got to Brandi's bedroom door and pushed my way in.

In the time that I'd left her, Brandi had gotten dressed, done her makeup and flat ironed her hair down.

"Ma, what are you doing?" Brandi said turning around to face me, out of breath.

"Nothing....I...just...your...father." I said grabbing my side and leaning forward.

"Branson is here?" She asked with excitement in her voice.

"I think."

"How do I look?" Brandi said as she held both of her hands to her side to allow me to see her get-up.

As ravishing as my daughter always seemed, to me, that night she looked extraordinary. Wearing a roomy, teal-colored three-quarter length sleeve dress that cuffed right past her knees, she looked dazzling.

I immediately noticed plumpness that had never been on her face before. Brandi had always been small in frame, but curvy as hell. Tonight, looking at her, I could see that my baby had gained some weight.

"What's this?" I asked grabbing onto her slight chubby cheeks.

"I know, right?" Brandi giggled as she slapped my hands away. "I blame Andrew. He's had me so stressed out with his Lisa stuff." She said turning back to the mirror so she could put the finishing touches on her hair.

"And what happened with that?" I asked zipping the back of her dress up.

"I told him that if he wanted to be with me he needed to be with *me* because I could have any guy I wanted and he was just about to be kicked to the curb!" Brandi laughed viciously.

"But you know...." I started.

Blitz

"I know, mommy… no dating for six months if Andrew and I break up. But he doesn't know that." She winked.

I had made Brandi a deal. She could date Andrew but only if she understood that after they broke up, she would not be allowed to date anyone else for six months afterwards. It was my way of teaching my daughter that jumping into a relationship, after one has just dissolved, is never a good idea.

In her mind, though, she and Andrew would never break up; but I knew better. As soon as Andrew got a whiff of the college girls at *Howard University*, where he was planning to go, Brandi would be nothing more than a simple after-thought in his mind.

"So is he coming tonight?" I inquired, hoping to keep the drama level down.

"He better be, if he knows what's good for him." Brandi laughed.

I locked arms with my daughter, partially because I was ready to go and partially because I needed her support if I saw Branson and fainted.

As we made our way down the stairs, I immediately noticed that the legs next to Charles weren't Branson's but rather Andrew's. He was holding a dozen roses in his arms.

"Look at our women, 'Drew!" Charles smiled widely at me.

Brandi took her flowers, hugged her boyfriend and made her way to the table. Charles pulled me to the side and whispered in my ear.

"Brandi's put on some weight, huh?" He said delicately.

"Blame that little knuckle-head next to her. He's been having her so stressed out she's eating everything in sight." I said just as the doorbell rang loudly.

My mouth went dry, my eyes began to itch and my palms seemed like they were shooting out sweat.

The moment of truth was here.

Rose opened the door and I was standing face to face with my ex-husband.
****

I don't remember the first couple of minutes after I saw Branson but I remember staring at him as Brandi ran to greet him, with her arms extended. All I could think was, "*this has to*

Ebonee Monique

be a dream". Charles stood beside me grinning and shit like he'd won the lottery. I couldn't tell if he was threatened by Brandi's father or actually glad that he was here.

I must have looked shell-shocked because after Branson was finished hugging and kissing Brandi, and meeting Andrew, he slowly looked up at Charles and I and held his head to one side. With a silly little smile on his face, he held out his arms like I was about to hug his trifling ass.

"Mia Bia!" Branson said chuckling as he rushed towards me with his arms out, ready for a hug. I hated his nickname for me when I was sixteen and I hated it now twenty years later.

I gripped Charles' hand tightly. I wasn't trying to make Branson jealous; I was actually scared for my life. I didn't know what the lunatic might have been holding underneath his denim blazer or, for that matter, in his pockets.

I stepped backwards as Branson got closer while I started to feel tears form in my eyes. All this time I had been thinking about whether or not Brandi was ready to be in her father's life but I'd never stopped to think about whether or not I was emotionally equipped to deal with seeing him.

I stared at his hands, almost in slow-motion, and remembered the times that they'd kept me in the bed for days. I hated those hands touching me then and I definitely wasn't about to greet homeboy like we were best friends. Had he forgotten what he'd done to me? What he'd done to our family?

I don't know how long Branson was standing in front of me, with his arms out and that stupid Cheshire cat grin on his face, but as I snapped out of my daydream I heard Brandi calling my name.

"Ma!" She yelled loudly before coming right up to me and nudging my side. "What?" I said looking at her with aggravation.

"Branson is trying to speak to you." She said smiling the same goofy smile that her father was smiling.

"B-Branson." I said sticking my hand out to let him know a hug wasn't happening.

With a confused look on his face, Branson obliged my request for a handshake instead and grabbed my hand tightly; a little too tightly if you ask me.

Blitz

After seeing that I wasn't budging with the small talk that he was trying to make of, "Your house is beautiful," and "You look great" he moved his introduction over to Charles.

Being the warm and personable man that he is, my boyfriend held his own as he spoke briefly with my ex-husband. As they spoke I felt Charles' grip tighten up on my hand to let me know he had my back.

I smiled warmly to myself as I finally peeled my eyes off of the ground and stared into the face of the man I hated more than my cellulite.

He looked okay, I guess. His once beautiful, thick head of hair was still intact but there were salt and pepper patches all through it; his skin made him look a lot older than I knew he was. It sagged a little too much, had some discoloration and scars on it and it just looked rugged. But he was still as charming as he was in high school. No matter what I wanted to say bad about him, I couldn't lie, he still had the swagger.

"Why don't we all have a seat at the table?" Charles said as he raised an eyebrow to Brandi and Andrew who were lagging around as Charles and Branson finished their introductions.

"Yes, sir." Brandi said as she pulled Andrew's hand towards the beautifully decorated table.

I looked over in the dining room and was shocked at the distance from where I was standing to the table. Everything seemed to be moving in slow motion and with extra emphasis on Branson's activity.

If I could just make it to the table, I thought, I'll be good. I just needed a distraction to keep Branson's eyes off of mine and mine off of his. Because, I thought, if I stare at him, I might cut him and there's nothing cute about a woman of my stature going to jail.

Quickly I rushed to the table and took the head seat and sighed. I glanced across the table, at the other head of the table chair, and smiled at Charles who winked his eye back at me.

I hoped that Rose and her sister would hurry up and bring the food to the table so none of us would have to talk or socialize; but before I could hurry her up, Brandi batted her eyes and started talking to her father.

"So…Branson…I mean, dad." She said uncomfortably as she looked back and forth at Charles and Branson.

Ebonee Monique

I'd never asked Brandi to call Charles her father or daddy, because, technically, he wasn't; she picked that up on her own. I really think that if a child feels like they have a father figure, then they'll call that person "dad" in some sort of way; Charles was just that, her dad.

But I could tell he didn't mind Branson being called "dad" as he looked on longingly at Brandi while she continued.

"What happened with the job you were telling me about?" She said excitedly as she crossed her hands together.

By that night, you would have thought that Brandi and Branson had a tight father and daughter relationship. Their discussions seemed so smooth, so entertaining and so lively; I was a little jealous.

"Oh, right." Branson smiled "I got the job and I start in two weeks."

"Where's this at?" Charles asked getting in on the conversation as I stared at him in awe. He was supposed to be on my side, not conversing with the devil.

"Um...Adams Jr. High school."

"Oh, yeah? What subject are you teaching?" Charles said as he eyed Rose and her sister bringing some salads around and placing them neatly in front of everyone.

Branson waited until Rose and Carmen finished placing our salads to answer the question.

"Nah, man. I got the head janitorial position over there. I can't teach no classes. Mia will tell you, I barely graduated high school. Ain't that right, Mia?"

Branson said pushing some of the greens around, in his bowl, before asserting his attention to me.

"You've never lied." I said not smiling, grinning or playing. I rolled my eyes and placed some food in my mouth and hoped that would ward off any more questions.

"Well, that's good," Charles said quickly "I know the principal over there, Mr. Laws."

"Oh man, that's who I interviewed with; he's a pretty cool brother."

"Yeah, we played ball together in college." Charles said.

I looked over at Brandi, who couldn't take her eyes off of Branson, and raised my eyebrows. I hoped she was happy; because I wasn't.

"So, did you all buy this house after you got married?" Branson asked politely.

"They're not married, dad." Brandi laughed as she glanced at everyone around the table.

"Oh, I just assumed that Charles had probably bought this house with his chump change; I mean, seeing how much money he's got." Branson said smirking in my direction.

What was he trying to say? I'd fallen into a rich man's lap and ended up with some money? Oh hell no. I'd worked hard to get everything I had.

"This is *my* house, Branson." I said finding the courage to raise my head and poke out my chest.

"Oh?"

"I purchased this two point five million dollar mansion with my *own* money." I clarified, emphasizing the dollar amount to make sure he knew just how well I was doing.

Charles cleared his throat and quickly gulped down some iced tea as Brandi stared at me with wide eyes. I could see Andrew chuckling, out of the side of my eye, as well.

"Oh…" Branson said sounding a little defeated. I'm not sure if anyone else in the room knew he was trying to play me, but I knew he was.

"But dad, like I was telling you my dad…I mean Charles, played football and so does Andrew." Brandi said sliding her hand on top of Andrew's. I could tell Brandi was reaching for some sort of attention or love from a father she didn't know.

"Oh yeah? What position?"

"Running back, sir." Andrew replied politely as he stared into Branson's eyes.

"Oh man, really? That's something else." Branson said playfully as he chuckled a little bit to himself.

"Why's that?" Brandi asked alarmed by his laughter.

"In high school, I played running back too." He said through his laughter.

"Really dad?" Brandi said with her eyes widened.

"Yep. I guess she really knows how to pick 'em, huh?" Branson asked raising his head to Andrew.

"You know it!" Andrew said as his arms relaxed around Brandi's shoulders.

Ebonee Monique

We tore through our salads and Brandi and Branson made small talk about Brandi's social life, her love for fashion and, most of all, how much she'd missed him.

I felt awkward sitting there listening to my daughter tell her abusive father how much she resented me for not telling her the truth. But, yet in still, Branson decided to leave out the whole "abusive" phase of his life and focus, instead, on co-signing with Brandi.

When the main course came out, I was just about ready to retreat to my bedroom and stay there until Branson left, when Brandi stood up and headed to the guest bathroom.

"Mom, come with me." Brandi whispered as she tugged at my arm.

Without hesitation I jumped up...anything had to be better than sitting across the table from Branson.

"What are you doing in there?" Brandi whined as she shut the door to the bathroom and leaned against the countertop.

"What do you mean?"

"You're being so rude to Branson. I mean, you haven't seen him in so long and all you can do is cut him down and throw stuff in his face?"

I stared at myself in the mirror and moved a piece of hair from my face.

"Didn't you tell me that the best thing to do was to kill someone with kindness? Can't you just be a little nice to him....for me?" She asked as she pouted her lips.

I nodded my head and chuckled,

"You're right; I guess I can only blame myself for raising such a great daughter, huh?" I kissed her cheek slightly.

We headed back out to the dining room table and the guys were already well into eating their dinner.

"So much for waiting on us." I joked as I winked my eye at Charles.

"Baby, you know I can't keep food in front of me smelling this good for too long." Charles said putting a piece of BBQ chicken in his mouth.

Rose entered the room and placed a bottle of champagne next to me.

"Thanks Rose." I said cracking the bottle open and pouring myself a glass of the chilled Veuve Clicquot Brut Rose champagne.

Blitz

The bottle circulated over to Charles and he poured a nice, hefty glass for himself before passing the bottle to Branson who held up both of his hands to block the bottle.

"I'm a recovering alcoholic." He said not skipping a beat. "I don't even need that near me."

"Would you like us to not drink as well? I mean, if it will make you uncomfortable..." Charles offered as he held the bottle close to him.

I could have smacked Charles for that offer; hell, I wanted *my* drink in *my* house.

"I mean..." Branson started "Only if it wouldn't be too much trouble. I don't want to be tempted."

Brandi looked at me, knowing me as well as she does, and pleaded with me-with her eyes- not to make a scene.

I blew out some air in frustration and regained my composure.

"That's cool; we can do without the alcohol tonight." I handed my glass to Rose as Charles handed his glass and the rest of the bottle to Carmen.

I wasn't shocked to find out that Branson had been an alcoholic. The only thing that surprised me was that he was recovering. I figured, in my mind, that when we saw each other again it would be at his funeral- dead from drinking too much.

"How long have you been clean?" I asked genuinely curious.

"About a year and a half; it's been a long road too." He dropped his head.

"So...what prompted....what made you..." I stuttered as I tried to figure out the right way to word my question.

"What made me stay sober?" He laughed, "Jail."

I could have choked on my food right then and there. Jail? I was expecting some sort of feel-good answer, like "my daughter" or "I needed to better my life." Not jail.

I guess the surprised looks on all of our faces helped Branson see that we needed further explanation.

"I was in jail for two years for theft; of course, while I was in I stayed sober but when I got out I was a mess." He looked into Brandi's eyes sympathetically hoping to find sympathy within them.

"I mean, your dad was out of his mind. I got arrested one time right after I was released, for D.W.I., and the judge

Ebonee Monique

was lenient with me and sent me to a rehab program; here I am."

"That's really admirable." Andrew said generically as Brandi stared motionless at the man she'd brought into our house.

"So, that's why I don't really blame your mother for keeping you away from me. I wouldn't have been *any* good to you as a father back then." He looked over at me and then back at Brandi. Shame oozed from his pores.

The rest of our night was relatively silent. Brandi tried to process the information she'd been given. I think, in her mind, she'd told herself that her father was this well-to-do, successful, stand-up guy that loved her and didn't have any flaws; but Branson was everything but that.

As we all sat around, rubbing our bellies and moaning in pleasure and disgust over how much we'd eaten, I noticed Charles checking his phone.

"Baby, I've got to go. I'll try to come back a little later." He didn't look up from his phone as he punched in numbers.

He leaned down and kissed Brandi on the forehead before coming to me and pecking me on the lips. And just like that, he was gone.

The four of us stared at each other, like our maestro had gone and we didn't know how to run the show. Before I had a chance to think of a way to get Branson out of my house, Brandi and Andrew were retreating to the backyard and calling for us to follow.

I loved my backyard, probably more than I did my entire house.

There was an oversized, beautiful gazebo and a stunning pool with clear blue water that stretched wide enough to cover almost an entire football field. We had wonderful walking paths throughout the backyard similar to a hiking trail.

I watched as Brandi and Andrew held hands and walked around the backyard grounds, seemingly in love.

"She's a good kid, Mia." I heard Branson say from behind me.

"Yeah, isn't she?"

"I know tonight was hard for you; it was…difficult for me too."

"Mmmhmmmm." I said still watching my daughter and her boyfriend as they leaned into each other for a small kiss.

"Really. I mean, do you think I like seeing the woman I loved all cuddled up with some other man?" He said slowly, as if he had to think about what he was saying.

"Well, it's over now so…"

I started to walk away from him, hoping he'd get the picture and just leave. But, soon enough, Branson was right on my tail still talking.

"So you've done alright for yourself. This little house of yours here is cute." He said staring at the pool closely.

I didn't even flinch when he referred to my seven bedroom, five bath mansion as a "little" house; I knew it was in Branson's nature to be jealous and try to put me down. And I think I'd mentally prepared myself for that.

"I like to think so."

He never asked what I did for a living, how I could afford the cars in the driveway or the pool he was admiring. I took that to mean he didn't care to know the details.

"I'm glad we have a moment alone, too." He said as he came closer to my ear and I began to cringe in disgust.

"Ever since I laid eyes on that beautiful little girl, Mia, I knew I wanted something more between us." He said as he talked with his hands.

"*Us?*"

"I mean, we are her parents, right?"

"I've been her parent for almost eleven years with no help from you." I said spinning around to face him.

"You kept my child from me."

"Branson, the truth of the matter is yes, I might have lied to Brandi and told her you were dead, but it was because, to us, you were dead. You might not want to admit that you knew where she was, but you did. And you never came looking for her, you never tried to contact her and you never even made an effort to see about her well-being, so…" I spoke in a hushed tone as I noticed Brandi looking over at us.

Branson dropped his head and stuffed his hands deep into his black slacks and sighed.

"I was never ready to be a father…not fully at least." He made his statement as if he were getting ready to reminisce over old times.

Ebonee Monique

"And now?" I asked raising one eyebrow.

"I mean, I'm trying. I've got a two-bedroom apartment, I've cleaned up and I *think* I'm ready but..."

"Branson you're here now, okay? You cannot come in Brandi's life and just leave her. Do you know what that will do to her? You cannot abandon her right..."

Branson looked a little startled at my words and held up one hand to stop me from finishing.

"The last thing I want to do is leave her, Mia." He said, "I love that girl."

His eyes met with Brandi's and he pensively stared at her and smiled widely before turning to face me again.

"And that's why I want Brandi to come and live with me."

Chapter 4

"**B**randi hurry up, we've got to get to the mall in an hour before they close." I shouted through Brandi's closed door as I checked my watch for the hundredth time.

Living with a teenager is like living with a senior citizen. They take so long to get ready, they're slow to react and they whine when you rush them.

I wasn't in the mood, though, to baby Brandi's hour-long hair and make-up session; we had to get to the mall in order to get to the bathing suit store that was holding a suit I'd agreed to buy Brandi.

It'd been two weeks since our dinner with Branson and while Brandi hadn't eased up on talk about her father, she also hadn't pushed for anymore family gatherings either, which I was glad about.

I'd held off on telling her the news about Branson wanting her to come and live with him. I kept quiet on that bit of information partially because I didn't know how and when to tell her. How would I drop the bomb that her father, who had been missing for nearly eleven years of her life, now wanted her to move to his cramped two-bedroom apartment in a sleazy part of town? My mind told me I had nothing to worry about, Brandi *loved* her room, her space and her things; Branson couldn't provide her with any of that. But my gut told me I did have a reason to be concerned because Brandi yearned to know more about her father. I cringed as I thought about her choosing to live with Branson over me, especially after everything he'd put me through.

"I said I was coming!" Brandi shouted back as she finally appeared from her room wearing a t-shirt and a pair of loose-fitting jeans.

"That was an hour ago." I joked as I started heading down the stairs.

"I think Rose has been washing all of my clothes wrong, ma." Brandi said as she followed me.

"Why do you say that?"

"My jeans aren't fitting like they used to and I won't even start on my shirts."

I looked back at Brandi and noticed she was wearing a pair of jeans that she hadn't touched in months, all because they were "too big" for her.

"Well, honey, maybe it has something to do with that weight you said you'd put on." I said cautiously as we walked towards the car.

Brandi shrugged her shoulders and looked down at herself. "I guess."

I thought about Branson and Brandi, and the moments I would be missing out on if my daughter left me for her father and I got a little sad. I didn't want to share my parental bond with Branson. I liked how life had been with me being the only parent Brandi had. I resented Branson for barging into our life and forcing Brandi to make choices she never had to make before and for his forcing me to share her love with him.

"So, what's new with you and school?" I asked as we pulled out of the gate that kept our home safe.

"Nothing." Brandi said crossing her arms and looking out of the window to the right.

"So, this talk I hear about you and Andrew breaking up is *nothing*?" I asked as I kept my eyes on the road in front of me purposely avoiding unwelcomed eye contact.

I'd overheard Brandi on the phone with one of her little friends, replaying the details of how she broke up with Andrew, during lunch, after finding out he'd been sneaking to see that Lisa girl.

"How'd you....How'd you know?" Brandi asked more shocked than upset.

"Mama knows everything." I said looking over at my child as she fidgeted with her shirt.

"I'm sorry mama. I know you liked Andrew a lot and...but he was treating me bad and cheating on me and..."

"Brandi the only thing I want is for you to be happy. I don't care about Andrew; I care about someone making *you* happy. There will be a thousand Andrews out there." I stroked her cheek lightly.

"You think?" She asked unsure about the possibility of a handsome, popular, boy wanting her like Andrew had at one point.

"I don't think, I know." I said smiling widely.

When we got to *International Plaza*, we rushed into the store and quickly found the bathing suit that Brandi had eyed a month earlier and had finally talked me into buying for her.

"Oh, this is really cute Bran." I said taking the hanger from the employee as she held it up in the air.

It was a cute terry cloth bandeau bikini in tangerine and tan that didn't show too much skin but still had a playful side to it. It had a small string that wrapped around the neck and had horizontal stripes on the bottom of the suit.

"This will be perfect in Aruba, right?" Brandi smiled at my reaction to seeing the bathing suit.

"Absolutely; don't you want to try it on?" I asked holding it up to Brandi.

"Miss, we close our dressing rooms a half-hour before the store closes; I'm sorry." The associate said as she eavesdropped on our conversation.

"Well, let's just get it I'm sure it'll fit!" I said putting it on the counter in front of the cashier.

"I'm going to look so cute in Aruba wearing this!" Brandi smiled at me as I pulled out my credit card.

I had agreed, well, actually I'd decided to take Brandi, Katrina, myself and Charles to Aruba for Brandi's upcoming fifteenth birthday. I thought of it as, not only a birthday gift, but also as a last-minute plug for Brandi to stay with me after I told her about her father's idea, after all.

We would spend five days and four nights in a bungalow condominium, which slept five, had two bathrooms, a full kitchen and full maid service. I'd found the bungalow on-line and was ecstatic about it being right on the white beaches of Aruba. I'd planned to give Brandi a beautiful Rolex watch with her name engraved on the center of the inside. I knew Charles was planning on getting her a Yorkie-Poo puppy when we returned to the states. I, literally, couldn't wait for the relaxing trip.

When we got back to the house Brandi ran up to her room, with her cell-phone to her ear, as I retreated to the kitchen where I found Charles sitting at the kitchen table.

Ebonee Monique

"Hey baby." I said throwing my purse on the countertop and rushing over to see him.

"Hey." Charles said looking up and smiling. "You look pretty today."

"Thanks." I said kissing him deeply on the lips.

I couldn't wait for our trip to Aruba and the nights alone with my man.

"Where are you two coming from?" Charles asked pulling me down into his lap.

"Nordstrom's. I just bought Brandi her bathing suit for the trip."

"Oh, does it cover up everything; because you know I envisioned her wearing a potato sack to the beach." Charles joked as he pulled me closer to him and began nibbling on my neck.

"It's a cute little bikini, Charles." I said laughing at the thought of Brandi in a potato sack.

"Bikini?" His eyes widened.

"Yes…" I said slowly "A bikini; but it's tasteful."

Charles looked at me for a couple seconds before standing up from the table, forcing me to stand up as well as he walked to the kitchen door.

"Brandi…come here!" He yelled loudly.

I didn't say anything; I just stood still with my hands on my hips-ticked off at the audacity of Charles-as I heard Brandi come racing down the stairs.

"Sir?" She asked as she came into the kitchen, phone still glued to her ear.

"Hang the phone up." Charles said seriously.

Brandi told whoever she was talking to that she had to call them back and stood confused as she looked back and forth between Charles to me.

"Go try that bathing suit on; I want to make sure it covers you up." Charles said.

"But I tried it on before and…"

"Brandi, obey your dad." I said.

I could see Brandi sulking as she stomped up the stairs towards her room.

"She's only fifteen Mia; you think she's ready for a bikini?" Charles lowered his voice as he turned to face me.

Blitz

I didn't see anything wrong with Brandi wearing a bikini; she'd worn one every year of her life since she was born. The only difference, I guessed, was that she was more developed than ever this year; Charles knew the vultures would be out.

"It's not a bad bathing suit-Charles; I wouldn't have her out there looking like she's hooking. I *am* her mother." I reminded him of the fact that I always had Brandi's best interest at heart.

I heard Brandi's door shut and I heard her slowly come down the stairs.

"Ma, I think we needed a bigger size." She said as she opened the kitchen door and showed us the bathing suit.

I could have screamed when I saw Brandi in her bathing suit. Everything I'd told Charles about her being covered up-and that the suit was cute and tasteful, went right out the window as soon as Brandi stepped into the kitchen. I didn't know what to say and I could feel Charles steaming as he stood next to me with his arms crossed.

Her body was...different, to say the least. Her breasts were slightly bigger, causing the top to droop and sag, and the bottom of the bathing suit seemed to be a little too tight. Her stomach, though, was in a ball park of its own. Slightly bulging out, I wondered how long it would take Brandi to work the weight off and get her old body back. I stared at her body, a body that I'd known for almost fifteen years, and I wondered where the time had gone; where I'd been. She looked like a grown woman, a fully grown, developed woman. While she still looked beautiful, I couldn't take my eyes off of the bulge that was, mysteriously, at the center of my attention. Where had it come from, why was it irking me and, most of all, what the hell was it? I knew she had been eating a lot lately, but the bump seemed to be a little more than just fat.

"Go on upstairs and change, Bran, your mother will take it back to the store tomorrow and get another one." Charles spoke through gritted teeth.

Brandi walked away quickly towards her room with her arms covering her back side.

Moments, maybe even minutes, passed by before I decided to ask Charles what he was thinking.

Ebonee Monique

"It looks too small, right?" I asked sitting down at the table as he joined me.

Charles didn't speak to me and barely even acknowledged my presence; he just got up from the table, grabbed his keys and left the house. I was a little pissed and highly concerned as I sat at the table with my head in my hands. The last thing I needed, at that point, was a fight with Charles over a bad judgment call on my part.

I was fixing a glass of tea ten minutes later when Charles returned with a plastic bag in his hands.

Turning to face him, I rolled my eyes and looked down in my tea.

"I can't believe you left because of that damn bathing suit...I *agreed* with you that the bathing suit was too small, all you had to do was..."

"This isn't even about you, Mia." Charles said sitting down at the table and setting the plastic, white bag in front of him slowly.

I eyed the bag closely and tried to make out what Charles had purchased.

He reached into the bag and placed the box in front of me and kept his eyes on it, almost as if he were trying to explain with his eyes what it was.

"You think I'm pregnant?" I asked raising an eyebrow as I eyed the pink and white pregnancy test box "I've been taking my..."

"I think Brandi's pregnant." Charles said cutting me off.

I dropped my glass, allowed it to shatter, and began shaking nervously.

In some sort of sick, twisted way, everything was starting to make sense.

Brandi's bulge, her weight gain and her attitude changes were all clear signs that I had ignored. But couldn't there be another diagnosis for all of her issues? Maybe she was just constipated or stressed; I rationalized as I tried to register the information.

Could it be true? My fourteen-almost fifteen-year old baby, pregnant?

My hands shook as I grabbed the box and gawked at it.

Blitz

"She…she can't be." I said as my eyes filled with tears. "She would have told me if she was having sex Charles; I know it."

"Maybe she didn't." He sighed. "And maybe I'm wrong. Maybe Brandi is just going through a rough patch and just gained a little weight. I *could* be wrong."

"Yeah," I said clutching to the small grain of hope that I wasn't about to be a grandmother

"She did say she and Andrew just broke up and she's been really stressed about that." I looked up at Charles who was nodding his head in reluctant agreement.

"And maybe that's it." He touched my hand,

"But, as she stood there in that bathing suit, I saw everything I needed to draw an assumption."

"This can't be true…" I said still eyeing the box in my hand.

My mind didn't want to believe what my heart already knew was true.

"Mia, I can give you all the reasons in the world about why she *could* be, but the only way to know for sure is if we test her." Charles said as he exhaled loudly.

Could it be? My baby, *having* a baby? Charles was right; the only way to know was to go through with making her take the test.

Holding the small pregnancy test kit close to my heart, I began my journey up the stairs and towards Brandi's room; it seemed like the longest, most intense trip of my life.

Life, as I knew it, was about to take an immediate change; I didn't know if I was ready for it.

****

I gawked at the pregnancy test that stared back at me from the bathroom sink.

"This can't be happening," I griped, as I ran my fingers through my mangled hair.

But there it was, clear as day, two bright pink lines indicating that a baby was, indeed, coming.

Ignoring the wetness on it, I gripped the urine-soaked test for a closer glimpse.

This is one of the lowest points in my life, I thought to myself, but even in my confusion, I knew I'd been through worse.

Ebonee Monique

When I fled from Branson, with Brandi in tow, I had promised myself that I'd never allow myself to feel as useless and horrible about myself and my existence as I did back then.

More than a decade later, I was one of the most successful realtors in Tampa. I lived in a lavish mansion, drove luxurious cars and had a wardrobe that confirmed my million dollar lifestyle; yet, here I was feeling lower than ever before.

With my hands shaking uneasily, I opened the bathroom window for air. I felt like I was about to pass out and needed to breathe fresh air.

"How could you?" I roared furiously to the sky.

God had been so good to me for years, and now this? There had to be some sort of mistake. I was too old to raise a baby.

As I prayed, I thought about the trip I'd planned to Aruba for Brandi's birthday.

Guess I have to cancel that, I thought as I closed my eyes tightly; hoping I was in the midst of some bad dream.

Taking a deep breath, my heart spoke to my cold mind, which was suggesting that I subject my daughter to the unthinkable, an abortion. My mind begged for another look at the situation.

Maybe the baby would be a blessing. Maybe it would find the cure for HIV or cancer. My mind tried to rationalize why God would add a baby to the situation at hand, but I didn't care about any of that; the only thing I could think about was everything I'd worked for, in order to better Brandi's life, going down the drain slowly as her stomach quickly grew larger.

I exhaled and turned to face Brandi, who was sitting on the toilet with her knees pulled into her chest. Silently I started to cry.

"You're going to have the baby...." I said kneeling down to my child as she, also, silently wept. Brandi's cat eyes grew large as the reality of what I was saying started to hit her.

"I'm h-having it?" Brandi asked, confused.

We'd been through worse together, I reasoned.

"*We're* having this baby." I said as I nervously patted Brandi's slightly protruding belly.

****

When I finally came out of Brandi's room, down to the kitchen where Charles was sitting quietly waiting the results, I

Blitz

think my face said everything. I was done crying and I was done asking why; I was just tired. I stood in front of him with a blank, pale face and he immediately knew the answer. Brandi was having a baby.

I'd never seen a man cry as passionately as Charles did when he faced the reality that his little girl was about to become a mother, before she could even drive. I needed my space and my time to process everything, and so did Charles. He jumped into his car and went for a long, long drive to clear his head.

This wasn't what we'd prepared ourselves for, or what we'd expected from Brandi. I knew teen pregnancy happened; hell, my mother had me when she was only eighteen, but this wasn't supposed to happen to *our* daughter. When I thought about teen pregnancies, I thought about children who didn't have any guidance in their homes, no structure and who were desperate for love. Brandi had all of that and then some, or so I thought.

It was a Saturday night and the sun was lightly touching the surface of the earth as it prepared to set. I nestled on one of our beach chairs next to the pool, watching everything develop around me; all I could think about was Brandi and the baby she was expecting.

How had I *not* seen this? Had she known? When and where had she had sex? Why hadn't she come to me? I wiped my cheeks as a couple of tears fell from my eyes and I ducked down as I heard the sliding glass door, from the house open.

"Ma?" Brandi almost whispered as she approached me.

I couldn't say anything. Not a response, not a moan...nothing.

Shutting my eyes, I prayed that Brandi would just leave me alone for a second, so I could try to understand everything that was happening.

But, being my child, Brandi came and joined me in the seat next to me.

She was wearing a pair of baggy sweat pants and an oversized sweat shirt. I wondered if, since finding out she was with child, she felt ashamed about her body and decided to cover up. She pulled her wrists into the shirt and opened her mouth to speak.

One look into my red eyes and Brandi, herself, began sobbing.

Ebonee Monique

"I'm so sorry, mommy." She said as she threw her head into her hands.

I didn't do anything to comfort her; nothing at all. What was I supposed to do? Tell her everything would be okay? I wasn't sure if it would be and I certainly wasn't about to lie to her. Was I supposed to hug and soothe her with some sort of heart-felt anecdote? I didn't have anything to give her. I watched her and felt sorry for her. I felt sorry for the fact that she would have her childhood snatched right from under her. My heart ached to know that she would never experience what it's like to truly be a carefree teenager. I also felt sad at the certainty that people would look at my daughter and point and stare. I mean, she was *Brandi Robinson*, after all.

Her shoulders were hunched over and her body was moving with every sob she produced. I wanted to take her into my arms and cradle her, the way I'd done since she was a baby, but everything was different. She was still my baby; but she had crossed the threshold of womanhood the moment she'd had sex.

Looking away from Brandi, I wiped a few tears from my face and fixated my eyes on a tree in the distance.

"Mommy, please don't hate me! Please don't hate me." She wailed as she flung herself onto me and wrapped her arms around my neck.

Even if I wanted to ignore her cries and words, my heart wouldn't let me. She was *still* my child and I had a duty to be her mother.

I slowly clasped my arms around Brandi and pulled her tightly into me and began crying deeply into her shoulder as she did the same in mine. As the tears continued to fall, my body shook and I tried to remember a time when Brandi was innocent. Where had I gone wrong? What kind of mother had I been not to notice that my own daughter was not only having sex, but pregnant as well?

"I don't hate you baby. I never could hate you." I said through tear-induced hiccups as I smoothed Brandi's hair down towards her scalp.

Brandi gulped for some air and laid her head on my chest.

"I didn't know, mommy. I swear I didn't know." She remorsefully chanted over and over again as she continued to cry.

Blitz

We sat there, mother and daughter, intertwined in one another, allowing ourselves to accept the painful reality of the situation completely.

By the time Charles came home, the sun was completely set and Brandi and I were still holding each other on the beach chair. Little words were spoken between the two of us as I tried to think of what else could be said. Taking a seat next to us, Charles hung his head and exhaled loudly.

"Dad, I'm…I'm sorry." Brandi said frowning as she moved towards Charles and threw her head into his chest and wept. She knew, by the look on his face, that he was disappointed in her and I could tell it hurt her.

Charles wiped a few tears from his eyes and hugged Brandi tightly.

"We're going to get through this, Bran." He said clearing his throat.

"But we need to talk first." I chimed in as I sat up and crossed my arms.

Brandi dropped her head and nodded.

Before Charles or I could try to formulate our questions, Brandi was talking in broken gasps for air. I watched her as she looked down at her little pooch of a stomach and back up at us with a look of disbelief plastered on her face.

"It was only one time." She said biting her bottom lip.

"When?" I asked getting slightly agitated at Brandi's admittance.

"About three months ago." She said looking down,

"But I told Andrew I didn't want to do it anymore because it hurt too much; that's when he started getting with Lisa."

I could see Charles cringing as Brandi recounted some of the details out loud.

"How could you let something like this happen, Brandi?" Charles screamed, finally blowing his lid. His chest was puffed out and the wrinkles in his forehead were more prominent than ever.

Brandi seemed to be caught off guard by Charles' reaction and opened her mouth to speak, but no words followed.

"Haven't your mother and I tried our best, to give you everything you ever wanted? And from the first time you got your period we talked to you about safe sex." Charles was talking with his hands.

I looked over at him and shook my head; *this* was her father.

"Yes, sir." Brandi finally replied as she wiped her tears.

"Then, why? What's your reason? I know you're not stupid and I know you know about the birds and the bees so why did this happen?"

"I loved him and he said if I loved him I'd prove it by having sex with him. Daddy, I didn't want to lose him." Brandi said through her tears.

"You didn't realize your period had been late?" I asked joining in the conversation as Charles exhaled again.

"I did, but I didn't think anything of it. I never thought this kind of thing would happen."

"Dammit, Brandi." Charles said, rubbing his hands together.

If there was ever a time where I questioned whether or not Charles was in this parenting thing with me, as I stared at him and visibly could see the care in his eyes, all my questions were answered.

Brandi stared at the both of us with huge, crocodile tears streaming down her beautiful little face and in that moment, I could see my daughter for what she really was; a little girl, in a grown woman's body, with no idea or clue of what to do.

"Have you told Andrew yet?" I asked knowing that she'd had plenty of time to call someone and break the news, since we'd found out the results.

"No but that's what I was coming down here to talk to y'all about." Brandi said holding her head up.

"You let us worry about telling him and his parents." Charles sternly responded.

"No...I don't think I'm ready for a baby." Brandi said looking down at the ground.

It had never even crossed my mind that Brandi would want an abortion. Everything in me wanted to agree with her, she *wasn't* ready for a baby, but regardless of whether she was ready or not, the baby was coming and it hadn't asked to be here.

"Brandi, abortion is not a form of birth control, okay? If you lie down and make a baby you need to stand up and raise one; that goes for you and Andrew. What if I had chosen to have an abortion with you?" I said somewhat sympathetically.

I couldn't tell if that hit home or not, but Brandi was taking a defeated breath when Charles stood up in front of her with his arms crossed.

"Brandi go on up to your room and let your mother and I talk." Charles said not looking in Brandi's eyes.

"I'm sorry," Brandi said getting up and preparing to head back into the house.

Charles and I didn't speak at all after Brandi left. We, instead, just held hands and geared ourselves up for the aftermath in the whirlwind of news.

I begged Charles to stay with me that night; he obliged, knowing I needed his touch to fall asleep. Normally he would wait until Brandi was asleep, we'd watch television and I'd fall asleep and he'd make his exit to his house across town.

I wasn't sure why we hadn't moved in together, but I liked the space between the two of us at certain times; this wasn't one of those times. I needed Charles badly and I needed to know if he blamed me the way I blamed myself.

"How do you want to handle Andrew's parents; you know they aren't going to be thrilled that their son is about to be a father." Charles whispered in my ear as I snuggled into his arms while we lay in bed.

I shrugged my shoulders, unsure of how I wanted to handle any of it. Would I have Rose prepare a batch of cookies and go over to their house, with Brandi and Charles in tow, and give them as a gift while I broke the news?

"We should do it soon." Charles said closing his eyes and running his hands through my hair.

"I guess." I replied, not at all enthusiastic about the A-bomb I had to drop.

"What are you thinking about?" Charles asked softly.

My eyes were wide open, staring into the dark, as I thought about his question.

I was thinking about a lot; too much to say in one sitting.

When Brandi would disobey me, I would discipline her immediately. When she got a bad grade in school I took away

Ebonee Monique

her cell phone and room phone; when she got suspended for talking back to her teachers in elementary school, I spanked her until my hand was sore. What kind of punishment could I dish out for this? She was already paying the price of being solely responsible for a human being for the next eighteen years; yet, I felt like I should have been doing more to reprimand her.

"I just don't know how this happened to Brandi, you know? She's smart, she's a bright girl; I've always talked to her about sex." I said.

"But it only takes one time of getting caught up..." Charles replied.

"I know, but...this kind of stuff doesn't happen to people like us." I said as I flinched at the "people like us" comment.

"What do you mean, people like *us*? Teenage girls, all over America-regardless of race or financial status-are getting pregnant. We aren't exempt- because we're wealthy, Mia."

"I didn't mean it like that. I just meant...how is Brandi going to function in a society that has never been in contact with a teenage mother-at least one that was in their same bracket? What about her friends? Her teachers? Her obligations?"

"It'll all come secondary to the baby, now. This was a choice that Andrew and Brandi made and now they're going to have to adjust."

"I'm going to have to pull her out of school, cancel the trip to Aruba and call Katrina's mother and the PTA...God how am I going to face them with..." I rattled on as I thought of the extra things I was going to have to do to accommodate my pregnant daughter.

"Shhhh!-We've dealt with enough unexpected for one night, let's schedule a doctor's appointment for Monday. We'll tell Andrew's folks after we get confirmation and then take care of everything else after that."

I pretended to shut my eyes and I breathed heavily to let Charles think I was sleep as I turned on my side and just stared in the darkness.

I kept trying to tell myself that I would wake up in the morning all that we had been through would just be one big joke or mistake. In the midst of the darkness all around me, I prayed that the pregnancy test had been wrong and the bulge in

Blitz

Brandi's stomach was nothing more than a bad case of gas. I knew I was reaching and even a bit delusional in my thoughts, but none the less, I prayed and prayed that God was going to somehow change the events of the day and a miracle message would be delivered to us that there would be no baby *in* my baby.

I turned over and faced Charles' back and smiled to myself. A few moments later, I heard small sobs coming from him as his chest began to shake with each whimper from his being. Remaining silent, I listened closely as the sobs became muffled and more consistent. There was no one else in the room and I knew I wasn't crying; I realized my man was in just as much pain as I was, if not more.

My heart burned in pain as a huge lump took up residency in my throat. I reached out and touched Charles' wet cheeks and startled him.

He sat up in bed and kept his back to me. Following his lead, I sat up and placed my arms around his bare back and squeezed him tightly, as I lay my head on his skin.

Just like that, more tears and crying came out of nowhere; this time he wasn't trying to hide them.

I couldn't help but cry as I felt my man's pain. The little girl he'd watched grow up had become a woman in a matter of minutes and in a not-so-exciting way. I wondered if events were flashing before Charles' eyes; the moments that we'd planned together for Brandi's life. Like Brandi's sweet sixteen, her first car, her SAT's, her college acceptance letter, college graduation and even her first real job. What would happen to it all?

"It's okay, baby." I said softly as I cuddled him tighter.

"Is it?" Charles asked not turning to face me.

I sat against my pillow, frozen by his thought-provoking question. I dropped my head into my hands and a blood-curdling scream escaped.

The dread in not being able to answer his question was more paralyzing than anything else.

Would it be okay?

Ebonee Monique

Chapter 5

I jumped as the phone rang and startled me out of my sleep.

"Hey Ms. Mia, is Brandi awake?" I heard Katrina say in a giddy voice.

I wiped the drool from my mouth and took a second to wake myself before answering.

"Why didn't you call her room phone, Katrina?" I asked through a deep yawn.

"I did and it's just ringing busy." She said pausing "So, do you think she's up?" She asked again, in a pestering manner, as I wondered why my talk-aholic daughter would be on the phone so early in the morning.

"Let me get up and go check and see. I'll have her call you if she is." I said as I threw the covers back and cradled the phone on my shoulder.

"Well, just ask her if she wants to go to the movies today. My mom said she'd take us, if that's okay with you."

I thought about it for a second, and tried to figure out how I was going to handle things like this. Inside, I felt like Brandi should be confined to her room, doing things like reading the Bible or knitting, instead of out having a good time.

"I'll have her call you." I said again before I hung up.

Charles was already gone, leaving an empty spot in my bed that screamed his name. Our night before had been one that made us, undoubtedly, closer and had, still, left us in an unknown spot.

I tossed on my robe and tightened the stings around my waist and headed towards Brandi's room. Just as I reached the door I stopped and thought about how different things were going to be between the two of us. Would I trade pregnancy secrets and tips of the trade, which I'd learned while pregnant with her? Or would we have a simple, two ships-passing-in-

Blitz

the-night type of relationship? I didn't want to feel resentment towards her and I didn't want her feeling resentment towards me, causing both of us to keep our distance. It was a long shot, but the thought ran through my mind.

"Bran?" I said as I put my hand on the door knob and turned.

I looked around the neat room and smiled at the little memories that were plastered all over her walls. Her recital pictures, celebrity posters and even her tiara and sash from her "Miss Princess" title; regardless of all else, I was still a proud mother. It wasn't something I could turn off or on at will.

Glancing at the corner of the room I saw Brandi curled up in her bed, barely moving. The navy blue and tan comforter cloaked her body so much that I hardly noticed her.

"Brandi?" I said again just as I saw her turn over on the opposite side.

The cover was moving, non-stop, as I heard the sniffles and soft crying underneath the cover.

Every other time that Brandi was crying, in trouble or needing me, I knew exactly what to say. I mean, in everything else Brandi had encountered in life, I'd been to some of the same places she had been so I knew how to handle her issues. But this was different; I'd never been here before and I didn't know what to say or do to comfort her or myself.

I took a seat on the edge of her bed and bit my bottom lip profusely before speaking.

"Brandi." I said slowly, "I love you."

I couldn't think of anything else, more meaningful, to say that would get through to her. Would I tell her that the baby inside of her would be a blessing when all she could see was the turmoil and stress that it was causing her?

I heard Brandi wipe her nose and cough a little bit, before I turned around to stare at her covered up body. I looked at her outline and tilted my head to the side as I noticed her phone, which was off of the cradle and sitting on the nightstand.

I guessed that Brandi must have gotten so frustrated and confused that she just wanted to block out the entire world. It was something she did when she was studying, upset with a friend or whenever she just wanted to be alone. I picked the phone up and placed it back on the cradle.

Ebonee Monique

"Sit up, baby." I said caressing her back as she shifted her body away from me.

"Ma, please just leave me alone." Her words stung with a bitterness that only a confused woman could deliver.

But I wasn't going anywhere.

Insistent upon seeing my daughter's face, I pulled the covers back and stared at her half naked body sprawled out on her bed. She was wearing only a cotton bra and underwear and her hands were rested, tightly, on top of her protruding belly.

"Sit up." I said slightly pushing her back up until she obliged and sat up against her headboard.

I'm not sure if the myth of "once you announce you're pregnant your stomach doubles in size" was true or not, but looking at Brandi, that morning, was like seeing someone I'd never seen before. Her stomach was poking out, more so than it had seemed to the day before, and her breasts seemed to be larger.

"Ma, *please* I just need to be alone."

"Honey, your alone time is gone." I said cracking a smile as Brandi stared at me with a stone face.

Sensing that my joke hadn't gone over too well, I took a seat back on the bed and placed my arm around her shoulder. Brandi looked away from me and stared at a wall.

"Look at me." I said placing the other hand on her chin and pushing it towards me. "I *love* you. Okay?"

"Okay." Brandi replied dropping her uncertain and confused eyes.

"There's nothing you can say or do that will stop me from loving you. Ever!" I said as I got a tad misty eyed at my own words. I knew I loved Brandi, but it took me facing the situation-in this case her belly- and accepting it for what it was, for me to know just how much I loved her.

Brandi slowly brought her eyes up to mine and I watched her lip tremble.

"I know you and dad don't even want to be seen with me. Mommy, I'm fourteen what am I going to do with a baby?"

I thought about her question and nodded my head as I responded.

"You are my daughter and I love you; being seen with you pregnant is the same as me being seen with you not pregnant." I smiled, "And, what you're going to do is raise your child, okay? You're going to give this child every ounce of love that you possibly have inside of you to give. Bran, when I had you I was twenty two years old and didn't know what to do with you...until you came along. This child is going to be dependent on you for love, protection and guidance. All you can do is give it all that you have." I smiled as I thought about the little baby that would be joining our family.

Although I wasn't thrilled about things, I was suddenly excited for Brandi.

"Were you scared?" She asked me as she fidgeted with her fingers.

"Terrified, honey. I looked over at you in that hospital bin and I remember asking the nurse how to make you stop crying." I laughed as I remembered the day of Brandi's birth.

"But it'll get better. You will come to think of all of this as a blessing." I said hoping I could convince myself of the same.

"I'm scared mom." Brandi said finally looking me directly in the eyes.

I knew that Brandi had made a mistake...a huge mistake. But still, I realized that she didn't need reprimanding from me. She was already dealing with enough on her own. It would've been easy for me to yell, scream and cry over and over for the rest of Brandi's pregnancy, but I hated the thought of stressing her out for something that neither of us could change.

Laying her head on my shoulder, I held Brandi's hand tightly and promised myself that I would at least *try* to have a pleasant disposition in our current situation.

"Trina called and wanted to know if you wanted to go to the movies with her this afternoon." I said matter-of-factly.

"Hmmm" Brandi said as she shrugged her shoulders.

"I know you want to go to the movies." I smiled widely as I turned towards my only child.

"I don't think so. I feel huge."

"Did you tell Trina?"

"No. I just took my phone off the hook and went to sleep. I think I'm going to wait until I'm showing more to tell everyone."

"You know we have to tell Andrew and his family sooner than later, right? Charles and I were thinking about Monday night."

Brandi shrugged her shoulders, again, and changed the subject.

"How is dad?" she asked politely. "I know he was really mad at me last night."

"He wasn't mad *at* you, honey. He was disappointed in you. This isn't the path we'd planned on you to be on right now in your life." I said blowing out air.

"But we'll adapt and accept the change." I smiled, remembering my promise to myself.

"What about Branson...I mean dad? Are you going to tell him?" Brandi quizzed.

I hadn't even allowed myself to think about Branson since he'd left our house a couple of weeks before, with dreams of Brandi living with him dancing in his head. Just as she brought his name into the conversation, I remembered my own secret that I was holding off on telling Brandi; the secret that her father wanted her to move in with him.

Now, I figured, still wasn't a good time to have that discussion.

"I think that should be something you should think about telling him...if and when you want to."

"Can you drive me over there next Friday after school?" She asked without missing a beat. "Branson says he has the weekends off, so maybe, I can stay the weekend with him?" She asked digging the guilt knife deeper into my heart.

I heard the front door shut loudly, and I patted Brandi's hand as I rushed out to see what kind of mood Charles was in. Before I could look, though, I heard him scream.

"Brandi!" He yelled loudly, just as I reached the banister.

Brandi covered herself up and stood beside me. "Am I in trouble?" She asked with wide child-like eyes.

"Just go down there." I said as she made her steps towards the staircase. I was close behind her and wanted to see what Charles was all in a tizzy about.

When we reached the bottom of the stairs, I saw Charles with both of his arms crossed over his chest.

"Hhhey dad." Brandi stuttered as she kept her distance from Charles.

"Have a seat." Charles motioned for Brandi to sit down on the living room couch.

I stood at the bottom of the stairs and watched as Charles kneeled in front of her and took a deep breath.

"When you were nine years old, you asked me if I would be your father." Charles reminded her of the day almost five years earlier.

"And I told you it would be a pleasure; that's just what it's been. I've seen you stumble and fall but I've also seen you triumph in the face of adversity. I've watched you blossom into a beautiful young woman and, even now, I'm amazed at your strength." Charles grinned as he placed his hand on top of Brandi's stomach.

"You're having a baby." He said forcing a laugh out of himself.

I could see Brandi tearing up as she put her hand, slowly, on top of Charles'.

"And, even though we were shocked by everything we found out yesterday, I've had a chance to think about things and...well...I recognize now that I have to be your father, your protector and your provider in good *and* bad; in happy times and scary ones. I made a vow to you that I'd always be there for you and I'm not going to bail on you now; especially when I know that you need me most." He said swallowing as he pulled out something from behind his back.

Brandi wiped a few tears from her eyes and glanced over at me, as I eyed Charles admirably. How had I been blessed with such a wonderful man?

Reaching from behind himself, Charles pulled out a blue box and held it tightly in his hands. Picking up one of Brandi's hands, Charles placed the box in her hand and closed it tightly.

"This is just to let you know that I've got your back, regardless." Charles said finally standing back up.

I came and stood next to Charles and placed my arm around his waist and leaned my head against his chest. We both watched as Brandi slowly opened the box and squealed loudly.

"Oh dad! It's beautiful." She said taking the silver necklace out of the box and opening up the heart shaped locket to reveal two pictures; one of Charles and one of Brandi as a little girl.

Tossing the box to the side, Brandi stood up and wrapped her arms around Charles' neck and hugged him tightly. "I love you guys."

This, I thought, was what would've happened on *The Cosby Show* if *Bill Cosby* had scripted *Rudy* to get pregnant by *Bud*. But, even I knew, that once the cameras and lights went off there would be nothing but a real, gritty situation to deal with.

I just wanted this scene to last a little bit longer.

****

Brandi and Charles went to the store, as I prepared dinner and worked on a couple of major real estate deals. I was dreading going into work the next day, but I knew the only way the bills would get paid was through my non-stop hustle and grind work mentality.

As I cooked, I tried not to think about Brandi's pregnancy; only because I never knew how I was feeling about it at any given time. Sure we'd all said our peace earlier that morning, but I had a feeling the smiling faces and comfortable attitudes would soon fade.

I dropped a couple of onions into the bowl of tomato soup, beans and turkey and stirred it up quickly. With the final touches to my tomato turkey soup down, I mentally checked off my to-do list and prepared for the next thing.

"Soup. Check. Bread. Check." I said looking around the kitchen at the various burners that were red hot on the stove.

I heard laughter in the foyer and stuck my head out to get a quick glimpse of Charles and Brandi coming through the door.

"Hey, ma we got the...." Brandi said just as she quickly covered her mouth and dropped the white, plastic bag in her hands.

"What's the matter?" Charles asked placing his hand on her back as I rushed over towards her.

Sooner than either of us could diagnose the problem, Brandi was emptying the contents of her stomach all over the marble floor. Charles and I jumped back, to avoid the pinkish orange substance from hitting our feet, and watched as Brandi rushed up the stairs towards her bathroom.

"What the hell was that?" Charles asked looking at the throw up and me.

"Morning sickness, probably; or maybe something I'm cooking isn't agreeing with the baby."

"But she didn't even eat anything."

"The smell could trigger anything." I said remembering my days of avoiding beef when I was pregnant with Brandi.

Charles rushed into the kitchen, grabbed a towel, and came back and began cleaning it up.

"I guess I've got a lot to learn, huh?" He asked while looking up at me.

"Well, honey, you don't have children so you wouldn't know these things." I smiled as I rubbed his back.

Charles looked like he wanted to say something, in regards to my comment, but ended up biting his tongue and walking away.

"What was that all about?" I said curiously as I eyed his back facing me.

"Nothing; maybe you should go check on Brandi."

"Charles…" I replied, knowing that whenever I said his name, in a particular tone, he knew I needed an explanation.

"Don't you think about the fact that our daughter is having a baby before we are? Do you know how that makes me feel? I've been asking you for almost five years now, to marry me and start a family of our own. But all I can get is a 'maybe next year' from you."

"And what? You want me to drop everything, right now, and marry you? Charles I can't believe you are bringing this up now…right now…of all times!" I said in an aggravated tone.

I wasn't as aggravated, though, as I was making Charles think I was. I would have given anything, really, to marry Charles; but only on my own terms. I was so terrified of marriage and the great relationship it would screw up between Charles and I that I played it to the left as much as I possibly could. All I could picture was Brandi being without a father and me being left with two divorces under my belt and nothing to show for it. I knew Charles was getting frustrated with me and my excuses, but I didn't want to be pushed or coerced into doing anything I wasn't ready for; besides, I knew Charles wasn't going anywhere.

Ebonee Monique

"Keep your voice down." Charles said turning around and facing me.

"Sorry." I said obeying him by lowering my voice.

"We'll talk about this later." He said leaving me standing in my spot.

Brandi retreated from her room half-an-hour later with her hair in a high bun, her dark chocolate skin looking more radiant than ever and wearing a one-piece long nightgown.

"Feel better?" Charles asked as he put a spoonful of the tomato turkey soup in his mouth and looked over at Brandi who was fixing a bowl of the thick orange soup with juicy pieces of turkey seasoned ground turkey and a healthy serving of fresh vegetables for herself.

"Much." She said shortly.

The three of us sat there, eating our warm soup, in silence as the news blared loudly on the television in front of us.

"Mommy, if you had to look at me and take a guess, how far along would you think I am?" Brandi broke the tension-filled silence with an awkward question that I wasn't sure I even wanted to try and answer.

"Well, based on when you said you had intercourse and the size of your belly, I'd say somewhere in the three month area, maybe twelve weeks or so."

I returned my attention back to the warm bowl of soup that sat in front of me. It provided me with an inner comfort our current situation lacked.

"When do you think you're going to tell Katrina?" Charles asked.

"I told her about fifteen minutes ago. I think she's in shock because she just sat there on the phone speechless, like she was mad at me or something. Then she said something about being the baby's god-mother and being happy." Brandi said smiling widely.

I was anxious to know that Brandi had finally, told one of her peers about her condition. That was a huge step, but I also knew how *these people*, (i.e. teenagers) operated; it was rarely pretty. I expected one person to shun Brandi, one person to accept it and one person to just be indifferent, but knowing that Katrina was in the "accept it" boat made life that much easier. I was so sure that Brandi didn't even realize how grateful she should be for the support of friends; she actually *expected* it.

"Do you think she'll tell anyone at school before you have a chance to go to the doctor?" I asked.

Brandi shook her head and looked at me like I was crazy.

"Trina is my best friend ma; she wouldn't do that to me. Plus I told her to keep it a secret until I broke the news to Andrew." She said slightly rolling her eyes.

"Okay, just asking." I replied trying to smile.

Even if I tried to hold on to my happy, normal life, with every strand and ounce of my being, I knew that change was stronger than any strength I *thought* I had. I exhaled a pessimistic sigh. One upper punch to my jaw, and my pride would be splattered all over the ring. Two jabs to my rib cage and my ego would crumble in pain.

Knock Out!

Change is a winner.

Change = One. Mia = Zero.

Chapter 6

For some reason, I woke up the next morning rejuvenated and ready to begin the day. I stood in front of my mirror, wearing a camisole and a black pencil skirt, and thought about my semi-fight with Charles the night before. I ran my hand over my stomach and wondered when and if I would ever be ready to give Charles the family he so desperately desired to have. It wasn't that I didn't want more children, but the thought of giving up the little bit of freedom I currently had was, just short of, petrifying.

How could I tell Charles that I wanted him around, I wanted to love him and I wanted all of him, but that I couldn't bear to think about giving him a part of me that he yearned for?

"Ma, are you ready?" Brandi said sticking her head into my door and staring at me for a minute.

"In a second." I said, not taking my eyes off of my image in the full-length mirror.

Remembering the importance of the day, I spun around and faced Brandi and raised my eyebrow in suspicion.

"You sure are excited to get to school this morning; what's the rush?" I asked plastering a smile on my face.

Brandi shrugged her shoulders and jumped on my bed and lay back against the plush pillows as she smirked.

"I'm just ready to get the day over with, I guess." She responded nonchalantly.

"Let me see what you're wearing." I said reaching for my jacket and slipping it on.

Brandi stood up and smoothed out her burnt orange, roomy tunic that she was sporting, along with a cute pair of jeans and matching flat shoes. Her hair was bone straight and parted down the middle and she had smoothed her fingers through it effortlessly to give it that care-free look. I'd always wondered where Brandi had gotten her thick, long, luscious hair from. When she was growing it out, at one point, it had reached to the middle of her back. I loved the look of her jet black hair against her deep chocolate skin. That morning she looked more beautiful than I had ever seen her before. The pregnancy glow was definitely in full bloom and very becoming on her.

"You look really cute, honey." I said walking towards her and placing my hand, nervously, on her stomach.

"Dressing with this is not fun at all." Brandi said pointing to her stomach.

I wanted to say something about Brandi referring to her child as "this", but I decided to leave that part of the conversation alone.

We got into my silver Range Rover and headed towards Brandi's school, Chamberlain High school, as she held her oversized purse directly on top of her baby bump and sighed. I wasn't sure if she was feeling anxious, knowing she had to face a school that had no idea she was pregnant, or if she was actually excited about the social aspect of school.

"Are you feeling okay? You know, if you get sick, just call me and either Charles or I will come and get you." I said keeping my eyes on the school, which was coming up on the right.

"I know." Brandi said sitting up in her seat and fixing her shirt as she grinned at the school.

Sometimes, I thought, Brandi enjoyed school way too much for a teenager. I'd heard so many different horror stories about teens *hating* going to school, and here was my daughter, practically begging to walk through the halls. I knew part of it was so that she could socialize and be with her friends, but another part of it had to do with her genuine love for education.

I pulled towards the front of the school and slowed the truck down and threw the gear into park. Normally, I would just drop her off, while the car was still rolling and blow her a kiss as she jumped out of the car and joined her group of friends who awaited - her arrival, but today was different. We both sat still, waiting on the other one to speak first.

"If anyone asks you anything, tell them to call me." I said looking at her in a serious manner.

"Ma, how would they even know? You, Charles and Trina are the only people who know." She turned her back to me as she undid her seat belt and waved to a couple of people who passed by the window.

Ebonee Monique

"I know, I'm just saying." I sighed an over protective exhale, not wanting Brandi to leave my truck. Something in the pit of my stomach didn't feel right. I wasn't sure if it was the soup from the night before or mother's intuition. I hoped it wasn't the latter.

"Everything will be okay, ma." Brandi slightly laughed as she leaned over and hugged me tightly.

For some reason I felt like Brandi was five-years-old, all over again, and starting Kindergarten. I hugged her petite body tightly and prayed to myself that she would have a productive, wonderful day.

Brandi pulled away and looked at me closely and smiled before opening her door and bolting out towards her circle of friends who seemed to look her up and down, as they normally did, to check out the threads she was wearing for the day.

I checked my rearview mirror, and prepared to pull out into the stream of other parents who were dropping their children off, when I remembered Brandi's doctor appointment had been scheduled for 12:30 p.m. that afternoon.

I honked my horn summonsing Brandi to come back to the car. Letting my window down, I leaned over the seat and watched as Brandi and Katrina approached the car with smiles on their faces.

"Bran, remember I'll be here at noon to pick you up for your doctor's appointment." I said quietly as Brandi nodded her head.

"Right."

Katrina leaned into my car window and widened her eyes and smirked slyly.

"So y'all getting a sonogram and everything at this appointment?" She a bit too loud for comfort and Brandi and I looked at her like she was psychotic.

Katrina stared back at us until Brandi rolled her eyes at her friend.

Like a light bulb had gone off in her head, Katrina dropped her mouth open widely and covered it with her hands. In that moment, I wanted to strangle that little girl.

"My bad, Brandi; I totally forgot. I'm just so happy for you!" Katrina said softly as she leaned into the car, away from the crowd.

Blitz

"Plus no one heard me." She said pointing to the crowd of girls who looked to be gawking at a group of guys who were passing by.

I ignored Katrina and looked back at Brandi, who was rightly aggravated, and asked her directly. "Are you okay?"

"I'm fine mommy. I'll see you at noon." She walked away leaving Katrina standing at the car alone.

Before Katrina could walk away and follow behind her leader, I called her name and directed her to walk around to the driver's side window.

"Yes ma'am." Katrina said nervously as she played with her chipped nail polish.

"Right now, your best friend needs you to be a *best* friend to her. She needs you now more than ever, Trina. Be there for her!" I looked Katrina right in the eyes, with no smirk or smile anywhere in sight.

"This might all be exciting to you, but Brandi is juggling a lot and she really doesn't need any additional stress, so just remember that before letting your lips get too loose."

Katrina didn't respond to me or even acknowledge that she'd been listening to me at all. Her reaction was just to somewhat roll her eyes and walk away.

I would have been surprised at her reaction, had it not been for my previous encounters with Katrina's bad attitude. She was a nice enough girl, just like her mother, but if I had my choice of friends for my daughter, Katrina would not have made the list.

There had been the times when Brandi and Katrina would fight and, somehow, the whole school would turn on Brandi because of Katrina's manipulation and skewed version of the events. Still, Brandi cherished the friendship she had with Katrina and refused to see the bad in her. I, on the other hand, couldn't trust anything the little girl did or said to me. She'd lied to me, on numerous occasions, about her mother giving her permission to go somewhere with us, only to find out later that her mother was pissed off at me for "kidnapping" her daughter. I knew how much Katrina looked up to Brandi and desired to be like her and I could tell from the day Katrina entered Brandi's life to now, that she'd adapted every part of Brandi's style and personality. Anything that Brandi liked, Katrina liked; anything that Brandi wanted, Katrina wanted. I wasn't sure what the underlying competition was all about, but since Brandi was able to overlook it, so was I. Katrina was skinny; almost skeleton skinny with a deep cinnamon skin tone, complete with dark acne scars, big-bug eyes and a slight overbite. Her hair always stayed in a gelled down ponytail, with a bunch of scrunches holding the horse hair in place while her wardrobe wasn't as exclusive or extensive as Brandi's. Katrina tried to hang with Brandi and her upper class counterparts, but she always fell a little short. Katrina's parents had been prominent in Tampa for a period of time, but after Katrina's mother and father divorced, leaving them little more than a house and a car, Katrina had to rely on Brandi to let her borrow the hottest fashions, in order to keep up. It wasn't something I was proud of allowing Brandi to do, but I also didn't know how to approach Katrina's mother about it; so I left it alone.

I rolled my window up and watched, in silence, as Brandi and Katrina laughed with one another and walked into the school. I smelled 'drama' looming in the air, even to my unsuspecting daughter.

I wondered what stories Brandi would have to tell me when I picked her up, because, as I drove away, the funny feeling in the pit of my stomach became more and more prominent; this time I knew it was a sign that something was about to happen.

****

I arrived at work and smiled as Cecil greeted me with a cup of gourmet coffee and a crumb cake. It wasn't a requirement of his job, but he was definitely learning quickly.

"How was your weekend?" He asked, taking a seat across from my desk as I put my things away.

Minutes went by, as I tried to think of something to say to answer his question. Normally I would have a full-length story about what Charles, Mia and I had done and what our plans were for the upcoming weekend. The past weekend, however, didn't afford me the luxury of some entertaining story. All I had was that I was about to be a grandmother and my fourteen- year old daughter was about to be a mother. And that was a piece of juicy gossip I was not prepared to share.

I shrugged my shoulders as I looked back at Cecil who had his eyebrows raised.

"It was…interesting." I said taking a seat and turning on my computer.

I took a sip of the coffee and broke off a piece of the crumb cake and ate it slowly.

"What'd you do?" He inquired.

"Nothing much, honey." I smiled politely as I danced around his questions and typed my password to log onto the computer.

"What about you?" I asked while I leaned back in my leather chair acting as though I was oblivious to his natural curiosity.

"I started looking for my own place." He said with a proud grin on his face for having joined the realm of making adult choices and decisions.

"Really? What prompted that?"

"I figure, if I have my own car note, now, I can handle paying my own rent. Plus mom's said she wants me out in six months." He laughed loudly as he rubbed his hair.

"Well, you know she means well. It's time for you to make your own place in this world, obtain your own life; see the real world."

"Right; I found this place on Waters Avenue that looks pretty nice. I was thinking about getting a two-bedroom place, only because you never know…I could start a family soon or something. It's better to be prepared." He said averting his eyes away from mine.

I sat back and crossed my arms across my chest and stared at Cecil before speaking.

"A family? Cecil, you're only nineteen; you have your whole life ahead of you. Why do you want to tie yourself down with a family?" I asked as I burrowed my brows suspiciously in his direction.

"I'm not saying I'm going out actively looking to start a family, but if it happens, it happens and I won't fight it. Especially if it's with someone that I care about." He said slowly as he looked away from me.

The office phone began ringing and Cecil darted out to answer it, leaving me and the air around us filled with confusion. I felt horrible even thinking about it, but was there a possibility for Cecil and Brandi to have slept together? To me, anything was possible. I hadn't even known Brandi was having sex, so I couldn't help but weigh the possibility that she and Cecil had slept together.

No, I thought as I shook my head, Cecil wouldn't risk his job by sleeping with my underage daughter. Or would he? Maybe he knew that if Brandi did get pregnant by him, I wouldn't fire him because I would know he needed work. My mind was playing all kinds of tricks on me with the scenarios it was presenting. Before I could think of another one, Cecil stuck his head in and motioned for me to pick the phone up.

"It's Mr. Donaldson on line one,"

I shook myself out of the daydream and picked up the line with a smile on my face.

"Good morning, this is Mia." I said as cheerily as possible.

"Mia, good morning beautiful." Mr. Donaldson said, "I thought we had a business lunch this weekend. What happened? You stood me up."

I slapped my forehead and silently cursed myself for forgetting my extremely important meeting with the city Commissioner who was considering selling his eight bedroom six bath mansion through me.

"I'm so sorry, Lee." I said hoping my kindness would be taken into account.

"It's perfectly fine; I had an unexpected emergency with one of my children, so I would have had to bail anyway." He joked as he laughed in a husky tone.

Lee Donaldson was one of the most well-known City Commissioners in Tampa and he had the reputation and money to make sure it stayed that way. After winning a lawsuit against a major amusement park due to a city police officer unfairly assaulting him, Lee had more money than he knew what to do with. I'd seen Lee around, for years, at various fundraiser functions that the City of Tampa hosted, but we were never properly introduced. Women seemed to flock to him, although he was nowhere near as handsome or charming as they wanted to believe. He was close to 50 and had salt and pepper hair that carried down into his perfectly trimmed moustache. In a lot of ways, he reminded me of *Steve Harvey*, with his dress, attitude and impeccable style and, just like *Steve*, he'd been married three times and was currently going through divorce number three. He had light chocolate brown skin, with a beautiful smile and delicious looking lips that would make any woman's mouth water.

"Whew!" I said playfully as I wiped my brow of sweat.

"I just wanted to play around with you, girl." He said still laughing,

"That wasn't funny, Lee."

"It was to me! I bet you were thinking about ways to make it up to me, huh?"

I shrugged my shoulders, like Lee could see me through the phone, and tried to keep my professional demeanor intact.

"We can definitely re-schedule the meeting and get together whenever you'd like." I replied clearing my throat.

Whenever I talked to Lee, I felt like he thought there was something between us, but I never allowed myself to go any further than a friendly flirtatious comment. I loved Charles with everything I had within me; Lee was just an *after-thought,* nothing more and nothing less.

"Great. I'm free this afternoon at noon; is that good with you?"

"It's perfect..." I started, just as I remembered Brandi's doctor appointment.

"Actually, I have to take my daughter to the doctor at 12:30, so maybe we can do it another time?" I said quickly, hoping Lee would be accommodating.

"Mia..." He said sounding stern "I really want to get this house sold as soon possible and you've been highly recommended by a number of my associates." He started and then paused, as if he was reflecting on something.

I took this as my chance to jump in and defend myself. I knew I was asking a lot for a customer to reschedule an appointment because of my personal excuses; but I needed the leeway. Normally, I never ran any personal errands, especially when I had a client meeting, nor had I routinely stood a client up; but with everything I had going on, I'd allowed myself to slip outside my norm.

"I really apologize for this, Lee. We, here at Robinson Realty, take pride in our customer satisfaction and I just want to make sure you have my undivided attention..." I said swallowing a dry lump of pride and trying to sound humble.

"And I want *your* undivided attention as well." He said deviously. "And that's why; I'm following your lead. If you want to meet tonight, tomorrow night or, hell, next weekend in Paris, I'll do what you say."

"We don't need to travel to Paris to talk about your property here in Tampa." I laughed.

"But we *could* take a separate trip there, sometime, if you'd like."

I was taken aback by Lee's forwardness and ignored his statement completely.

"So, can you meet tomorrow at 8:30 p.m. at the Columbia Restaurant in Ybor? I know the owner, Richard Gonzmart, and I can call and place some reservations." I said as I name-dropped.

"That sounds wonderful." Lee replied, "But don't forget my offer."

"Have a good day, Mr. Donaldson." I said as Cecil approached my door and stood with a file in his hand.

"Mrs. Chambers just called and said that she'd like to schedule a meeting to go over some of the properties that you went over with her. She said she's had a chance to talk with her husband and they have their favorite three picked out." Cecil seemed excited about delivering the news.

"Should I schedule a 1:00 p.m. with her?" He pulled out a pad and started jotting down notes.

I swirled my mouse around and stared at the fifty e-mail messages that I had to open and respond to and I sighed.

"Huh? Oh, no. I have to take Brandi to the doctor at 12:30, so clear my schedule from 11:45 until about 2:00 p.m." I said not taking my eyes off of messages from satisfied clients who were sending me pictures of their decorated homes.

Cecil stared at his notepad for a second before lifting his head up. He hesitated before speaking, but finally spit out what was on his mind.

"Is everything okay with her?" He asked in an off-handed kind of way.

"Who?" I said not remembering my previous comment to him.

"Brandi. Is everything okay with her?"

I glanced around the computer at the nervous kid and nodded my head.

Blitz

"Everything's fine. Why do you ask?"

"No reason. No reason at all." We both knew he was lying.

I acted like I was making a call and Cecil headed back towards his desk to file some information away and answer the phone, which was ringing non-stop.

"It's Charles on line four." Cecil announced through the intercom system.

I smiled and picked the phone up. I'd only been without him for a few hours, but I still missed his voice.

"Hey there handsome." I sweetly stroked my man's awaiting ears.

"What time was Brandi's appointment?" He asked without greeting me back.

"Twelve thirty; why? Were you planning on coming?" I said, sensing a shift in his normally jovial attitude.

"I *was*. Is that a problem?"

"I didn't say that, Charles."

"Fine. I'll see you at Doctor Valdez's office." He said hanging the phone up.

There were days when, without warning, Charles would have a major chip on his shoulder that no one in the world could soothe. He'd bitch, moan, scream and shout about nothing in particular until he felt better. I hoped this was one of those days and he wasn't still hung up on our conversation from the night before.

I took a deep breath and hung the phone up. All I needed was yet another issue to deal with, I thought, as I sorted through my e-mail.

All I need was another heavy item on my emotional plate. I felt like I had eaten from the biggest buffet of emotions and I was fuller than I'd ever been.

****

"Hey Ms. Robinson!" A perky, high-pitched voice echoed as I walked down the hallways of Brandi's high school.

"Bree?" I said astonished at how beautiful she was.

She had butterscotch skin, wide-set eyes, and her short hair was bumped lightly hitting the nape of her neck. She had the deepest dimples I'd ever seen and was dressed as neatly as I remembered.

Breeann Thompson-or Bree as we called her- had been Brandi's best friend from Kindergarten on through to the sixth grade. They were inseparable. After she and Brandi graduated from elementary to middle school, Brandi started hanging out with the "cooler" crowd and the shy Bree pretty much stayed to herself. The two of them remained close friends, but they'd never regained the bond that they once shared when they were younger. Breeann's family consisted of her mother and father and seven old brothers, who were all successful in their fields. One was a doctor, the other was an attorney, one worked in advertising and one of them was the Superintendent for the Hillsborough County School Board. I hadn't seen Bree for a couple of years; so today was a pleasant surprise.

"Yes!" She said squealing as she walked towards me and continued grinning.

"Come here and give me a hug, girl." I bent down to embrace the tiny little girl.

The two of us walked, and caught up on old times, as I headed towards the front office to sign Brandi out.

"You make sure to tell your mother and father that I said we *have* to get together for dinner one evening, okay?" I said as I scribbled Brandi's name on the sign-out sheet.

Bree excitedly nodded her head and clasped a book in her hands as she stared at me.

"That'd be great. I don't think I've been to your house in so long." She smiled politely.

One of the office runners sped out of the room, with Brandi's blue excuse pass in his hand, and told me he'd be back with her in a second.

Bree stood in front of me, her smile slowly fading, and rocked from side to side before dropping her head.

"I heard about Brandi..." She said softly, like she didn't want anyone to hear us.

My face grew flushed and hot as I wiped my forehead of sweat buildup.

"You heard what about Brandi?"

"Oh wait...you don't know? You...never mind." She said waving her hands in the air as she nervously laughed.

"Bree, what are you talking about?"

Realizing I was serious, Bree opened up.

Blitz

"I heard a rumor that she was pregnant and going to have her sonogram done today." She said leaning in towards me.

I don't know if I made any faces or sounds, but my body was shaking from the inside out. How in the hell had Bree, someone who wasn't deep within Brandi's circle, found out about the pregnancy?

"Bree, where did you hear that?"

"I heard some girls talking in the library about it. They said that Brandi thought about having an abortion but that you were making her have it and…" Bree said as if she felt free by letting it all out.

"Stop." I said holding my hand up. "Who is spreading this?"

"I don't know, Ms. Robinson." She said shrugging her shoulders.

As Brandi rounded the corner, I took one look at her red, puffy eyes and swollen face, and I could tell that my prayer for a drama-free day had not been answered.

****

We sat in Dr. Valdez's office quietly as we waited on Brandi's name to be called.

"How do you think everyone found out?" I asked, knowing the culprit but wanting Brandi to say it out loud.

A few tears escaped her eyes and she shook her head over and over.

"I only told Katrina, ma. I swear. But she told me she wouldn't tell anyone and…I believe her." She said sniffling.

Brandi described how one whisper turned into another, which then turned into a huge discussion between everyone in the school. She didn't know for sure if the news had reached Andrew yet or not, but she was pretty positive that it had.

"I feel so stupid." Brandi said clasping her hands together and placing them in her lap.

A young nurse came out with a clip board in hand and called Brandi's name, "Brandi Robinson!"

"Right here." I said pulling Brandi's hand towards the open door.

Charles was running late and I just hoped that he would hurry up so that we could get everything over with.

Ebonee Monique

"Why don't you change into this, and the doctor will be right in to see you." The Hispanic nurse said, in her light accent, as she handed Brandi a white paper medical dress.

I took a seat in one of the chairs and crossed my legs and Brandi stared at me like I was loony.

"Ma, can you excuse me while I get dressed?" She said putting her small purse on the counter.

I stared back at her, to find out if she was serious, and once she didn't budge I stood up and chuckled.

"Brandi I've seen everything you have."

"So? I still want to get dressed by myself; I'm not a baby."

I wanted to, so badly, tell her that she *was* a baby; my baby. But I inhaled and exited the examination room just as Charles was asking a nurse where we were.

"Hey there." I smiled widely extending my arms for a much needed hug.

"Where's Brandi?" He replied patting my back.

"In the room dressing; she told me she needed her privacy." I laughed.

Charles didn't even look me in my eyes; instead he focused on his phone, which seemed to engulf his attention as he typed rapidly.

"Charles?" I said softly as I pulled him away from the door and towards the empty hallway.

"What?" He asked, irritated by my interruption.

"What's   wrong   with   you?"

"What's wrong with me? What's wrong with me, Mia?" He repeated.

"Yeah, you're acting like something is bothering you and I just want to know what it is." I responded in a defensive manner.

"You *know* what it is, but you don't want to deal with it right now, right?"

"Oh gosh, here we go again. Is this about the marriage and family little thing?" I asked rolling my eyes back into my head.

Charles didn't say anything; he just looked at me with a blank stare and sucked his teeth in irritation.

"I think we should just…" I started, not sure of where I was going with my statement.

Blitz

"I'm done letting you decide what *we're* going to do, Mia...calling my wish for a wife and family a *'little thing'*." you've shown me exactly what you feel about us. Charles placed his *Blackberry* back into its holder on his hip.

"You knew coming into this, that I was looking for a woman who wanted to be my wife and have my children. But now, when the time comes to actually live up to what I'm asking from you, you come up with every excuse in the fucking book." His tone was hushed, yet filled with anger.

"I'm   not   making   excuses   I'm...."
"I'm not done talking." He said harshly

"I'm over and done with letting you ruin a perfectly good relationship because you don't want to live up to your end of the bargain. If you don't want to marry me and have my child, fine, someone else will."

"What are you saying?" I said jerking my head back. I knew Charles was and had been upset about the topic for a very long time, but I didn't think it was enough for him to call things off between us; definitely not like in such an abrupt manner.

"I'm saying you don't want all of me. You want *some* of me, and only when you want me. Everything is according to your need. Well, I need *all* of you, but you're nowhere to be found. All that stops here Mia! It's been almost six years and I'm tired of trying to *make* you see that I'm not Branson. I'm not him and I shouldn't have to pay for his fuck-ups." He said shrugging his shoulders.

"Charles I..."

"Mom, dad, they're ready." Brandi said sticking her head out and quickly popping it back in.

Charles made his way towards the door and I stuck my hand out and jerked his body as hard as I could.

"Don't just walk away from me like that; we've got to talk about this."

"We can talk about this later, remember?" He mocked me as he removed my hand from his arm and walked into the examination room, leaving me alone in a room full of people.
****

"Why is dad meeting us at Andrew's house?" Brandi asked me as I zipped up the back of her dress.

"Because he had some business deals to work out." I lied, not wanting her to worry about *our* issues.

Ebonee Monique

I walked toward my mirror and made sure my makeup and hair looked okay. My black slacks and black and white shirt fit my stressed out body perfectly.

"Do I have to take these pills with food?" Brandi said holding up the big white bottle of pre-natal vitamins that the doctor had prescribed for her to take.

"That would probably be a good idea, but go eat some crackers or something and take it before we get to Andrew's house." I said fixing the collar on my shirt.

Dr. Valdez had confirmed what Charles, Brandi and I already knew. Brandi was, indeed, with child. Dr. Valdez said that based off of Brandi's information, period dates, date of intercourse, etc., that she was about thirteen weeks pregnant. As our fears were verified, Charles and I spoke briefly about how we'd handle Brandi's necessary doctors' appointments.

I turned and watched Brandi twist out of the room and exhaled. I still hadn't thought about a game plan, or even a strategy for telling the Whittaker's that their seventeen-year-old son was about to become a father in six months. I didn't like not being prepared for things like this; but, then again, I'd been blindsided by the news myself. In my head, I hoped that the Whittaker's would take the news, process it and allow it to sink in. In a perfect world, I thought to myself as I picked up a pair of pearl earrings, we would all embrace this sudden change with open hearts and minds. But I was having a hard enough time opening my eyes to see that my *baby* was going to be a mother herself. As I checked myself out, again, I thought about Charles. Was he really serious and our relationship was over?

No, he couldn't have been serious, I thought.

How could he just up and throw away six years of love and devotion because of one silly argument? Truth be told, while his speech in Dr. Valdez's office had pissed me off, I hadn't thought much more of it since then. See, Charles and I were like that; that was our *thing*. We both loved passionately and endlessly, which was why I knew he couldn't have been telling the truth. He said he'd love me forever, so how could he just walk away? I made a mental note to make my way to Charles' house later that night, so we could fully discuss the situation. With everything else on my plate why was Charles doing this *now*? I knew it had a lot, if not everything, to do with Brandi's pregnancy. The fact that our fourteen-year-old daughter was starting a family before we were must've been the straw that broke the camel or, in this case, the Defensive End's back.

"You look cute, ma." Brandi said reappearing in my room with a glass of water in her hand.

I smirked and gave her the once over. "You too." I smiled.

Brandi was sporting a black and red wrap dress and another pair of flats that coordinated perfectly with the dress. Her silver hoops and accessories, paired with her perfectly styled bun, which sat at the back of her head, was impressive.

"You ready?" I asked as I turned to pick up my purse off the bed.

"I guess."

Brandi had expressed all kinds of hesitancy about telling Andrew that she was pregnant and I understood her nervousness. Shoot, I was Branson's *wife* when I got pregnant with Brandi and had still been worried about telling him the news. Of course, he took it wonderfully, but for two or three weeks I was completely on edge.

Our ride, over to the Whittaker's, was filled with sounds of *R.Kelly* saying he believed he could fly. Brandi didn't say much to me and neither did I to her; but as we turned into Andrew's neighborhood, she began twiddling her thumbs.

"Are you okay?" I asked, knowing she wasn't.

She looked over at me, shook her head and returned her glance outside of the window. I wondered what was going through her mind as I approached their driveway and my cell phone rang.

"Is their address 2415 or 2615?" Charles asked.

"2415. We just pulled up." I said looking around at my surroundings.

"Okay, I'm right behind you." He said as he flashed his lights at the car.

"I see you..." I began before Charles hung up the phone in my ear.

Looking at the phone, I thought a couple of horrible things about Charles and immediately turned to face Brandi.

"You ready?" I asked rubbing her hands softly.

"I don't want to do this. We don't have to tell him, do we?"

Ebonee Monique

I widened my eyes, in confusion, as Brandi continued giving her rationale.

"It's not like we need their money, right? We have our own; we can raise the baby, ma."

I laughed a little bit at Brandi's assumption that my money was *her* money.

"Brandi, honey *you* don't have any money. Now, I said I'd help you out with this baby but that doesn't mean I'm going to fully take care of you. This is *your* child. You need to find a way to support the two of you, and your child's father plays into that equation." I said as I stared at her seriously.

"Fine. I'll get a job and I'll take care of the baby myself. We don't need Andrew." She said getting snappy with me.

"I never said I wouldn't *help*, honey, but this is both of your responsibilities. I'm sure Andrew's family will agree that he needs to step up to the plate and do the right thing."

"I don't think we need to tell him. I can do it by myself." She said shrugging her shoulders. "You did it; so can I."

I dropped my shoulders and shook my head at the things; Brandi had no idea what I'd gone through to provide for her when she was a child. It had never been easy and I'd never taken the easy road; but all she saw was the money, the house, the cars and the clothes. She was clueless to just how hard raising a baby alone could be.

"It was hard, Brandi; really, really hard." I sighed remembering the nights where all we had to eat was stale bread and peanut butter. Those nights, I cried myself to sleep at the life, or lack thereof, that I was giving my daughter. But, as a child, Brandi didn't understand the concept of being poor. She got toys for Christmas, through the *Toys for Tots* program, and had pretty cool clothes, donated from churches or bought from *Goodwill*, and had trendy sneakers, which I'd manage to negotiate from flea markets vendors. She didn't know the struggle I'd gone through to give her a normal life on a poverty budget.

"I can do it, ma. I know I can." She said finally looking over to me.

Blitz

"I'm not saying you can't because if you *have* to, I know you can. But, this *is* Andrew's child too; he deserves the right to know about his child, don't you think?"

"Not the way he's treated me. No."

"See, this is where being a parent becomes tricky. You have to put aside your personal feelings and do what's best for your child; regardless of how you feel about the other person."

Brandi rolled her eyes and sucked her teeth before replying.

"Like you did with Branson?"

She had me there. As Brandi's parent, I had allowed a portion of my personal feelings, toward Branson, to affect my decision in keeping her away from him. But, in my defense, I'd also done what I felt was best for my child; I made no apologies for that.

Brandi sat with her arms crossed and pouted as I turned the car off and got out. Before I closed the door, I stuck my head in and raised my eyebrows.

"Either way it goes they're finding out tonight. You can either tell them yourself, like a woman, or you can let Charles and I do your dirty work."

Brandi looked over at me; rolled her eyes, again, and opened her car door.

"Hey Bran." Charles said as he was greeted with a cold stare.

"What's your problem, girl?" He asked as he pulled her towards him.

She looked over at me and replied through her pursed lips, "Nothing."

I joined the two of them, on the other side of the car, and sighed as I looked at the comfortable size house we were in front of.

We got to the door, rang the bell and within seconds Mrs. Whittaker, a beautiful former model, was at the door with a wide grin on her face.

"Why hello!" She said wiping her hands on her red and white checkered apron.

Taking one look at her was like looking back at an old 50's movie, where the mother stayed home and baked pies, cookies and bread all day waiting for the father and son to get home. Something about Teresa Whittaker was reminiscent of

Ebonee Monique

that. She was beautiful too; a little too beautiful for my taste. Where I saw myself as completely flawed and just a tad cute, Teresa Whittaker was drop-dead gorgeous to me. She had the highest cheekbones I'd ever seen, the smoothest caramel skin, long flowing hair that fell just below her shoulders and a megawatt smile that I would've killed for. If you glanced quickly at her, you might have gotten her confused with actress *Lynn Whitfield.* Yes, she was just *that* beautiful.

"Hello Mrs. Whittaker." Brandi said leaning in for a hug.

"Teresa." I said leaning from one side and then to the other, pecking both of her cheeks lightly with my lips.

"Mia, you look wonderful." She said genuinely.

"And you remember my friend Charles, right?"

"Of course; Charles and I go *way* back." Teresa smiled broadly.

I wasn't sure what "*go way back*" meant, but I was pretty sure that it required an explanation at another time.

Charles and Teresa hugged and chatted, while Brandi and I made our way into the large living room and took a seat on one of the couches. I glanced around the room, taking in the beautiful Italian tile that I'd seen in interior decorator magazines I'd scoured when I'd toyed with the idea of redecorating my home. I admired the oversized grandfather clock that sat directly across from us as it quietly ticked to, what seemed, like the exact speed of my heartbeat. The Whittaker's had immaculate taste and it was shown in every square inch of their home; from the tile, to the furniture, right on down to the expensive Faberge eggs that sat on their end tables.

"My husband should be down in about 5 minutes, he just needed to change into some comfortable clothes." Teresa said kindly "Would you all like anything to drink?"

"I think we're good." Charles said.

All three of us sat there, in silence, as Teresa retreated towards the stairs and disappeared.

"Dad, what did she mean y'all went way *back*?" Brandi asked breaking the silence, as a grin appeared on her face.

I turned to catch Charles laughing and nodding his head, not making eye contact with me, and waited for the answer.

"We used to date in college; long before she was Mrs. Whittaker." He revealed. "That was a long time ago."

I wasn't upset, so much, but I was a little taken aback that Charles had never told me that Brandi's boyfriend's mother had, at one time, been his girlfriend-even if it was in college.

"I didn't know you knew Teresa like *that*." I said as I put a fake smile on my face.

"There are a lot of things we don't know about each other, right?" Charles shot back, with the same fake smile on his face.

In the nick of time, my cell phone began buzzing, and I looked at Charles and rolled my eyes. I knew it was childish to be mad at him for something that had happened years ago, but I didn't care; I was upset.

"Hey Lee." I said loudly, so Charles would know I was still being contacted by other men, as I stood up and went to the other end of the room.

I could feel Charles' eyes all over me and something about it turned me on. Knowing that Charles was upset about another man contacting me made something click inside of me; it made me feel wanted.

I wasn't sure if it was a coincidence or a sign, that Lee had called at the time he had. Whatever it was, I was grateful.

"Hey, there." He replied.

"I'm getting ready to step into a meeting; is there anything you need?"

"I just wanted to call and confirm our dinner date for tomorrow." He playfully responded. I had to give it to the man, he was persistent.

"That's my job; I'm supposed to confirm our dates." I said loud enough for Charles to hear me.

"Well, I thought I'd make your job a little easier."

"Why thank you," I giggled playfully knowing, full-well, the idea Charles was getting.

"And yes, we are confirmed for our dinner date at Columbia tomorrow night at 8:30."

"I'll see you tomorrow." He said slowing down.

"And make sure you wear your dancing shoes."

"I don't know what dancing shoes are but I'll wear something comfortable." I said smiling before I hung up and headed back towards the couch.

Ebonee Monique

"Who was that?" Brandi asked, suspiciously raising one eyebrow.

"A client." I said sticking my phone back into my purse.

"So, you're having dates with your clients now?" Brandi asked with attitude.

"Not that I have to answer to you but, yes. I do have occasional dinner meetings with my clients."

"But you said dinner *date*, ma." Brandi countered.

"I meant meeting, then. That was my mistake."

Charles sat back in the chair and looked in the opposite direction and nodded his head to whatever was running through his mind.

"Good evening, all." Mr. Whittaker emerged from the stairs with Mrs. Whittaker close behind him.

Leonard Whittaker was older than all three of the adults in the room. He was in his mid-sixties and not much of a looker, either. With his gapped teeth, bulging belly and beady eyes, I didn't trust him at all. When I'd see the two of them out at events, I often wondered how he attracted such a kind-spirited, beautiful woman like Teresa, then I'd see the Bentley that he drove and reality would slap me in the face.

"Why don't we go into the dining room?" Teresa smiled as she directed us all to the conservatively decorated room.

A crystal chandelier hung from the ceiling and shined perfectly as the light switch was turned on.

"This is a beautiful room, Teresa." I said taking a seat next to Charles at the table.

On one side there was me, Charles and Brandi; opposite us was Teresa and Leonard, along with an empty chair where I assumed Andrew would be sitting.

"I'm so glad you all came over for dinner; we haven't seen Brandi in so long." Teresa said as she stood up from the table and headed towards the kitchen.

Teresa set the table and placed a full plate, with chicken, mashed potatoes and broccoli, in front of every seat, except the vacant one where Andrew was supposed to sit.

"I'm so sorry Andy couldn't be here tonight. He had a group meeting for one his classes." Teresa said taking a seat and looking at the three of us and our shocked faces.

Blitz

Charles was the first to speak.

"We were kind of hoping to have all of you here; Andrew included."

"Is something wrong?" Leonard said wiping his mouth after drinking from his glass of water.

"We just needed everyone here, that's all." I said trying to think of something else to say.

I could see the fear slowly creeping over both of their faces as they ran the possible worse-case scenarios through their minds.

"Since Andrew can't be here tonight, why don't you just tell us whatever it is you need to tell us?" Leonard said, sounding as if he was getting agitated with our presence.

"Brandi..." I said looking over at her, as she dropped her head and then quickly picked it up.

"Um..." She said clearing her throat "I'm pregnant."

Teresa dropped her jaw and quickly covered it up, with her perfectly manicured hands, while Leonard sat back in his chair and threw his napkin on top of his food.

"We didn't want to tell you over the phone or through e-mail; we wanted everyone to sit down and figure out a plan of action..." I began before Leonard cut me off.

"What do you mean a plan of action? Are you trying to tell me this is my *son's* baby?" Leonard said squinting his eyes in our direction.

"Yes. He's the only boy I've ever been with, sir." Brandi said speaking up. I could tell she was thrown off by him insinuating that Andrew wasn't the father.

Teresa just sat there, with her hand still over her mouth, with tears starting to form in her eyes.

I could see the fumes coming from Leonard's balding head and the anger in all of his actions as he stood up and walked towards a telephone in the next room. He punched a couple of numbers and tapped his foot nervously before the person on the other line answered.

"Andrew, get your ass home NOW!" He screamed, slamming the phone down to its cradle before rejoining us at the table.

Brandi had her head dropped and Charles could sense that things weren't going the way any of us had planned. We didn't think they'd be thrilled about the news, but Leonard was one step away from being overly irate. I knew Brandi didn't need to hear the things he was going to say.

"So you're...you're keeping it?" Leonard asked finally sitting back down at the table. He nervously clasped his hands together as he strained to keep his attention on Brandi.

"Yes, she's keeping it." I interjected; horrified that he would even suggest that my daughter have an abortion.

"She and Andrew created this child and they should take responsibility for it."

In less than five minutes, Andrew came bounding through the door with panic smeared all over his handsome face. He took one look at Brandi and shook his head as he looked over in disgust.

"What kind of lie did she tell you?" He said ignoring Charles and I sitting at the table.

"Is what she's saying true? Is this your child?" Teresa said carefully as she wiped a tear from her eye.

I knew the fear and the horror that was running through their minds; I'd been there. I knew the disappointment, the disbelief and the anger that had to be shooting through their veins. Everything they'd provided for their son and, still, he had fallen into this life-altering situation.

"No mother! She's a liar." He said not looking at Brandi "I've never even slept with this girl; I'm a virgin."

Brandi's eyes grew large as she stared at the boy she loved, and listened to the things he was saying.

"Andrew, why are you lying? You know you took my virginity." Brandi said softly, as if she didn't want to get Andrew in any further trouble.

"I've never been with anyone else but you."

"That's a damn lie." He said not caring about the vulgarities spewing from his mouth.

"You know you were sleeping with half the guys in the school and now you want to pin that kid on me because you know how rich my family is."

I couldn't tell if the tears, streaming down Brandi's cheeks, were from pain, hurt or disbelief.

"My mom and dad have more money than both of your parents; why would I need your money?" Brandi asked as her voice cracked. "You told me that you'd always love me; that if I loved you I would have sex with you."

Blitz

"You're a liar. I never touched you, Brandi. I can find at least five guys in school who have hit that, dad. I bet one of them is the father." He said turning to his father.

Charles and I were so stunned at the things that were being said to Brandi that we didn't know what to do, but I could see Charles revving up to defend his daughter.

"Andrew…" Brandi whined as she stood up from the table "Why are you lying? This is your baby and I didn't do this by myself."

"You can't pin that child on me, Brandi. You know you've slept around with everyone. What about Stewart, Terrence and…oh yeah…I bet you thought I didn't know about that cat Cecil, huh?"

Charles glanced to me, I glanced at him and then we both looked at Brandi who gasped and covered her mouth and ran out of the room.

"I can't believe you!" She screamed in her retreat.

Andrew shrugged his shoulders and sat down next to his mother and gave me a challenging look.

"You should really be ashamed of yourself." I said pushing my chair away from the table.

"My son says he's not the father and I trust him on that. There are always little girls around him trying to trap him up in some way; I'm sorry your child became one of them." Leonard said matter-of-factly.

It took everything in me, including Charles holding me back, not to reach across the room and lay all kind of hands on that man. I knew my daughter and I also knew what she was capable of. If she'd been sleeping around, I would've known it…right?

"Stop it!" Teresa said loudly as she waved her arms in the air, while I tried to give Leonard a piece of my mind and hands.

"We're going to excuse ourselves right now; but Andrew, you want to be taken seriously as a man? Stand up and raise your child like one." Charles said as he pulled me away by my waist.

"That's not my baby." Andrew said defiantly.

Brandi was standing, hiding her tear-soaked face in her hands from embarrassment. Neither of us knew what to do or say, so we just wrapped our collective arms around her and hugged her tightly.

"You were right, baby; *we* can do this without him." I said as I laid my head on top of hers.

Our drive home was as silent, if not more, than our trip over. With every red light, turn and yield, I thought about everything Andrew had said. I hadn't raised Brandi to be the type of person Andrew was describing and yet, something was nagging at me about what he'd said. I hadn't brought Brandi up to be a teenage mother either, but somehow that had happened. I had to rethink everything about my child. Were there more surprises, about her that would be coming to the forefront? How had Andrew known about Cecil? To my knowledge, Andrew had never meant, seen or talked to Cecil, so how had his name been thrown in the mix? Had Brandi and Cecil really consummated their flirtatious relationship? Had I been duped right under my nose? I didn't want to discredit what my daughter was telling me but with secrets coming out left and right, what was I supposed to think? Was Brandi fooling us all into thinking that Andrew was the father and if so, why?

I glanced over at Brandi's stomach and hoped that there *was* light at the end of the tunnel in six months.

Chapter 7

The days following Brandi's admission to Andrew and his family about her pregnancy, were what one could only describe as pitiful. By the time I got home each night, Brandi was already in her bed and had been there since she'd gotten home from school. Her bed was her comforter and shield of protection against the world and all she did was cry. I had never seen someone cry so much and each night before I went to bed I tried to get a smile on her face, but nothing worked. Rose, who had agreed to help out a little more now that a new addition was joining our family, kept me updated every step of the way; whenever I couldn't be physically there, Rose was my eyes and ears.

Charles and I, on the other hand, were more distant and out of touch with each other than we had ever been. Part of me wanted to pull him to the side and say "Yes, I'll marry you; I'll have your child." But the other part of me-primarily my pride- wouldn't let it happen. In my mind, I wasn't wrong. How could I be? I'd been too busy raising my daughter, growing my business and trying to ensure that I never ended up poor again, to worry about starting a new family. Charles *was* my family. Brandi *was* my family. Why did he need more than that? Why wasn't that enough? I didn't think we needed an official marriage, piece of paper, or baby together to seal the deal. For me, the deal had been sealed the first time he called my child *his* child, or when he followed through on things he said he'd do.

"Señora, she's been crying in her room and screaming at someone on the phone." Rose said as I came through the door with my mounds of paperwork underneath my arms.

"Was it Andrew?" I quizzed, setting the papers down.

Rose shrugged her shoulders as she looked at the stairs longingly.

I had secured Lee Donaldson as a client and boy, did he have me working. Not only was I supposed to sell his beautiful home, but he'd also asked me to help him find a new resting spot. I was overwhelmed; I had three major clients that needed my immediate attention, and over twenty non-major-but still important-clients that were pretty demanding as well. I had planned on staying at work until midnight, until Rose called and said Brandi was packing a bag and that I needed to get home.

The entire way home, all I could think about was what disaster I was going to be walking into when I got home. Charles was nowhere to be found so I had to bring my work home with me, which I hated doing.

"You said she was packing a bag?" I pushed my hair behind my ear to make sure I was hearing Rose right.

"Si." Rose said looking worried. "But I talked her out of it, I think."

I made my way up to Brandi's room, and pushed open her door.

I heard soft music playing in the dimly lit room and observed white candles lit all over the room, which filled the space with a soothing Vanilla scent. Searching around Brandi's humungous room, with no luck, I finally went into the bathroom and found Brandi sitting in the bathtub filled with bubbles.

"Hey ma." Brandi said through a sigh as she lifted her head up and slowly laid it back on the padded tub pillow.

"Is everything okay? Rose told me you were packing a bag." I said taking a seat on the tub's ledge cautiously.

Through the water, I could see Brandi's hand sitting on top of her continuously growing stomach.

"I just got mad, that's all."

"Mad at who?"

"Andrew. He called and told me he was going to make my life miserable if I kept telling people I was pregnant by him."

I rolled my eyes. I couldn't believe the audacity of that little boy; still I wondered why Brandi was so damn calm.

"So where were you going?" I asked leaning over to stroke her hair.

"I don't know; I just wanted to leave and go somewhere that I couldn't bother people. I know you and dad are mad at me..."

"Honey, we're done being upset and angry. We just have to deal with this situation." I tried to sound loving as I rubbed the stray ringlets of hair out of her face.

"But, I know I'm a burden and I just wanted to…I just wanted to leave." She exhaled.

"How was school today?" I questioned as I stood up.

"Worse than the day before; but I'm not going to give Andrew the satisfaction of pushing me out of school."

"Pushing you out of school? What do you mean?" I asked spinning around to face her.

"He said his dad was passing around some petition to get me kicked out of Chamberlain for being pregnant with *his* child." She laughed calmly "Well, he didn't say the "his child" part because he's still denying everything."

As angry as I had been about the things Andrew had said about Brandi, when we'd told him was about her being pregnant, I was livid that he was trying to take away her education; all for *his* reputation. What kind of man was Leonard Whittaker anyway? It was no wonder his son had turned out to be the person he was, I thought, as I shook my head in disbelief.

"Did you see the petition?" I asked curiously.

"Bree said she saw it; didn't sign it. I didn't see it though." She said calmly.

"I can't believe him."

"I heard that some students were getting their parents to sign the petition too."

"I'm going to set up a meeting on Monday with your principal, the school board, all those parents who signed the petition and Charles and I. This has gone too far."

Brandi shrugged her shoulders. It was like none of this mattered to her; like she wasn't fazed at all that everyone was against her and her baby.

"Why are you so calm about this?" I asked.

"Because it's going to pass and Andrew will come to his senses and realize that I'm who he wants and we'll all be a family." She said with her eyes closed and a grin crept on her face.

"What?!" I yelped, allowing my voice to echo in the bathroom.

Brandi's eyes shot open as I continued.

"Why would you even want to be with him after everything he's said about and to you, Brandi?"

"It's all one big misunderstanding, ma." Brandi said waving her hands calmly in the air. "Once I talk to Stewart and Terrence and have them talk to Andrew, and tell him that I didn't sleep with them, it'll all be straightened out." She said as she smiled again. "And Andrew will love me again."

"Brandi, honey, that isn't going to straighten anything out."

"How do you know?" She shot back with a look of anger in her face.

The last thing I wanted to do was fight with her but everything she was saying sounded warped to me.

"I don't but..."

"See." She said like she'd figured out a puzzle "Trina said she was going to talk to Andrew and tell him the whole truth."

"Why can't you talk to Andrew yourself?"

Brandi bit her bottom lip and sighed.

"Because he won't talk to me; so it's easier to just have Trina handle it. I mean, she is my baby's god mother."

It was the first time Brandi had uttered the words "my baby" and it made me feel funny. The pit of my stomach dropped as I digested her words. It was almost as if Brandi wasn't grasping the severity of what the two of them had gotten themselves them into. This wasn't just a baby doll that Brandi could toss into her toy chest or a baseball that Andrew could discard of. This was a baby... *their* baby.

"When did you make this decision?"

"She is my best friend, mom."

"I know but..."

"So then she's my baby's god mother."

"So you want to stay at Chamberlain? You don't want me to hire a home schooling teacher? I can, you know." I said raising both of my eyebrows.

I knew that as time went on and Brandi's belly got bigger, things would start to become more difficult for her. The stares would get longer, the whispers a little louder and her self-esteem would possibly plummet. I prayed that I was wrong, though.

Blitz

"I'm staying at Chamberlain, ma. No one is tripping that I'm pregnant." She said slowly as if she had to verify what she was saying was factual.

I stopped myself before replying to her naïve comment. She hadn't lived like I had, she hadn't experienced the things I had and she couldn't understand the advice I was giving her. This part of her life, I thought, she'd have to experience on her own.

As I made my way down the stairs, I heard some rustling coming from the kitchen and slowly crept around the corner and peered in. I didn't have a weapon or anything, but I was ready to go to war with anyone or anything that was in my home.

"Charles?" I said as I saw him bent over the lower cabinets in my kitchen.

"Oh." He said turning around like he'd been caught doing something he shouldn't have "I didn't think you'd be home."

"You saw my car out there, right?"

"I didn't know which one you drove today." He said turning back to the cabinets.

I noticed that three of his red pots were on the counter and he was still fishing for something else.

"What are you doing? What are you looking for?" I inquired as I placed my hands on my hips.

"My pots and pans; that's all."

"Why do you need *all* of your pots and pans tonight; what are you cooking a big meal?" I joked as I approached him playfully.

"We've already gone over this, Mia." He said dropping his head slightly before returning to his search.

"Been over what?" I said "And what do your pots have to do with anything?"

"I'm leaving."

I stood still, in my tracks, and tried to make sense out of what he was saying.

"What do you mean, you're leaving? You're leaving Tampa?"

"I'm leaving you. I can't do this anymore and I don't feel like trying." He said as he located his black skillet and placed it inside the other pots.

Ebonee Monique

I couldn't have been hearing right, could I? Charles, the love of my life, the dose of reality I craved and needed, was leaving me?

"Wait, wait a minute." I said as I felt my voice tremble. "I thought we were just fighting and we'd come to a common ground and work it out. Why are you leaving me?" I said finally screaming.

"Mia, what common ground can we come to? You don't want to marry me and you don't want to have a child by me. Where's the common ground in that?"

"I do." I said wiping a tear as fear ran straight through my body.

"I'll marry you; I'll have your baby, Charles. I don't care. I'll do whatever you want me to do. If it'll make you happy, I'll do it." I wailed as I wrapped my arms around him tightly.

I could see the tears in Charles' eyes that he was trying to fight back, as well. He didn't want to let me go; I know he didn't. He loved me just like I loved him and all of this was coming out of left field for me.

"That's the thing, Mia. I don't want you to do something because I want it. I want *you* to want me as your husband and the biological father of your child. I want you to want those things; but you don't." He said as a single tear fell down his muscular cheek.

"And I *want* those things, baby. I want someone who wants it too."

"But what about Brandi?" I asked throwing my daughter in for sympathy. Surely this man, who'd promised to always be her father, wouldn't leave her too, would he?

"Nothing is changing with Brandi and me. I'm still her daddy and I'm still going to be there for her. I just can't do *us* anymore. I can't." He said breaking away from our hug.

"So just like that, it's over?" I said loudly as I trailed him up the stairs towards the bedroom.

Brandi stuck her head out of the door and watched, in silence, as I begged Charles for an answer.

"Dad, what's happening?" She said while I cried nonstop.

"Go back in your room, Bran."

Blitz

Brandi listened to her father and shut the door back; but I knew she was listening on the other side.

When we got to the bedroom I threw myself in front of Charles' path until he was forced to say something to me.

"What?" He screamed loudly. "What do you want me to say? If you think this has been out of the blue, then you haven't been paying attention to me at all." He said looking me dead in my eye.

"This isn't fair." I cried, feeling like a baby.

"Life isn't fair." He shot back.

"Charles…"

"I love you woman, do you know that?" He said cupping my face in his hands as he stared at me and allowed tears to stream out of the corner of his eyes.

"But I don't see us going anywhere past boyfriend and girlfriend; I want more and you don't." He said as I sobbed heavily.

"I do, Charles, I want it." I lied as I gasped for air. "I want you."

"No, you don't." He said letting my face go.

Charles was right, too. I didn't want to marry him and have his child. I just wasn't there, yet; but I figured he could at least give me some more time to warm up to the idea.

We stood across from each other, trying to compose ourselves, and silently trying to figure out something to say.

"Can't we talk about this? Why do you have to just up and leave?"

"Because I don't want to be *that* guy." He said as he plopped on the bed and continued.

"I don't want to be that guy that continues to give a woman an ultimatum and finally gets her to agree to what he wants only to figure out that she never wanted it too and was only doing it because it would make him happy. I don't want either of us wasting time on each other if we can't make one another happy."

"But you make me happy, baby. You make me happy." I said sitting next to him.

"But you don't make me…" He said slowing down before he finished his sentence.

I held up one hand and stopped him.

"I don't make you happy?" I asked. "Since when? I could've sworn that when we made love you were screaming "*I love you*" and telling me how beautiful I am and..." "I do love you and you are beautiful." He replied "But you aren't ready to give me the things that will make me happy, Mia."

Both of us sat in silence as I thought about all the times I'd told myself I had the perfect relationship. How had I overlooked this? I'd, somehow, ignored Charles' constant appeal for my hand in marriage and baby in a baby carriage. I'd swept it all under the rug with ease, and hoped we could deal with it at another time; I just wasn't sure when that time would come. I could easily ignore my own hesitations and be Charles' wife and the mother of his children, but would I really be happy?

As if he was reading my mind, Charles chimed in as he stroked my hand.

"I don't want you to resent me one day. I don't want to coerce you into marriage and motherhood and then you're miserable with everything."

I nodded my head as I thought about what was happening. Why couldn't I keep Charles and still give in to at least one of his requests? I needed this man, I thought, but not as much as I needed my pride and independence. I couldn't let go of my own selfishness long enough to see that I was letting something wonderful slip through my fingers.

"I just need to get some things and I can come back later, and get the rest of my things." Charles said standing up from the bed and heading to the closet.

"No. I'll leave; I need to clear my mind anyway. You can take whatever you need. Just call me when you're leaving; you can explain everything to Brandi." I said not looking back at Charles as I headed towards the bedroom door.

I didn't know where I was going or what I was doing when I got there, but I needed to get out. I needed to drive until my gas tank was begging for more fuel. I wanted to run away; far, far away.

"Wait." Charles said rushing towards me. I knew it, I thought, Charles couldn't leave me. He couldn't just up and leave the one thing that made sense to him; I knew because I couldn't stand the thought of him leaving me.

As he reached me, he extended his arms and wrapped them tightly around me. His hug felt like goodbye; my body didn't want him to pull away for fear that it would *actually* be over. His lips reached down to mine and I sucked on each one of them delicately. I knew this was a farewell kiss. I could sense it the way he flicked his tongue in every crevasse of my mouth. I grabbed his head and locked my hands behind it and sobbed as we kissed. When we were done, I stood back wondering if the kiss had been enough to keep him and I tilted my head to the side.

"Goodbye?" I asked softly as Charles positioned himself against a wall.

"Yes." He said hanging his head. "Goodbye, Mia."

****

My entire weekend was completely shot, to say the least. Brandi and I lay in bed and watched re-runs of *A Different World* and ate delicious, yet fattening, Ben & Jerry's Butter Pecan ice cream. She continued to grow by the day and I was impressed at how calm and well she was handling things. That is, of course, until my phone rang on Sunday afternoon, four days before Brandi's fifteenth birthday.

The unexpected call caught me by surprise.

"Ms. Robinson?" The older woman said as she cleared her throat.

"This is she." I replied.

"This is Beulah Hopkins; I'm President of the *Alpha Beta Sigma* sorority."

"Yes, I know who you are." I said smiling widely as I looked over at Brandi.

Maybe they were about to cut Brandi's scholarship check and I could go ahead and deposit it in her savings account.

"We need to schedule a meeting with you and Brandi, along with the principal of her school-tomorrow evening at 7:00 at our sorority house." She said plainly.

She didn't sound excited or upset; her tone was monotone and as she kept talking I grew sleepier.

"What is this about?" I asked.

"Brandi's scholarship."

"Okay. Well let me get the address."

Ebonee Monique

I grabbed a pen off the nightstand and wrote the address down and smirked.

"We'll be there." I said sighing.

I could only pray that the meeting would be a beacon of light in the middle of all of our darkness.

Charles had been on my mind every moment of every day of the week. With Brandi and Charles being so close, I wondered if he gave her any hints into if he was missing me too; because I missed him like hell.

I hadn't been able to focus, completely, on anything. My clients were getting their first-rate attention and all, but it definitely wasn't the focal point of my life.

I'd hesitantly agreed to go out on an actual date with Lee and was already dreading the time I'd have to tell Brandi. She was so attached to the relationship that Charles and I had, and rightfully so, that she couldn't stand to even think about me with another man.

But I had to at least try to move on; even if it hurt like crazy.

As *Whitley Gilbert* made some crazy joke about *Dwayne Wayne*, I stared at the ceiling and tried to think about Charles' face. It had been so long since I'd seen him, two days to be exact, and I was starting to forget things on him that I took for granted. Like his chipped front tooth, his soft-like-butter hands and the beauty mark on his abs.

Disturbing me from my daydream, Brandi rolled over and smiled at me.

"You're thinking about dad, aren't you?" She teased as I rolled my eyes.

"No, not at all."

"Yes you are; I bet he's thinking about you too."

"Well, he shouldn't be." I said trying to sound hard.

"I ain't thinking about him."

Brandi sucked her teeth and returned her glare to the television.

I hoped that I could fool Brandi into thinking I didn't need a man, but I was lying. I needed *that* man badly.
****

Monday came and went, without little excitement. Brandi sulked into the house, as usual, complaining that

Blitz

Andrew wouldn't hear her out about the baby and I daydreamed about Charles.

Brandi dressed conservatively, in black slacks and a beautiful teal button down shirt with a pair of black pumps, and I kept on my pant suit from that day's work.

"Don't you look spiffy?" I said as she came down the stairs with a somber look on her face.

I didn't want to hear about the drama or he-say-she-say that had gone on at school; I wanted to focus on the goodness of the Ms. Princess title and scholarship that she'd won.

"Thanks."

We boarded into the Mercedes truck and headed towards the address that Beulah had given me. It was in a shady part of town, and the location was extremely dark, so I hoped the entire trip would be in and out. Maybe the principal wanted to present the check to Brandi while the sorority photographed it? I was giddy with excitement as we pulled into the driveway of the sorority house.

"Ms. Robinson." Beulah said as Brandi and I entered the traditionally decorated house slowly. Walking in the building made me feel like I'd taken a step back into the 50's, into the home of Donna Reed; they kept the home so immaculate, I was scared of *walking* wrong, in fear of breaking something. The hardwood floors gleamed brightly as the outdated furniture stuck out like nobody's business.

Looking around, I would've thought they were the ones who needed money. They had old raggedy furniture; the house reeked of moth balls while the carpet looked like it belonged in a 1970's *Shaft* movie or some other type of black exploitation film. I wasn't the least bit impressed.

"How are you this evening?" I asked courteously as Brandi and I followed the lady into a back room.

"I'm well." She said standoffishly.

Brandi kept quiet, behind me, as we all walked in silence.

"Why don't you have a seat?" She said pointing to a long folding table with six chairs. There were two seats on one side and four on the other.

Brandi and I sat motionless as the cold air hit both of us harshly.

"It's cold in here." I said to Brandi as she nodded in agreement.

Shortly after we'd sat down, three ladies, including Beulah, came out in a single file line and sat in the three seats across from Brandi and me. I smiled at each one of them, kindly, but they all seemed to look past me. Ignoring their obvious disrespect, I sat up straight and stared straight ahead.

Seconds later, Brandi's Principal, Mr. Hemmings, entered the room and took the remaining seat across from my daughter and me.

In that instant, I knew we weren't there for the scholarship check; their faces said everything I needed to hear, loud and clear.

One woman, an old grey-haired looking winch, kept shaking her head softly as she looked back and forth between me and Brandi. She looked to be in her mid-seventies and had trifocals that were attached by a chain to her shirt. The other woman was closer to my age and she looked like she had been through some rough times in life. The nearly black circles under her eyes told a story of hard times that she didn't have to verbalize, and her hair seemed like it was matted down to her scalp due to neglect. Then there was Ms. Beulah; she was a character in and of herself. She had bluish grey hair, was overweight and completely snobby in both word and appearance; in a nutshell she was everything I prided myself on not being. There was a certain air about her, the way she held herself and talked to people, that made me realize that she *knew* she was better than us.

"We've called this meeting tonight in regards to a couple of rumors that we've heard." Beulah said as she read from a piece of paper avoiding direct eye contact as if it was unnecessary from a woman of her prestige.

Brandi immediately tensed up and grabbed my hand. She was afraid. I squeezed her hand back to reassure her that I would protect her. I had always been there for Brandi and now, in the times she needed me most, I was not about to turn my back on her. She was *mine* and she was given to me to protect; I was going to do just that.

"Okay." I said holding my head high.

Blitz

"Is it true that you are pregnant young lady?" Beulah asked as the two hens and principal stared on with intrusive, prying eyes.

Brandi seemed to be at a loss for words. When it came to telling Andrew's parents, she hadn't been as scared because she knew Andrew had played a part in the situation as well; staring at these three women, and her Principal, Brandi froze.

I cleared my throat and clasped my hands together on the table.

"Why, may I ask, is that any of your business?"

"It's our business, Ms. Robinson, because our name is on the scholarship that your daughter was awarded."

"Okay and..." I said raising one eyebrow as the younger hen spoke.

"We reserve the right to select the *type* of student who receives our scholarship money."

"And Brandi was chosen; so what does that have to do with her being pregnant?"

"So she is pregnant?" Mr. Hemmings said shocked at my admission.

"Yes, I'm pregnant." Brandi said joining in.

The three ladies looked at each other, then to me, then to Brandi and finally to her stomach. Their eyes made a circle of shame that started and ended with my daughter. I could feel it; their judgmental eyes pierced right through my daughter's self-esteem and pride, and I hated it.

"As a Chapter we've met and decided that Brandi Robinson shall have her title of Miss Princess revoked as well as having the award of the scholarship money agreement nullified." Beulah said staring at me with a defiant look begging me to check her.

"What!! What are you talking about?" I asked as I felt my face growing hotter and hotter. Did they have the rights to do this? Could they take away Brandi's scholarship and crown because she'd made a mistake?

"Like we said before Ms. Robinson, we have the right to decide if a candidate is eligible to receive our scholarship and title. Both are awarded by us and we reserve the right to decide if we deem the recipient worthy." The younger woman said as she crossed her legs.

"I know what you said," I commented as I looked over at Brandi who was crying in disbelief, "But you chose my daughter based on her grades, her desire to go to college and because her peers all recommended her for the title, right?" I shot back with my eyes widened.

"This type of thing just isn't something that we can overlook and ignore. Brandi can't represent our sorority and be a pregnant teen." Beulah replied, ignoring my question and challenging of her authority. "We have an image to think about."

"My daughter has had high honor roll *every* year of school since she was eight. Now, because she makes a mistake, you all decide to take away something that she's dreamed about and worked hard for her entire life, because of your image?"

The three ladies listened with stone faces, as I continued.
"Miss Princess doesn't even do any type of promotional work for you nor does she represent you."

"She would be required to ride on our Spring Formal float, ma'am." The nest-headed woman said like she knew it all.

"The *high school* parade? You've got to be kidding me." I said as I slammed my fists on the table. "You're worried about your image at a high school parade?"

I wasn't mad because they were taking away money, because we obviously didn't need it, I was angry because my daughter had worked hard for something, was awarded it, and now was having it snatched away because three country hens decided she wasn't worthy of receiving it. Though I shouldn't have, I wished harm to people like them.

"We're really sorry." Mr. Hemmings said as he eyed an inconsolable Brandi who lay with her head on my shoulder sobbing.

"I'm sorry. Please don't do this. It was a mistake and I swear I'll cover up." Brandi sobbed

"People will still know." Beulah said coldly.

"But…But I know you all have children and they've made mistakes before, right? And you've forgiven them. You've allowed them to live their lives with that experience and grow from it." Brandi said as she spat off knowledge and words I didn't know were in her heart. "Just forgive me, please!" She wailed apologetically.

Blitz

"Our children would never…they'd never…."

"Have sex? Get pregnant?   Or make a mistake? Exactly which one of those would your child not do?" I said angrily as I stood Brandi up by the arm.

"Which one Beulah? Answer that! Because, as I hear it, your slut bag of a son has more than enough illegitimate children sprinkled around town." I said jerking my head to the side. If they wanted to play dirty, I was ready to do just that. In all actuality, I hadn't heard that Beulah's son, Raymond-a flirtatious construction worker-had any illegitimate children, but it was the first thing that popped into my mind. When people sling mud, you grab for what's around you, who cares if it is mud or rocks.

"How dare you?" Beulah said, shocked at my words.

"Go to the car, Brandi." I handed her my car keys. Brandi listened and slowly moved towards the front door.

"So, are you going to take away the crown of Mr. King, from Andrew Whittaker? Because he's the father of her baby."

"We've spoken with Leonard Whittaker and he assured us that the DNA of this child has yet to be determined; so, no."

"You all are unbelievable; you make it so easy for people to call you snobs and bitches, you know that?" My anger took control and spoke for me.

The three women sat back, with their hands over their mouths and eyes widened, as I got closer to their faces. I wasn't about to harm them but I damn sure wanted them to be scared.

"Mr. Hemmings, I want you to know that I've heard about your little petition to have my daughter removed from school." I said heading towards the door.

"I can explain…" He said trying to raise his voice.

"Don't. I want you to know that both the sorority and the high school will be hearing from my lawyer." I faced Brandi who shook her head in disbelief and shame as she dashed out of the sorority house towards my car.

Within seconds, Brandi was dashing back past me and into   the   house.
"What happened?" I asked.

"I left my purse."

I sat in the car, with my head in my hands, wanting to know when the madness would end. I knew my child had made a mistake and I was aware that she would have to live through the consequences of that mistake for a very long time, but people were sure making it hard for her to see the "blessing" of her baby. Everything happens for a reason, I kept telling myself.

When Brandi returned to the car her body crumpled and wept in my arms. The moment she'd stop crying, she'd look up at me and say "sorry" and start bawling all over again. I looked at my child and I knew I couldn't take it on for her, but I sure wanted to.

I drove and Brandi cried the entire way home. I wanted to stay strong, for her, but I knew how hard she'd worked for that crown and how long she'd talked about getting it and now it was nothing more than a distant memory.

"Ma," she said, through gasps of air, "I want to be home-schooled."

I snapped my head towards her in confusion. Where was all this coming from? She'd told me, weeks earlier, that she was facing the rumors and whispers head on.

"Why? What changed?"

"I can't do this." She sobbed "I can't handle these people or others like them."

"What?"

"When I went back into the sorority house, to get my purse, I overheard them saying, '*What kind of mother would raise a girl like that?*' Right then, I knew there was nothing I could say or do to change their minds about me or to make them stop thinking about me the way they did. I'm just tired of everyone judging me. I don't want to see anyone from school." She curled up in a ball and allowed her tears to soak her shirt. "I've been acting like I don't care that people are pointing, staring and about me, but I do care ma. I do!"

Of course they hadn't known what kind of mother I was the kind who worked three jobs to put food on the table, made sure my daughters' grades were up and loved her daughter unconditionally. They knew nothing about me or my daughter, just that she was another teen who got pregnant. But I knew one day, those old hens would remember Brandi for being more than just a bulging-bellied teen; and I couldn't wait for that day to come.

****

Blitz

The next day, I withdrew Brandi from Chamberlain High School.

I ran into Mr. Hemmings, who tried his best to explain the petition and its intentions, but I ignored every one of his pleas. I knew I'd placed fear in him when I'd mentioned my lawyer; I was glad about that.

"Did you see...anyone?" Brandi said when I returned home that evening with the things from her locker.

I knew the "anyone" she was talking about had to have been Andrew.

"No." I said tossing the stuffed plastic bag on her bed. Brandi had the covers pulled up to her chin and she looked disappointed as I gave my answer.

"Oh." She said sighing.

I turned to walk out of the room and Brandi sat up and called my name.

"What are we doing for my birthday?" She asked as she bit her lip.

With her trip to Aruba being cancelled, I'm sure she was wondering what she could expect for her big day.

"I don't know, Brandi." I exhaled as I turned back to face her.

To say I was stressed would be an understatement. I hadn't been able to sleep much, my work wasn't doing itself and I was just agitated for plenty of reasons. Charles had yet to call me back, so we could talk; one of my clients was giving me a hard time; and I had three showings to prepare for the following week. Simply put, I was spent.

I hadn't had a chance to even think about Brandi's birthday and adding it on my list of "things to do", had me feeling overwhelmed.

"What do you want to do?" I asked as I tried to mask my frustration.

"I don't know; maybe have a party at the house or something this weekend?"

"A *party* Bran? How am I supposed to get something like that together?" I shot back.

"It was just a suggestion, dang."

I blew air out, calmed myself down and slowly walked to Brandi's bed. Taking a seat next to her, I smiled.

Ebonee Monique

"I'm sorry." I said "It's your birthday; if you want a party let's try to get some things organized. You get your list together, call your friends and I'll get Charles to throw something together from the restaurant." I said calmly as I thought about the dozen or so other things I needed to conquer before resting my head on the pillow that night.

"He's out of town, ma." Brandi said like she was confused that I didn't know Charles' whereabouts. "I thought you knew."

"Oh, right." I said trying to sound like I was in the know.

"I forgot. Well, he can still get someone at the restaurant to bring something over."

"What about music?" Brandi smiled getting excited about the party.

"I don't know." I said trying to rack my brain of deejays I knew.

"You know Cecil deejays, ma." Brandi said as a small smirk came upon her face.

"Is that right?" I said raising one eyebrow "And why do you want Cecil all up in our house?"

"Because he's a friend."

"Is he?" I asked before throwing my arms across my chest "Or is he *more* than a friend like Andrew said?"

Brandi stared at me, with a look of shock on her face. I could tell I'd hit a sore spot, but there was no backing up from what I'd said. I hadn't meant to insinuate that Brandi and Cecil had been intimate, but with everything else going on in my life, I'd allowed it to boil over.

"What's that supposed to mean? He's a friend." She lividly screamed as she threw the covers back and stormed towards her bathroom.

"I can't believe you would even think to say something like me. I told you already that Andrew is the *only* boy I been with. So, now you believe him?" Brandi screamed from behind the bathroom door. I heard things being tossed around.

I shook my head, why had I gone there with her? The one thing I needed, in my life and in my home, was peace; having an angry pregnant teenager definitely didn't give me that.

Blitz

"Honey, I apologize." I said walking towards the door and placing my hand on it. "I was wrong to say that; you know I believe you."

Brandi didn't say anything after that, even after I continued to apologize to her; so finally, I left the room and headed into my office.

I dialed Charles' number and sat back in my black, leather chair, waiting to hear his voice.

"Hello?" He said sounding like he was in the middle of a laugh.

"Ch-Charles?" I said smiling.

"Hey, Mia; is everything okay with Brandi?" He asked clearing his throat.

"Oh, yeah; everything's fine. I was just calling you to…I'm sorry, are you busy?"

"I was out with a friend, but if you need to talk…"

"I'm sorry. I didn't mean to interrupt your boys' night out."

"It's not boys' night out, but it's okay. What's wrong?"

I silently sat, with the phone to my ear, trying to think about who Charles could be out with, in another town, on Tuesday night.

"Hello?" He remarked snapping me out of my daydream "You there?"

"Yeah, I'm here; sorry." I said. "I was calling about Brandi's birthday. She wants this party at the house this weekend and I was thinking you could cater it; but I know you're out of town and everything so…" I trailed off.

"I'll take care of it. Is that all?" He asked.

I wanted to tell him, no, it wasn't all. I wanted him to tell me that he missed me the way I missed him; I wanted him to say he forgave me and would accept me and my little quirks. But as I heard him talking to someone else, I knew it wouldn't happen, at least not then.

"Yeah, I mean…unless you needed something." I added as I crossed my fingers.

"Nah, not really; I think we've covered all our bases." He said coolly.

"Where are you?" I blurted out before I could censor myself

"I came home to Alabama to check on my mother."

Ebonee Monique

"Is she okay?"

"Yeah, she's alright; I just needed to check on her that's all."

"So you're out with your...mother?" I said knowing I was reaching into his business.

Charles chuckled, "No, I'm not out with my mother; I'm out with a friend."

"What's her name?" I blurted out, knowing it was another woman with *my* man. I could envision her sitting next to him, probably telling corny jokes in his ear and rubbing his hand slightly as he ordered more wine for her. I could imagine them, with their hands intertwined, his lips upon hers and their breathing becoming heavy. He would probably take her back to his mother's house, or maybe to a hotel, and make passionate, never ending love to her the way my body was crying for him to do.

Charles seemed to hesitate before answering my question slowly.

"Her name is Anita."

"Oh." I said as I tried to catch my breath.

Was he really dating already? We'd only been broken up, separated or whatever, for a few days and he was already moved on?

Before I could make a sound or comment on Anita, the phone beeped; someone else was on the other line. Saved by the freaking bell.

"Well, I've got to go; I have another call..." I said as I clutched my chest.

"Let's talk about this..." Charles said before I clicked over and, finally, gasped for air.

"Hello?" I said through my deep breathing.

"May I speak with...Mia, is that you?" The deep voice said.

"Who is this?" I said trying to catch my breath. If I thought I was hyperventilating then, hearing the name of the person on the line could've sent me into a cardiac arrest.

"It's Branson; are you okay?" My ex-husband asked curiously.

"I'm fine; what do you want?"

"Excuse me for asking." He snickered "I was calling to speak to my daughter."

Blitz

"Why didn't you call her line? You know it."

"I'm actually at my girl's house and I left Brandi's number at my place."

I could have screamed at the irony of everything. I didn't have anyone and the man who'd caused me years and years of agony and stress did.

"She's in her room; I can give you the number."

"Please." He said shortly "And I promise I won't ever bother you again." He joked.

"It's 380-1952." I replied.

"And Brandi told me about you withdrawing her from school; I just wanted you to know I thought that was the biggest mistake you could've made. Brandi should be in school with other kids, just like her. Just because you all have more money than everyone else doesn't mean she should be treated differently."

"More money? What are you talking about? I didn't withdraw Brandi from school because of our money." I said cocking my head to the side.

Something was telling me that Brandi hadn't told her long-lost pappy that his little fourteen-almost fifteen-year-old daughter was having a baby and that he was going to be a grandfather.

"Well, then why'd you pull her out?" Branson asked boldly.

I didn't know if I was crossing, yet, another line by telling Brandi's business, but at this point I didn't care. I'd given her ample time to tell Branson about her pregnancy and she had him thinking I'd allowed money to go straight to my head.

"Brandi's pregnant." I said shrugging my shoulders.

I could hear the thud of the phone as Branson dropped it, along with a bunch of muffled cursing in the background. It was minutes before Branson returned to the phone, obviously pissed.

"What the hell do you mean she's pregnant?" He screamed loudly.

"I mean, you know about the birds and the bees, right Branson? A man sleeps with a woman; his sperm goes inside of her and…"

"Mia, don't play with me, obviously I know what being pregnant means. Are you playing about Brandi being...pregnant?"

"Do you, honestly, think I'd lie about something like that?"

"Was it that Andrew boy? It was him; wasn't it? I could tell that boy was up to no good."

"Is that right?" I said smirking. Branson had only met Andrew once and had, mysteriously, been able to call that he was no good. Look out *Ms. Cleo*, I thought.

"The way he was all up on her and...how could you let something like this happen?"

"Wait a minute! You know what? I'm tired of everyone blaming *me* for this."

"You are her mother, Mia. Who the else are we supposed to blame!"

"I don't know, maybe the person who got pregnant; the one who opened her legs. Or maybe we can blame her sperm donor of a father for not teaching her the proper way a man should or shouldn't treat a girl. It's obvious she wants badly to be loved by a man to make up for not being loved by you." I said out of breath.

"So this is my fault, now Mia?" Branson shouted loudly.

"Hell, I didn't lie up and get her pregnant. Brandi is a young woman now, Branson. If you bothered to be in her life you'd know that! You come into her life like some fake ass Super Hero and think you have super-human powers to fix everything with the snap of your fingers. You're running around here like you have a cape of protection all of a sudden. But where were you when it mattered? Where was Brandi's Super hero then? You pretend like you've done such wonderful things in your life; like you've had valid reasons for missing out on eleven years of your own child's life...do you know how much of a sorry ass excuse of a man you are for the things you put Brandi and I through? You ought to be glad I even let your raggedy ass near my daughter. Yes, I said it...she's *my* daughter. I'm the one that put her to sleep every night for fifteen years. I'm the one that clothed and fed her and was the only parent she knew. That was me! ALL me not you

Branson!" I screamed as I stood up from my desk and paced the room like a mad dog.

"And if you ever want to blame me for anything-with your sorry ass-make sure you blame me for being the best mother *and* father to my daughter. Blame me for doing the best I could to play *both* those roles. That's what I'm guilty of Branson...playing two roles at once."

There was silence on the other end of the phone, but I knew that Branson was still there because I could hear the television in the background.

"Are you finished?" There was little emotion in his voice.

"I could go on for days, Branson. Don't get me started!"

"Look, have you talked to Brandi about moving in with me? I think now, more than ever, that she needs to stay with me."

I couldn't believe the nerve of that man. He'd come back into our lives out of nowhere, posed himself as Mr. perfection and he wanted to pour salt in the wound by taking the only thing left in my life: my daughter.

"Are you crazy, man? Have you lost your freakin' mind?" I held the phone further from my lips and I shouted into the receiver while my eyes bugged. "My daughter is pregnant...do you hear me? Pregnant! And you want me to allow her to come live with you?" I laughed sarcastically.

"I'd be better off leaving her with a dog, than you!"

"How about we let Brandi make that choice." Branson replied as he sucked his teeth.

Something in me wanted to prove, to Branson, that my daughter loved me the most. I had, after all, been her sole provider and supporter for the majority of her life; she wouldn't leave me. I was convinced of it.

"Brandi! Get down here!" I shouted as I stuck my head out of the door.

I pushed my hair out of my eyes and paced the room frantically, as Branson talked to someone in the background.

"What?" Brandi said appearing in a tight shirt and plaid boxer shorts, which were rolled up. Her stomach was obvious as it poked out of the bottom of her shirt.

"This is your...Branson is on the phone." I said stopping short of calling him her father. What a joke.

A smile lit up on Brandi's face as she inched closer to the phone I was holding.

"Hey dad!" She said loudly into the phone.

"Brandi, we need to talk to you." I said motioning for Brandi to take a seat on the couch in my office.

"What's wrong?" She asked taking a seat and crossing her legs at the ankles.

I swallowed, put the phone on speaker and took a seat at my desk.

"Honey, your father wants you to come and live with him." I said as I eyed Brandi's reaction, which seemed to be a mixture of bewilderment and shock.

"Uh huh..." She said raising an eyebrow.

"And you know how much mommy wants you to stay here, but we want this decision to be yours." I said clasping my hands together trying to remain calm. Brandi bit her bottom lip and looked at me and then the speaker phone.

"Brandi, sweetie, I just want to make up for all the lost time and since your mother told me about the...the baby, I thought this would be the best time." Branson said tenderly.

Brandi's eyes shot over to me and the fire in her eyes told me I *did* have something to worry about. Not taking her eyes off of me, Brandi started shaking her head.

"You told me I could tell him, ma! Why did you go and tell him before I had a chance to? You had no right to do that!" She screamed loudly as she rushed towards me and pounded on my desk.

I sat back in my chair and tried to think of something to say; but I was lost.

"This is my life and my decision. Did you think I wasn't going to tell him? Who do you think you are to just up and tell people my business? This is *my* baby; not yours!" Her face was flushed as she screamed louder and louder with each sentence.

"I thought you'd already told him." I tried to interject. "I'm sorry."

"Whatever!" Brandi stormed of the office towards the stairs. "This is so not fair!"

Blitz

"I guess her decision is made up, huh?" Branson laughed, sounding as if he'd won the lottery.

"She didn't say anything about moving in with you. Besides, she's hormonal." I shot back before picking the phone up.

"If you want to talk to my daughter, you can call her line. Don't call here again." I slammed the phone down and stood staring at it in disbelief.

What the hell had I gotten myself into? Maybe Brandi moving with Branson wasn't a bad idea after all, I thought as I fell back into my seat and threw my hands against my forehead.

My heart was gone.

My baby could actually be leaving.

I had to get a grip.

Chapter 8

"**M**a, I'm bleeding!" Brandi frantically screamed as she flung open my bedroom door with her underwear in her hands.

I was knocked out, with crusty sleep in the corner of my eyes and breath strong enough to knock out *Mike Tyson*, but my body automatically reacted when I heard her voice. In seconds, I was in a *Nike* t-shirt, sweats, sneakers and a camouflage hat and was slowly ushering Brandi to the car.

"Do you think something's wrong?" Brandi asked stroking her stomach and looking at me.

"Everything is probably fine." I said sharply turning onto the interstate.

"Should we call Andrew or dad?" Brandi asked sounding like she was expecting the worst.

"We'll just see when we get there." I said not taking my eyes off of the road ahead of me.

I prayed that everything was okay, but I knew the possibility of it was diminishing as the traffic in front of me came to a standstill.

****

By the time we got to the emergency room, Brandi was in tears.

Wanting to be safe, I called Charles and also Andrew's parents who politely asked me never to call their house again; I hesitated as I dialed Branson's number. Charles said he'd just landed and would be there as soon as he could.

"Brandi is at the emergency room, she was spotting." I said quickly "We're at St. Joseph's Women's Hospital."

The nurses were efficient and extremely helpful; even when they saw Brandi's age.

"Aren't you the cutest little thing?" An older black woman said as she pinched Brandi's tear-stained cheeks. "And it's your birthday, too. Happy Birthday baby!" She exposed the large gaps in her teeth as she smiled.

"T-thank you." Brandi said trying to be polite.

That's when it hit me. We were spending my baby's fifteenth birthday in the ER because of her baby.

"Happy Birthday, honey." I reached over and hugged her tightly "Everything will be okay."

Brandi nodded her head and continued to massage her stomach.

Just like he'd flown into our lives, Branson blew into the hospital emergency room calling out both of our names loudly, embarrassing the hell out of me.

"Mia! Brandi! Where's my baby? Mia? Bran?!!"

"We're over here, Sherlock." I said as the woman called Brandi's name and I helped her up.

Branson took one look at his daughter and covered his face in disbelief. Maybe he thought I *was* making the entire thing up; but as he saw it with his own eyes, he knew it was real.

"My Lord." His voice was lower than before as he gasped while following us into the room.

Brandi went into the examination room first and I turned and stopped Branson before either of us could take a step further.

"Just so you know... that little girl is going through a lot right now. She doesn't need your criticism or harsh words right now. Her friends have turned on her, her ex-boyfriend is denying he's the father and the things she's worked very hard for are all being taken away from her. So, if we can just *pretend*, for one moment, to have a united front in there, I'd really appreciate it." I said taking a deep breath.

"We don't need to pretend. Look, I'm sorry about last night; I was wrong to say the things I did about it being your fault. You've been a wonderful mother to our daughter and I can't fault you for anything."

I looked into Branson's almond eyes and wanted to cry. I'd never heard those words from him before. It was like he was speaking French, but I understood him completely. I nodded my head and turned to go into the examining room. One part of me felt like I was walking on air, but the other part of me felt like I shouldn't have let him off with a simple apology. I wanted to make him pay, but I was conflicted with feeling thankful for his words.

"Interesting" was the only way I could describe what was to come.

****

"You are going to be fine, Ms. Brandi!" The nurse said as she removed her latex gloves and tossed them in the trash.

The doctor came in next, examined Brandi, and told her everything was fine. I have to admit that it never got easy seeing my teenage daughter with her legs in stirrups, being poked and prodded by a doctor. My eyes wanted to stay focused on what the doctor was doing, but at times, it became too much to view. After we all confirmed that everything was A-Okay with the baby, we all let out a unified sigh of relief.

Branson and I quickly hugged Brandi.

"So, my baby is okay?" Brandi asked raising her eyebrows.

"Perfect. In fact, there are a lot of women who experience the same light spotting as you." She said as she turned to wash her hands off.

"What causes it?" I asked stroking Brandi's hair.

"Normally it's because of the increase in the supply of blood to the cervix and pelvic area." She smiled.

"So we're free to go?" Branson asked clapping his hands together.

"Well, this is optional, but we can give you an external ultrasound just to put your mind at ease; plus we can try to find out the sex of the baby…that is if you want to know." The nurse smiled as she looked at Brandi who was looking at me. "You are eighteen weeks along now and we *should* be able to determine the sex."

"It's up to you, baby." I smiled, knowing I *did* want to know.

"Okay." Brandi smiled eagerly as she looked down at her stomach and shrugged her shoulders.

I hadn't noticed it before but Brandi's stomach was pretty large. It stuck out enough that it was noticeable to any and every one; I wondered if Brandi was starting to understand the gift in being pregnant.

Blitz

Branson sat by the window and I stayed close to Brandi, as the woman spread the clear jelly on her stomach.

Placing her hands behind her back, Brandi watched everything the woman was doing with a close eye.

"What's that for?" She asked as the nurse placed the jelly goop on the wand in her hand.

"This will go over your belly and will help us see how your baby is doing."

"That's cold!" Brandi squirmed a little on the table, giggling as a child would do. I couldn't help but smirk at her action.

I watched as the black screen in front of us, became muffled and contorted in nature. My maternal instincts were in full form as I watched the nurse slowly place the wand over Brandi's stomach. She swirled the wand around in the jelly, looking for a good spot. Once she found the perfect position to give everyone within view a Kodak moment they would never forget, she stopped, punched some numbers in the machine then turned to Brandi and me as she smiled knowing the info she had was priceless to our waiting ears.

"There's your baby. The product of all the madness. Brandi, say hello to your child."

She smiled pointing to the screen where my grandchild lay. I could make out the features clearly. Before, the baby had been nothing more than an image in my mind; but now it was a reality. In that moment, I felt the same excitement about the new life as I had the day I saw Brandi's ultrasound for the first time.

"That's...that's my baby? It's gotten so big from when we were at Dr. Valdez's office." Brandi said covering her mouth.

"That was weeks ago, honey. Babies grow quickly!" I said trying to contain my excitement.

With all the hoopla and drama, everything seemed to calm down as all of us stared at the screen.

"Is it a girl or a boy?" Brandi asked switching her view to the nurse.

"If you look right here, you'll notice a little *thing*, if you will. This is your son's penis." She chuckled as she circled the baby's genitals with her finger.

Ebonee Monique

I gasped eagerly as Brandi strained her eyes to get a better view.

Branson jumped up and clapped his hands. "It's a boy!"

I stared at the screen and then at Brandi and I bent down to kiss her forehead.

She smiled at me and turned her head to get a better look at the baby on the screen.

"I can't believe that's my...that's *my* baby." Her eyes glistened and her mouth could not contain her grin.

Although my heart was still torn about seeing my daughter in the state she was in, I couldn't resist feeling a little happy. I'd always envisioned having a grandchild; of course in my mind it happened when Brandi was married and in her late twenties. Staring at her with a deep glow on her face and a beautiful baby bump and I felt overwhelmed with emotion; I had to leave the room.

"What's wrong, ma?" Brandi asked sitting up on her elbows.

"I'll be back; I just need to get some coffee." I lied as I kept my head down and exited the room.

My sneakers squeaked against the white and grey floor as I paced up and down the corridor in front of Brandi's room. Branson's words echoed in my ear. Had I been a neglectful mother, giving Brandi everything she desired but not paying close enough attention to her comings and goings? I'd always prided myself on my daughter's hospitality, her kindness, intelligence and determination to be somebody; yet here I stood getting ready to be a grandmother before the age of forty. I'd gone wrong *somewhere*, I told myself as I plopped down in a pleather chair down the hall from Brandi's room. I covered my face, in my hands, and sighed deeply. I couldn't take back Brandi's pregnancy, but I wished I could go back in time and talk to her before she gave herself to Andrew and tell her to be safe, if not to wait. I leaned my elbows on my knees and shook my head.

"Are you okay?" I heard Branson's voice say before I wiped my eyes and looked at him.

"What do you think?" I asked shoving some of my hair backwards and sitting back in the seat.

Branson took a seat next to me and exhaled. "I know."

Blitz

How did he know? How could he understand where I was coming from? To him, Brandi was merely a stranger; someone that shared his DNA but who he knew the slightest about.

Relaxing into the comfortableness of the pleather chair I had called home for more minutes than I had anticipated, I rolled my eyes and chuckled. "Oh you do?"

"Damn, Mia." He turned his to face me. "You think that because I wasn't in Brandi's life that I didn't think about her or *want* to be closer to her? I wasn't the best man back then, but I'm trying now." Branson stood up and stuffed his hands in his dingy jeans.

"Regardless of anything that happened before, between us, I want the best for her. I don't want her to end up like…well, like you."

I jerked my head to the side and gave Branson the evilest eye I could muster. I wanted him to feel the heat building up inside me.

"What's that supposed to mean? *Like me?*"

Seconds passed and I could tell he was thinking about my question as he gnawed on the inside of his cheek, something he did when he was nervous. Finally, he spoke.

"Look at you. You went through hell and high water as a single mother and I know it's been hard for you. I don't want Brandi to have to go through the struggles you did. Granted, she turned out wonderfully and you did a great job, but being a single mother wasn't the lifestyle I had in mind for her when she was born."

"We all had different ideas for our lives back then." I reminded him of the vows we'd both taken long ago.

"That's another thing; I don't want Brandi blaming all men for the fuck up of one. If we live long enough, someone will eventually hurt us. That's reality Mia; especially in matters of the heart. I want our baby girl to be prepared for that reality. I want her to recognize that fact without dwelling on it. I want her to know that the sour fruit of 'dwelling' muddies the water of forgiveness. I messed up Mia, okay? We both know that, so can we stipulate that as a fact? That's reality. Neither of us down plays that. I don't and day by day you make it painfully clear that you don't either. I can't change anything about my past; it is what it is. But you can't let go either, can you Mia?

You hate me for everything I was, and rightfully so, but you don't want to like me for the man I'm trying to be. You're hung up on what I used to be. I need you to see me for what I am now. I want to be in our daughter's life as I should have been all along. I want to pick up the slack I left behind when you left me." He took a seat beside me and let his words float in the air we both shared.

I stared straight ahead and tried to ignore what he was saying. Hating him and all he had done to me was easy. Ignoring him and concentrating on all that he had done wrong was easy; that came second nature to me. Hating him was as easy as the breaths I took, for me. Stepping back and giving him a second chance…well, that was harder than I was willing to acknowledge or recognize. Viewing him in the manner he was presenting was too perfect, too typical and, most of all, it made hating him that much harder. To be honest, I wasn't sure if I was ready to let go of my anger and hate for him. I didn't know if I was ready, just yet, to forgive him.

I thought about Charles as Branson continued his protest that I not blame all men for *his* mistakes.

Is that what I had done? Had I kept Charles at a safe enough distance so that I wouldn't risk getting hurt? I had to stop and question the validity of that possibility.

Snapping out of my side-line thoughts, I turned to face Branson and stared closely at the lines in his face.

"That boy doesn't know the damage he's doing by putting Brandi through this shit. Trust me, I know. If I could take back everything and still be with you and…" Branson said trailing off as I stood up and held a hand in front of his face.

"No. Don't start that kind of talk, okay?" My heart was fluttering and I couldn't tell if it was because of the things Branson was saying or because I was going into shock.

"I'm sorry." He said dropping his head.

I spun around from him and shook my head continuously as my eyes filled up with tears. I held them back as the growing lump in my throat changed my pitch.

"Do you know the things I had to put up with? Do you know the bruises I had to cover up and the nights I slept in fear, thinking you would kill me? Branson I was *scared* for my life when I was with you. Did you know that?"

Blitz

I could see his ego deflating, second by second, as I continued talking.

"And just like I was scared then, I'm scared now; I don't trust you. I don't trust you around me and I don't trust you around my child. But I'm trying to look past all the bad and see some good; it's hard. But that's my baby in there." My voice cracked as I pointed towards the door.

There was a piercing, sensation in my heart as I thought about the nights I swore up and down that I'd never forgive or forget what Branson had done to Brandi and me.

"And my baby wants to love you so I'm trying to start *liking* you. But it just scares me that she's going to be a mother. I don't know where I went wrong and what I didn't do that could've caused this. It's like you come back into our lives just as I'm trying to clean up a mess that I caused; and you want her to leave me to be with you."

"This *isn't* your fault, Mia. If Brandi and Andrew didn't want to be parents they should have used protection or, better yet, not had sex."

I nodded my head in agreement as he continued.

"And I wanted Brandi to come live with me so that I could lighten your load a little bit; you know, help with everything. She *is* my daughter too."

"I know." I said leaning against the wall and sighing.

"And regardless of what we'd planned for, *our* daughter is having a baby."

Hearing the words out loud, spoke by someone other than myself, caused tears to swiftly drop from my eyes onto my cheeks. I couldn't control them and, for some strange reason, I didn't want to. A freeing sensation came over me as I cried in front of Branson letting him know I was scared and seemingly alone. I dropped my head and shook as my sobs continued pour like a waterfall. I didn't try to cover the tears or wipe them clean. I allowed my face to feel the fear and nervousness in each damp tear that fell.

I closed my eyes and prayed for some understanding to my fear. Was I more scared of Brandi choosing Branson over me or about the way my life was changing?

Branson stood up and aggressively placed his arms around me and hugged me tightly. I tried to fight him, by slightly pushing him away, but as more tears fell, my strength aimed at stopping him diminished.

"Stop" He whispered tenderly in my ear as he pulled me into his chest and gently pressed his body against mine.

Laying my head against his chest, I felt his heart beating and with each deep breath he took, I allowed myself to be held. I didn't want Branson to be the one to comfort me; I wanted Charles. And as we stood in the middle of the hallway, in a frozen embrace, I thought about how surreal the moment was. I mean, I was hugging my ex; the man I hated with a vengeance. Who could've predicted that, I thought, as I shifted my head?

Slowly, I wrapped my arms around his waist and sighed. It felt comfortable to be in the arms of someone who knew me as Mia Bia; the silly, geeky little girl who just desired attention, love and not much more.

For moments we sat still until my tears dried up and I began to feel a little stronger.

"You feel better?" Branson asked as he looked down at me with his arms still around me.

"A little." I said not cracking a smile as I looked up at him.

"What room is Brandi in?" I heard Charles ask as he approached both of us with a serious look on his face.

I backed away from Branson's embrace and he did the same to me and we both looked at Charles who was breathing like an angry bull.

It was like God was playing some kind of joke on me; the timing of everything was just too convenient. I wasn't sure what Charles was thinking, as he saw me embracing and inhaling my ex-husband; the man I vowed to never forgive.

"Hey, Charles, man." Branson finally broke the silence by extending his hand.

Charles reluctantly shook his hand, looked over at me and shook his head.

"She's in that room." I said following behind him as he walked into the room quietly.

"Branson, give us a minute." I said turning around to stop him from coming in.

"Cool. I'll go grab a soda." He said digging in his pockets for change.

Blitz

"Hey, Daddy!" I heard Brandi squeal excitedly as she sat up in the bed and wrapped her arms around Charles' neck.

"Hey, there!"

I stood back, away from the two of them, and watched with a smile on my face.

"Did mom tell you the news?" Brandi said as she knelt down to tie her shoe.

"Nah, what?" Charles asked taking a seat on the bed.

"It's a boy!"

If I could've recorded the look on Charles' face, I would have. I could see the pride and joy that beamed from his eyes.

"Where's Branson?" Brandi asked me as she stretched her arms.

"He went to get a soda."

"Do you have a dollar dad? I want to grab some juice." Brandi smiled as she hugged Charles' waist.

"Here." He smiled, handing her two dollar bills. "Bring me one back too."

As soon as Brandi left the room, I turned to face Charles who was staring out of the window with a distant look on his face.

"Can we talk?" I asked

"About...?"

"About what you just saw and about your date in Alabama."

"You can talk about whatever you'd like, but I'm not discussing my personal life."

"What do you mean your personal life? Since when did we start keeping things from each other?" I asked cocking my head to the side and placing my hands on my lower back.

"I guess from the moment you started getting close with your ex." He said turning to face me.

"He was just comforting me. I was down about Brandi being pregnant and he was there and..."

"What if I hadn't shown up?" Charles asked raising an eyebrow.

I was insulted that he'd even asked me that; like I would have taken Branson to an empty bed and picked up where we'd left off eleven years earlier.

Ebonee Monique

"We would've stopped hugging and probably taken Brandi to Denny's for breakfast." I said angrily shrugging my shoulders.

"I bet." Disbelief surrounded his words.

"What the hell is your problem Charles?" I shouted loudly "Two months ago we were fine; you loved me. Now I don't know..."

"If you have to even question my love for you now, then you always had a question about it in the back of your mind." He said as he walked around me. "I do love you...I love you enough to tell you the truth."

I followed his movements with my eyes and listened closely to his words.

"You want to know what happened two months ago that changed everything?"

"Yeah," I said hesitantly, not sure if I wanted to know the truth of if I was prepared for what Charles was going to tell me.

"Someone came into my life that showed me that I didn't have to beg for what I wanted." He looked down at the floor as he spoke.

Was Charles telling me that he'd cheated on me? As my mind tried to wrap around what he was saying, I continued listening.

"And I got tired of begging you."

"So you cheated?"

"Nope. I've never cheated on you. Anita and I..."

"So this is about her? I should've known your ass was waiting on a way to get out of this." I said shaking my head in disbelief.

"A way out? You think I was *looking* for a way out? If anything I was looking for a way to ignore my feelings so I could stay with you. But Anita's willing to show me the flip side."

"I can't believe you."

"Well believe it. I'm ready to be happy."

"So you're with this Anita, girl?" I asked, not believing what I was hearing and sensing.

Charles hesitated before answering. He stared at the ground and kept his eyes there until I got closer to him and crossed my arms.

Blitz

"I asked you if you're dating this Anita woman now." I repeated knowing Charles had heard me the first time.

"She's someone really special to me." He said bringing his head up, to see my reaction.

My heart sank deep into my throat as I tried to make sense out what was happening. My life was unraveling right before my eyes. I wasn't as hurt as I was angry. There were no tears in sight as I turned to leave the room with Charles staring at my back.

"So you're just going to leave?"

"What else do you want me to do, Charles? You want me to wish you the best in your new relationship? Hell, I didn't even know ours had officially been put to rest, but now that I know…" I said as I chuckled angrily.

"This is so typical of you. You get a problem and you run away. You ran away from Branson and…"

I spun around and pointed my finger in Charles' handsome face and I couldn't stop shaking.

"Don't you even act like you know what I was going through back then; I did the best thing for my daughter." I said slightly screaming.

"You took her home to meet your mother, Charles? How *could* you do that to me?"

"You know, despite what you think, everything isn't always about you Mia. My relationship isn't about you. Branson wanting to be closer to his daughter isn't about you and Brandi's pregnancy isn't, at all, about you."

I rolled my eyes as I stared at the man that used to make me melt. I could tell he was reaching for something, anything, to hurt me.

"Stop being so fucking self-absorbed in thinking that everyone else has all the issues. Maybe then you would see that *you're* more screwed up than any of us." He said confidently.

I cocked my hand behind me as far as I could and slapped the taste out of Charles' mouth. I'd never, in my life, hit a man with as much urgency as I did that day. I could see the red mark starting to appear on his face as my hand started stinging.

Brandi and Branson reappeared, with drinks in their hands, and I grabbed Brandi's arm and pulled her towards the door she'd just come in.

Ebonee Monique

"What are you doing, ma?" She asked as she cautiously allowed herself to be pulled.

"We're leaving." I said not making eye contact with Charles who was rubbing his cheek.

"Leaving? No. Dad said he'd take me out to breakfast; I want to go with him." She jerked her arm away from me. "What's the matter with you?"

I stood back and looked at the three of them; one who was taking a positive turn, one who was altering her life with a new life, and the other one who was turning out to be just another sad chapter in the story of my life. All I could do was scream.

"Fine!" I yelled as I tripped on my shoestrings and stumbled backwards against a wall. Catching my balance, I grabbed my purse and darted out of the room.

I ran down the hallway, past several nurses and patients as I headed, deliriously towards the exit. I heard Brandi calling my name loudly, but I didn't turn around or even respond to her cries. I made it to my car, fumbled with my keys and finally got my car started.

Before I could pull off, Brandi rushed towards my window and began banging on it with her fists.

"Ma, what's going on?" She had a frightened look on her face.

How was I going to tell her that the man who'd caused me the most physical pain in my life was now more comforting than the man she knew as Dad? How could I tell her that Charles was causing me the most damaging kind of pain: emotional. How could I explain that I *was* more screwed up than she knew? I was on a downward spiral and I didn't know how to crawl out of my hole.

I opened my mouth to say something and I saw Branson and Charles rushing out of the hospital towards my car.

"I can't take this." I said to her as I shook my head and threw my car in drive.

"Have Branson drop you off at home when you're done." I said as I sped off.

Looking in the rear view mirror, I saw a concerned Brandi rushing to both of her fathers as she pointed to my car.

Blitz

Laying my head back on my leather headrest, I sighed. Charles had been right, none of this had been about me; I was about to manually remove myself from everything that I'd thought meant anything.

Chapter 9

B randi had *Ciara* blasting in surround-sound as we decorated the living room and back porch area for her birthday party. We hung pink and black streamers throughout the room as Branson directed the party planners I'd hired to decorate the back yard. As he supervised the set-up of white tents and colored lights, I couldn't help but smile. It was shaping up to be a pretty cool, yet low-key event; Brandi seemed extremely excited.

We hadn't talked about what happened in the emergency room, but I could tell that Brandi was still a little worried about me. I was fine, though.

"Ma, what do you think about this dress?" Brandi asked as she pulled something from the closet, where I kept all of my little knick knacks.

She was holding a white, pink and black dress that was adorably cute with its A-line bottom, which would fall to her knees, and a tasteful halter top. There were little ruffles near the edge of the dress and it had 'Brandi' written all over it.

"That's cute baby." I smiled as I tried to figure out how her belly would play into the dress.

"Try it on." I said as I returned my attention to the streamers, which needed one last piece of tape.

I wasn't thrilled about Brandi's party, partially because I felt a feeling in the pit of my stomach again, but more importantly because I knew Charles would be there.

Brandi quickly walked up the stairs to her room and closed her door behind her. I could feel the excitement as she bounced around the house like a mad woman. She blabbed on and on about seeing Katrina and all her friends; they, according to Brandi, had so much catching up to do.

"Wanna come see the tent and lights?" Branson shouted over the music to catch my attention.

I nodded my head and headed out to the backyard.

"Everything looks beautiful." I grinned as I saw the pink, green and blue lights circulating throughout my back yard. We'd purchased a temporary dance floor that would go underneath the tent where the Deejay and sound system would go. Naturally, we assumed, the children would be under the tent dancing their butts off.

We catered food from Charles' restaurant as well as some finger foods for any parents that might drop by. In short, Brandi and I had worked ourselves silly preparing for the party.

Balloons hung everywhere around the pool and as the sun prepared to set; I geared myself up for the drove of Brandi's friends that would be coming in the next couple of hours.

"This is really nice; I can't believe you did all this in three days!" Branson said picking up a piece of trash off the ground.

"Me either." I said walking towards the tent and sighing.

Against my better judgment, I'd allowed Cecil to be the Deejay for the party. Since his name had been dropped at the Whittaker's house, I'd taken a slightly off-handed approach with him. I wasn't as friendly, I didn't give him as much leeway and I definitely didn't see him in the same light as I had before. Something was different, I thought, as I approached Cecil underneath the tent, as he set up his equipment.

"Do you need anything?" I asked bluntly.

I knew Cecil could tell the change in my attitude towards him, but he never veered from being polite. I wasn't sure if I was upset with him because he possibly could have been linked to my daughter sexually or because he possibly hadn't been truthful with me.

"No Ma'am. We've got everything under control."

"You know I don't want you playing songs with a bunch of curse words for lyrics, right?" I said raising one eyebrow at him.

Branson stood back, giving me my room to be me, and looked in the opposite direction.

"Right; we'll make sure to keep it clean."

Brandi moseyed over to us and I could see her cheeks rising as she saw Cecil.

"How's this?" She posed the question as I turned around to see her party dress.

Ebonee Monique

It was perfect. Absolutely, positively perfect; her stomach, which was evident but under control, wasn't an issue. Her breasts, which were growing by the day, fit just right in the cups of the dress. She was sporting a black pair of heels which showed off her black and pink painted toe nails.

"This is beautiful, honey." I smiled as I rubbed my temples at the same time.

"Dad, what do you think?"

Branson walked over to her and placed his arm around her shoulders.

"I don't think God made a more beautiful little girl." He grinned.

I glanced over at Cecil, who hadn't been able to tear his eyes off of the birthday girl, and cleared my throat.

"Brandi, why don't you go up to your room and start doing your hair and finish getting ready?" I said breaking their staring competition.

"Okay." She said smiling at Cecil.

"You look nice, Brandi." Cecil commented as he hauled a heavy piece of equipment behind the Deejay booth.

"Thanks." She beamed as she skipped off to her room.

I rolled my eyes and exhaled as I headed into the house; I needed a nap to prepare for the night ahead of me.

****

I straightened out my black wrap top and positioned my breasts so that they peeked out slightly over the top. I knew I was dressing for a teenage birthday party, but with the possibility of seeing Charles, I knew I had to pull out all the stops. There's something intriguing about seeing an ex-boyfriend right after the two of you have broken up. He could've been the scum of the earth or-in my case-an asshole in disguise, but you can't help wanting them to take one look at you and say: "*Damn, I never should've let her go!*" It could be the extra bounce in your step, as you waltz past him, making sure to sway your hips as slow as you can, or the extra cleavage you show, letting him know, *yes, I am desirable and you, missed this train, buddy!* Even though I'd been wolfing down sweets and fast food like crazy for over a week, I hoped that I could pull off the *I-look-better-now-that-I'm-not-with-you* look.

I turned and checked out my rear and smiled. I looked good and wearing Charles' favorite shirt as ammunition, I was sure to evoke some sort of emotion from him.

Coming down the stairs, I caught Brandi looking out of the window down our driveway.

"They'll be here, honey, go sit down." I joked as I walked up behind her and patted her bare back.

She looked cute with her hair in a side ponytail curled in a tight candy curl, and her makeup just lightly done.

"The party was supposed to start thirty minutes ago, ma."

"No one comes to a party on time, Brandi. Give them time to get here. You know how people like to make entrances." I said smiling to her.

"Where's Branson?"

"Out back with Cecil."

"Oh…"

"Ma, can I talk to you?" Brandi asked as she smirked nervously.

"Always. What's up?" I asked sitting down on the love seat opposite of Brandi.

She sat down slowly and leaned forward with her hands clasped together like she was getting ready to break some news to me.

"You know dad is going to be here tonight, right?" She asked slowly.

"Yes, I know that. You told me last night, remember." I tried to play off my hurt.

"I know. I just wanted to remind you that he'd be coming and…he's supposed to be bringing a guest." She said flinching.

A guest? I thought to myself. He can't be crazy enough to think about bringing his new lover all up in my house.

I stood up and shook my head as I sucked my teeth.

"That's not going to happen. If he wants to come, fine, but his girlfriend will not be parading around eating my food and enjoying my house." I said as I started walking away.

As far as I was concerned, there wasn't a need for any further discussion.

Ebonee Monique

"Ma, please; for me…" Brandi whined as she chased behind me.

"Brandi, as much as I've done for you, I don't think I owe you this one…this is a little much to ask; don't you think?"

"He's my dad, ma."

"Then he'll understand that he's the only one invited; not his girlfriend."

"She's not his girlfriend."

"Brandi, we're not discussing this; she is not welcome in this house, okay?"

Brandi looked pissed that I wasn't giving in to her manipulating pleas. She turned to walk away, then stopped mid step.

"I invited Andrew here, are you going to tell me he can't come either?" She spat, spinning around to meet the shocked expression on my face.

"Why would you invite him here? He doesn't want anything to do with you or your baby."

"If I can just show him that we don't need his money and that I'm not trying to trap him, maybe if he can see the baby's sonogram he'll do right by me and the baby." She said with less of an attitude.

"Why are you trying to force this perfect family thing to happen? If Andrew wants to be a father, he will be; nothing you do is going to change that. And because he can't be man enough to treat you like the mother of his child, he's not welcome here." I wished I could make Brandi jump ahead five years and see that Andrew was, and would always be, a boy who wanted his freedom; not an instant family of a wife and kid.

"Why are you doing this? Why do you want to keep us apart? You, yourself, said he needed to be in his child's life."

"The courts are the only means of forcing him to be in your child's life and even then, that only takes care of the child financially, honey. I just wish you would stop being so naïve and wake up and realize that you can't make a man want to be a father."

"Well…well…" She stuttered as she shrugged her shoulders,

"I invited him and he said he might come."

Blitz

"Brandi, as many mean things as he said to and about you, you still want to be around him?" I earnestly pleaded with my eyes for her to understand how brainless she sounded.

"I love him, mama." She replied confidently.

It was eerie how much Brandi sounded like me when I was pregnant with her. I'd find any excuse, anything good, to hold onto Branson and our marriage. I prayed on my knees until they were bloody; begging God to make him love me enough not to hit me. When Branson would do something nice, I'd use that as ammunition to everyone who wanted me to leave him. He loves me, I rationed, if he didn't he wouldn't do nice things for me. But the moment I stood on my own two feet and realized how much I was worth, the second-rate B.S. treatment went right out the door; I saw Branson for who he truly was, an abuser, user and manipulator.

A knock at the door interrupted my train of thought and Brandi eagerly rushed past me to open it.

"Hey, girl!" Bree said holding a beautifully wrapped gift in her hand as she leaned in to give Brandi a hug.

"Hey, Bree!" Brandi happily squealed as she pulled her friend in by the arm.

The two girls headed out towards the pool. I shut the door behind them and began focusing my thoughts on how I was going to deal with seeing Charles and his new girlfriend.

Within minutes, two more adolescent guests showed up and joined Bree and Brandi underneath the tent. In the midst of bringing a tray of chips and other refreshments to the tent, the front door opened.

It was Charles.

"I guess we don't knock anymore." I forced a fake smile on my face as I eyed Charles' companion.

She was everything that I'd expected. Thin, beautiful and glowing because of the man she was with. She had light brown hair with, what I assumed were, expensive blonde highlights, which fit her butterscotch, flawless complexion. Her dark brown eyes were exotic and captivating and her smile, perfectly straight and white, brightened the entire room. In all reality, she was damn near perfect. Wearing a simple blue and white boat neck dress, her body was something to be envied. My eyes lingered, for a second, as I watched Charles rest his hand easily on her lower back; I cringed with anger. Everything

I'd worked hard for-to make Charles want me- felt like it had been done in vain. I was okay, but this Anita-woman, was stunning.

"Sorry, I knew it would probably be open." He said smiling.

I didn't know if I should've been upset or friendly towards Charles, following the stunt he'd pulled in the hospital But I remembered the *kill them with kindness* quote and decided that was my best route to take.

"Hi, I'm Mia Robinson; so nice to finally meet you. Charles has told me so much about you." I grinned as I held the tray with one hand and shook her hand with the other.

"Hi, I'm Anita Malone. This is a beautiful home you have here." She said generically as she looked around at my house and then up, lovingly, at Charles.

I tried my best to look thrilled to see Charles and Anita, but the whole scene was just short of a dagger being stabbed straight into my heart. I'd accepted that Charles and Anita would be present, but looking at them together made me physically ill.

"Brandi and her friends are out back; why don't you go out and say hello?" I smiled towards Charles and Anita as I pretended to head back into the kitchen.

"Do you need any help?" Charles asked as he approached me.

"I've got it. Thanks." I said as I shooed him away. "Brandi can't wait to see you, why don't you go see her?"

Charles hesitated before shaking his head and making his way outside to the tent and music. I slammed the tray down on the counter and cursed myself for not saying and doing what I really felt. What I really wanted to do was strangle little miss perfect, while I slapped Charles for subjecting me to his parading of his new girlfriend. I had been his everything for six years and somehow, he'd found it easy to move on so quickly from what we had; that hurt.

I propped my elbows on the granite counter top and did some breathing exercises to calm myself down.

"It'll only be a couple of hours." I said out loud, trying to reassure myself, as I ran my fingers through my hair.

But I knew a couple of hours, in this instance, would feel more like eternity. How could I focus on anything else when Anita's hands and eyes were doing the things I knew I should've been doing? I paced the kitchen up and down as I tried to figure out facial expressions and small pieces of conversation I could use to get me through the night. Suddenly, the kitchen door swung open.

"Hey…" Charles smiled picking up a chip and popping it in his mouth.

I didn't speak, I just stared at him. I wondered what happened to the man I'd fallen in love with, the one who seemed to love me back. Where was he; and who was the cruel imposter who had taken his place?

"We won't stay long; I know you don't want us here." He said making sure to put emphasis on the word *us*.

I cleared my throat and crossed my arms as I walked away from him.

"I don't have a problem with you being here, Charles. But did it ever occur to you that it is disrespectful for you to parade your new woman in my house? How do you think that makes me feel? Or do you even care?"

"How *does* it make you feel?" Charles let the words linger in the air as he walked towards me.

"How do you think it makes me feel?" I asked staring into his beautiful eyes trying to read his thoughts.

I didn't want to stop being mad at Charles. I wanted to hate him for abandoning me like he did. I wanted to be able to not think about him and more and just let it all go; but I couldn't. He walked closer to me and I stood frozen at the possibility of our bodies touching.

His hand went onto my face as he gently moved a piece of hair that had fallen forward. He ran his fingers up and down my face as he eyed my reaction of pleasure at his touch. My eyes were closed and my mind imagined the two of us naked, enjoying every inch of our bodies. I turned my head to the side and moved my head up and down his hands, enjoying the soothing touch.

"You look so beautiful tonight." He leaned down and whispered softly into my ear. The warmth of his breath made the goose bumps, which always appeared whenever Charles was near, creep slowly throughout my body.

His hands seductively caressed my body as he bent down and planted sensual, wet kisses on the nape of my neck.

The moment our lips met felt like a science experiment where two magnets are held across from each other, and their magnetic pull brings them together. I sucked on his lips eagerly and grabbed the back of his head tightly. I didn't want the moment to ever end. Hoisting me up on the countertop, Charles pulled away from me and stared deep into my eyes for a second, connecting my soul with his. In a hot flash, though, he was back to servicing my lips with his. I locked my legs together, behind his back, and pulled him closer to my open legs. I didn't care where we were or who was around; he was *my* man and I wanted him…all of him.

I lifted his button down shirt up, slightly, and caressed my cold hands against his warm body.

"I missed you." I said softly, between one of the kisses. It was like I couldn't say everything I needed to say and feel the way I wanted to feel, in the same sitting.

Charles stopped kissing me and embraced me tightly.

"What are we doing?" I asked as I bit my lip and held him close to me.

I wanted him to tell me that the charade of us breaking up, was over and he was back in my life.

He shrugged his shoulders and separated from our embrace, while readjusting his shirt back into position

"We need to talk." He said dropping his head.

"What about Anita? This is wrong to do to her." I said, jumping down from the counter and walking closer to him.

He grabbed one of my hands and looked worried, as he wracked his brain for something to say.

"That's what we need to talk about."

I looked confused and before I knew it, Branson was bursting into the kitchen with sweat dripping down his forehead.

"An…Andrew's here!" He said pointing to the front door.

I dropped Charles' hand and rushed towards the door, cursing the entire way there.

"I know that little girl didn't disobey me and let that bastard in my house!"

Sure enough, when I got to the door, I stood face to face with Andrew and Brandi as they made small talk.

Blitz

I glanced around and saw a small crowd around the twosome, including Bree, Katrina and a few other people; definitely not the crowd I'd been expecting.

"Brandi I told you he's not welcome in this house." I said, eyeing him up and down.

"That's fine; I didn't come here for Brandi anyway." Andrew said in his smart-alecky tone.

"Then you can go ahead and get your little ass out of my house."

Andrew turned to exit the house when Brandi jumped in front of him.

"No, don't leave, Andrew." She begged, "Take me with you, we can make this work; me you and the baby."

Charles stepped in and placed one hand on Brandi's back and she jerked away from him and walked closer to Andrew.

"Man, I told you already..." Andrew said ignoring Brandi's desperate pleas. "That ain't my baby!"

I could see the tears beginning to stream down Brandi's face as Andrew rejected her, again; this time in front of everyone she knew and loved.

"But Andrew..." She wailed like some love sick woman in a bad TV movie. This would be the point in the movie where I'd either opt to roll over and go to sleep or change the channel. Unfortunately, I didn't have an option for either.

"Man, everyone in the school knows that ain't my baby; you ain't nothing but a slut."

Branson and Charles walked up on Andrew who chuckled and turned to leave.

"I love you, Andrew. Why are you doing this?" Brandi cried loudly.

"Get the hell out of my house, little boy." I shouted as I tried to comfort Brandi.

"Leave me alone, ma! I want to be with him." She said trying to break my hold. "We're going to be a family; you're just mad because I'll have it all before you will."

Brandi didn't even look in my eyes as she spat her hurtful words out; I let her go as soon as I saw that she wanted this, regardless if it was right or wrong.

Ebonee Monique

Charles walked towards Brandi and held up his hands in her face.

"Wait a minute, now. You will not sit up here and disrespect your mother; obey her, Brandi! If she says he can't be here; he can't be here!"

Brandi cocked her head to the side and looked at Charles closely before she responded.

"Leave me alone! You aren't my real dad anyway; I don't have to listen to you!"

I felt like Brandi had kicked me in the stomach as she blurted out the words I prayed she'd never say. We all knew who'd donated the sperm that'd created her, but the man who raised her was Charles.

"Brandi!" I yelled.

"Why don't y'all just leave me alone and let me live my life? I know what I'm doing!" Her demands were both forceful and hurtful.

"Oh yeah? Do you? Is that why this little bastard is telling you, to your face, that he doesn't want you or that damn baby and you're still begging his ass for a chance?" I said matter-of-factly.

"You don't know what you're talking about."

"I know exactly what I'm talking about and if you knew what you were doing, like you said, maybe your dumb ass wouldn't have gotten pregnant and screwed up your life—and all of our lives up—like you did."

Before I could retract the statement that I obviously hadn't meant, Brandi was bum rushing me with her arms and trying to push me to the ground.

Andrew stood back with a little smirk on his face while he watched the mother of his child fight her mother.

While Branson and Charles got the two of us off of each other, I was focused on getting that demon child, Andrew, out of our lives.

"Consider yourself freed of duty; I don't want you around my grandchild or my daughter, okay?" I said shoving Andrew firmly.

"I don't care." Andrew said brushing himself off.

He turned to leave and Brandi rushed on his tail to get him to stay.

"I love you." She said over and over as she reached for something, of his, to cling to.

Andrew turned around and looked at Brandi and shook his head in repulsion and then quickly scanned the crowd of people watching the incident unfold.

"Katrina, let's go!" He yelled as he motioned for Brandi's best friend to follow him.

I grabbed Katrina's arm and hissed "You aren't taking her anywhere."

Katrina yanked her arm from me and rolled her eyes, as she walked past a wide-eyed Brandi, all the while looking like she felt sorry for her begging best friend. The look, which was a mixture of shame and disgust, angered me to the core.

"This is my boyfriend now, Ms. Robinson; I think you need to mind your own business." She said grabbing Andrews' hand and snuggling close to him.

****

I tried to catch my breath as I plopped down at my dining room table watching Brandi and Bree follow each other up and down the stairs gathering her things.

"I'm moving in with Branson." She screamed after Andrew and Katrina had finally left the premises. "I hate you!"

I couldn't believe that somehow, this thing had turned around and become my fault. Granted I knew what I'd said had been totally wrong, but in the heat of the moment, I just wanted Brandi to see the light. Andrew didn't want her and probably never did.

Bree reluctantly followed her friend as she stomped up the stairs and started throwing things in suitcases. I didn't stop her nor did I give Charles or Branson the green light to. Branson wanted her and now she was all his.

"Are you...are you sure about this?" Branson asked as he paced the living room nervously.

We'd called all the parents of the children who were at the party and had just seen the last of the bunch off.

"Yeah, I'm sure, if she's sure." I said eyeing Brandi as she lugged a duffle bag down the stairs while rolling her eyes violently at me.

Branson waited until Brandi had gone back to her room before he took a seat next to me and leaned in closely.

Ebonee Monique

"I can't…I don't think I'm ready for this Mia."

"Isn't this what you wanted?"

"Yeah, but…I just don't know."

"She's not staying in my house so, unless you want your daughter out on the street in her condition, I advise you to let her stay with you." I crossed my arms against my chest.

I'd begged Charles to stay and wait Brandi's anger out, but he and Anita bolted as soon as Brandi began bad mouthing me for causing Katrina and Andrew leaving together. I'd been so close to resolving my issues with Charles, I thought, and Brandi had gone and messed another thing in my life up.

I still don't think it had hit her that her ex-boyfriend, the apparent father of her child, was now dating her supposed "best friend". She was so caught up in me not letting Andrew in the house that she was overlooking the obvious.

"Bree, come here." I said as I motioned for Bree to take a seat with me at the table along with Branson.

Bree looked like she was torn between going back up to Brandi's room to help with the remainder of her things, or sitting and talking with me.

"Okay." Bree said sighing as she walked slowly towards me, "She's getting all her hair things together; I know that'll take a minute." She smiled briefly before biting her bottom lip.

"What's going on with your friend?" I asked, feeling a little silly that I was consulting with a fourteen year old.

"She's mad…"

"I know that much, but *who's* she mad at? I know it's not me; not after everything I did…" I vented as Bree began shaking her head, which made me stop mid-sentence.

"She's in denial about Katrina and Andrew but I know…" She said slowing down as she stared at the staircase, to make sure Brandi wasn't coming.

"…I know that they've been together for about a month and a half."

My mouth dropped. I had never pegged Katrina for a backstabber; a liar maybe, but not a backstabber.

"How could Katrina do that? Why would she?"

Bree rolled her eyes and pursed her lips tightly, as if she, too, had a problem with Katrina.

Blitz

"Katrina wants to be Brandi so badly. Now that Brandi isn't at school anymore, she's trying to be her. She started dressing like her, wearing her hair like hers, she got with Andrew and then she talked Mr. Hemmings into giving her the Miss Princess crown and title." Bree said.

"She's the new Miss Princess?" I asked shocked by what I was hearing.

"Yep; I haven't had the heart to tell Brandi, yet."

"Do you think she had something to do with the sorority and Mr. Hemmings finding out that Brandi was pregnant?" I asked playing detective.

Bree shrugged her shoulders just as Brandi's bedroom door opened slightly.

"Her mom *is* in the sorority." Bree said "And she was the first person to tell everyone in school. I think she was waiting on the perfect moment to make everyone hate Brandi."

Right then, it all made sense. Brandi had welcomed a wolf in sheep's clothing into her heart. Katrina had portrayed herself as someone completely different than who she actually was. She had single-handedly played a role in making sure my daughter's life was rocky; I hated her for that.

I wanted to rush up the stairs and cradle Brandi until she realized that this was all one big misunderstanding; but I knew that once she had her mind made up, she rarely changed it.

"What about the party? Why didn't more of Brandi's friends come?" Branson asked curiously as he watched my expression change from anger, to disbelief and ultimately sympathy all in a matter of thirty seconds.

"Katrina and Andrew have been spreading so many rumors about Brandi that nobody wants to be around her. They've been saying Andrew isn't the father and that she'd slept with all his friends and that she's a..." Bree leaned forward as she whispered the final part of her sentence.

"A whore." She said softly. "But I know that's not true. I know that's Andrew's baby; Brandi was crazy about him."

"Brandi still is crazy over that boy." I said shaking my head at how things had unfolded. "I can't believe any of this is happening."

There were five bags, filled to the brim, which Brandi had placed by the front door for Branson to load into his car. I viewed each bag closely and realized if I wanted to be a bitch, I could've been. Each one of those bags had been paid with my credit cards, my cash or my connections; Brandi wasn't entitled to any of them. I could have taught her a quick lesson in the hard knock life, but I knew she'd get a dose of reality soon enough.

"Do you think I should tell her...I mean I don't want her to hate me...?" Bree asked sitting back in her seat with her hands by her side.

"It's better that someone hate you for telling the truth than them hate you for lying." I said.

"I guess..." Bree smirked and quickly jumped up from her chair when she heard Brandi's door open.

I could see Brandi wiping a few tears from her eyes as she lugged her boom box on her hip. Her belly was the only thing that I stared at as she made her way down the stairs. I wondered what kind of treatment that child would get being brought up by an inexperienced mother and grandfather.

"You got everything?" Branson asked as he took the boom box from her and picked up a few other bags off the ground and headed towards his Honda Accord.

"Yeah." She said not looking at me as I stood up.

Bree and Brandi joined each other in the dining room as I saw Bree drop her head and say a couple of things to Brandi, to which she dropped her jaw and then covered her mouth with her hands. I figured Bree had just dropped the bombshell.

I grabbed a few of Brandi's school books, which her home schooling teacher would need to give her assignments, and handed them to Branson as he made his last trip.

"I'll give her teacher your phone number and address; you'll need to work out something so that you're home during her school time. She has her pre-natal medication that she needs to take with food. Her doctor's appointments are..." I said as I rambled off a list of things that Branson needed to know about his daughter.

I could tell he was overwhelmed, but this was the role of father; if he wanted it he had to know the ins and outs.

"Bree, we can give you a ride home." Branson said as he headed towards the front door and opened it slowly.

Blitz

Everything seemed beyond unreal. I couldn't seem to grasp the fact that my daughter was leaving on her own will, to live with her father. We'd come so far, just the two of us, and I always thought that we were in the easiest time of her life.

I thought about all the nights I'd prayed over my child for her safety, her dreams and her wellbeing; I felt robbed. I felt like I'd raised an ungrateful, self-absorbed little girl who was leaving me because of a temporary fight. She was mad at me but I felt even angrier at her. I was angry at her for her hurtful words, her actions and her betrayal to our fifteen-year union. Although she was only my child, I felt as horrible as I did when Branson and I divorced; I wanted someone to blame. How could she be mad at me-the person who'd given her life and protected and provided for her without thought of my own needs? Then there was Andrew who had shown, over and over, that he didn't want her or her child; the one that had disrespected her in her face was held in higher regard than me.

Brandi, Branson and Bree all headed towards the front door and Brandi slowed down, trying to contemplate whether or not she was going to say goodbye to me.

She folded her arms across her chest and sucked her teeth, like I needed to walk towards her. I chuckled out loud at her actions.

I was making her choice easy for her. I stood up and breezed past my only child, my flesh and blood, and made my way up the stairs towards my bedroom, with my nose in the air. I could feel Brandi's disbelieving eyes staring at me as I placed one foot in front of the other and didn't acknowledge her departure. If she wanted to do this on her own; then alone she'd be.

Branson yelled my name loudly and I briefly looked over my shoulder to see Brandi, staring at me with an angry gaze while Bree and Branson simply shook their heads.

"Don't do this." Branson said calmly as I threw my hands up and shooed them all off.

"Lock the door on your way out!" I yelled over my shoulder as I slammed my bedroom door.

Chapter 10

I strained my eyes as the sunlight pierced them with intensity. The beam of light felt like a freshly sharpened knife being drug deeply into the sockets of my eyes. I quickly covered the windows of my soul with my hands and rolled over on my back sliding up against the headboard.

"Damn," I said as I reached over to answer the blaring, ringing phone.

I'd never noticed, before, that the ring tone on my phone had been as loud as it was. Maybe the sound being louder had something to do with the empty bottle of scotch that was lying next to me on my Egyptian Silk comforter.

I rubbed one of my temples with my free hand and groggily answered the phone as I tried to clear my throat.

"Hello?"

"Good morning to you too!" I heard Charles say as he slightly chuckled.

"I feel like shit; nothing's good about that." I said as I leaned against the headboard and tried to remember the events of the night before.

I remembered leaving Brandi, Branson and Bree standing at the bottom of the stairwell and crying as I flipped through Brandi's old baby photo albums. I remembered thinking that I was to blame for everything happening in my life and as self-pity took over, I reached for the full bottle of Johnnie Walker for comfort. I only intended to have a small glass but after glass number four, everything became fuzzy. I *think* I called Branson's house and maybe Charles' as well. What I said, though, was a mystery to me.

My head was pounding like a pro basketball team dribbling on my forehead. I cradled the phone between my shoulder and face, shut my eyes and prayed for the uneasy feeling in my stomach, to go away. How could someone feel as horrible as I did and still be alive and kicking? My head felt like

I was swimming in a pool full of nothing and, yet, it seemed to weigh more than my shoulders could support. I could feel the uneasiness in my stomach swirling around as it made a swishy sound over and over. I ran my fingers over my face and inhaled; the smell of alcohol was almost too much to bear. I stared at my fingers, wrinkled and dirty looking, and sniffed them closely; just like I suspected, they were alcohol laced.

"Do you even remember last night?" Charles asked me softly.

"Oh...last night? Did I talk to you last night or something?" I asked as I tried, my best, to recall the previous evening. I remembered hearing Charles' voice, I remembered telling him I loved him and I remembered caressing his body with my dirty alcohol fingers; but I knew all of that was nothing but a dream. So what *had* happened last night?

"*Talk?*" He asked sounding shocked at my answer "You really don't remember last night?" I finally opened my eyes and saw the room spinning uncontrollably; the uneasy feeling in my tummy was having a field day, causing me to almost vomit. Immediately, I shut my eyes and covered them with my hands. I didn't care anything about the stench that was on them, all I wanted was for the hangover of the century to be done and over with.

"I *really* don't remember last night." I said as I turned on my side and pushed myself underneath the covers.

I could hear Charles pausing, like he wanted to say something but didn't know how to, and finally he sighed and pulled himself closer to the phone. I could hear his deep breathing getting closer to my ear. "Mia..."

Just then, I remembered my conversation with Branson and Brandi from the night before. I'd called the apartment and had reached Branson, who allowed me to speak freely to my daughter. I didn't remember our full conversation, but I did remember Brandi crying and saying she was sorry and loved me. I rolled over on the other side of the bed and felt dampness on my pillow. I figured, I must've been crying as well.

But with my side-splitting headache, there was no telling if what I was remembering was an actual event or just something I'd made up in my drunken stupor.

"I talked to Brandi last night...I think." I said rolling my eyes towards the ceiling.

Ebonee Monique

Whatever had possessed me to pick the bottle up would definitely never enter my thoughts again.

I hated being drunk and I hated not knowing what I'd done or what I was going to do. I called alcohol, especially scotch, the devil's juice because every time I drank it, I did devious things that I never would've stood for if I were sober. But my grandmother always said: *"A drunken mouth speaks a sober mind."*

"Humph." Charles said sounding as if he didn't want to hear the details of our call.

"I think I said she could move back…but I don't know." I said as I moaned at the continuous waves in my stomach.

"You told her what?!!" Charles shot back to me "Mia, she's made her bed now she needs to lie in it."

Although I reeked of alcohol and couldn't remember what I'd done or said hours earlier, it felt good to have Charles back in my life, even if the terms hadn't been defined. I knew he'd been extremely hurt by Brandi's words and actions, but he still loved her.

"I don't know, Charles. I really don't know what happened for sure."

"How could you *not* remember what you did? I know you were a little tipsy but I didn't know you were that gone." He said with a chuckle.

"How'd you know I was tipsy? Did I call you last night too?" I moaned as I thought about the things drunk Mia probably laid on Charles.

"We slept together last night." Charles said matter-of-factly. "I can't believe you don't remember."

I opened my sleep-filled eyes and covered my mouth with my hands. He was kidding, right? He had to be kidding. There was no way I'd slept with Charles and not remembered it. I mean, this *was* Charles we were talking about; he wasn't an easy thing to forget.

"You're…you're kidding, right?" I asked with my hands on my forehead.

"We slept together last night, Mia; more than once." Charles said sounding a little hurt by my memory loss.

I tried to think about Charles, in the sack, pleasuring me in every way I loved, hoping it would spark some kind of memory; but nothing.

Exhaling, he tried to jog my memory.

"You called me and asked me to come over. You said you were depressed about Brandi and needed me to...to fall asleep."

"Uh Huh."

"When I got there, you were naked at the door and told me *things* that you'd been thinking about."

"Things like what?"

Charles cleared his throat and took a deep breath before responding.

"You told me you were ready to be my wife and have my babies."

"What?!" I said with skepticism.

"You *said* it. You might not remember us having sex, you might not remember us taking a bath together and you might not even remember you asking me to move in with you; but you *said* you were ready to be my wife and have my children." He said as his breath slipped away.

"And you weren't drunk when you said it."

"Charles, if this is some joke of yours...you've really got me."

"I'm not joking with you."

"Then why don't I...I would've remembered if I...and I'm..." I stuttered as I tried to think of a rational explanation for Charles.

My mind was all kinds of jumbled as I struggled to think of something to say.

"You still don't believe me?" Charles asked.

"I'm not saying you're lying. I'm just saying..."

"You aren't wearing any underwear and you have on your purple and white *La Perla* bra that I bought you in Italy last year." Charles replied.

I looked down at myself and my favorite purple and white bra, and slapped my forehead. Holding the cover up, I noticed my nude vajayjay staring back at me and I could've screamed.

How could I have forgotten sleeping with the man I'd been thirsting for? My body tensed up, even at the mention of

Charles' name, and yet I'd apparently slept with him and didn't remember it?

"I know you remember saying it; I know you do." Charles said in a hushed tone. I could tell he was trying to convince himself, as much as me, with his words.

"Charles, I'm sure I did and said a lot of things last night, which I don't remember and that just might have been one of those things." I said as I yawned.

"So you're telling me you didn't mean it. That's what you're saying right?"

I paused and tried to collect my thoughts as Charles waited patiently. The same thing he'd done for our entire relationship.

"I'm not saying that." I vaguely responded.

"Whatever." He said sounding angry. "We need to talk, anyway."

"Ugh…can it wait until tomorrow. I don't think I'm doing anyone any good in the condition I am in." I said as I clutched my queasy stomach tightly.

"We can do breakfast tomorrow morning, if that's cool with you."

"Yeah, I'll call you tonight or something."

"Did you have a chance to reschedule your showing for later in the week?" Charles asked, sounding concerned.

"My showing? What are you talking about?" "You are showing a house for Commissioner Donaldson this afternoon, right?"

"What time is it?!" I shrieked remembering my obligation, which had totally fallen to the back of my list of important things.

"It's almost noon."

"Shit! Are you kidding me? Why didn't you wake me up earlier?" I screamed as I remembered that the showing was scheduled to start at 1:00 and was halfway across town. I'd never get up, get sober, dressed, pick up the catered platter of food and get to the house in time.

"I didn't know I was your personal alarm clock." Charles responded.

I flung the covers back and cupped the phone against my chin. As soon as my feet hit the ground, I was already trying to stabilize myself and my heavy head.

Blitz

"I've got to call you back." I said hanging the phone up in Charles' face and clutching my bed as I leaned over and took a deep breath. With my face in the covers, I took deep breaths in and out. My head continued spinning and my legs felt like they were about to give out on me. I pounded the covers heavily. No matter how bad I wanted to move, I couldn't. However, after minutes of trying to steady myself, I was finally at a point where I could stand up without feeling like I was about to pass out. I made my way to the bathroom, started a shower and stared at myself in the mirror as the room fogged up. Wiping away the moisture on the glass, I looked closely at all the lines, gray hairs and small pimples around my mouth.

I looked worn out; I was sure it hadn't come from the bottle of scotch. With everything that I was dealing with, I hadn't really slowed down to look at the affect that everything was having on me. But just like any other day, I didn't have time to think about anything else other than business.

I rushed into the shower and sighed heavily as the steamy water splashed onto my body and relaxed all the tension residing there. I leaned up against the limestone tile and allowed the water to do its job on its own. I breathed heavily as I felt all of the problems weighing heavily on my neck and back.

Even though I wanted to stay in the shower all morning, I knew I was already short on time.

I jumped out of the shower, dried off, lotioned my legs and quickly stepped into a casual, tan linen pant suit. Thank goodness you don't have to iron linen clothes, I thought, as I brushed my hair into a conservative ponytail near the nape of my neck. I threw on a beautiful pair of tan earrings and a matching necklace and headed out the door towards my car.

"Cecil, where are you?" I barked into my cell phone as I started up my Range Rover and backed out of the driveway.

"I'm at the Donaldson house." He said sounding a little more nervous than usual.

"Why the hell didn't anyone remind me of the showing?" I yelled to no one in particular. I knew it wasn't Cecil's job to remind me of my *own* showings; hell, if anything, I should've been reminding him about the showing.

"I'm sorry." He said sighing, "But I've got everything under control. I picked up the platter from *Publix*, I located some areas of concern and fixed them up and I'm sitting here with Mr. Donaldson browsing a few of the comps in this area." Cecil said confidently.

Inside, I was completely relieved that I didn't have to make all the stops along the way that I thought I would've had to; but outside, I was livid. How dare Cecil step on my toes and mix and mingle with my client?

"I'll talk to you when I get there." I said hanging the phone up.

As I turned my car down Bay Shore Boulevard, I revved up my engine and pressed down on the gas. I had fifteen minutes until the showing started and I needed to get there to repair any misunderstandings with Lee.

I saw my speedometer creep up to 45, then 50 and, before I knew it I was nearing 80 mph. Just my luck, a police officer's red and blue lights swirled behind me, letting me know that my joy ride in speed racer heaven, was coming to an end.

"Ma'am, do you know you were doing 80 in a 45mph zone?" The handsome black officer said as he approached my car.

I pushed my Chanel shades on top of my head and exhaled before staring deeply into his eyes. "It was my mistake. I was just in a rush; I'll take whatever the ticket is. Do you think we can just...hurry it up?" I asked raising my eyebrows.

I'm not sure if the officer was more caught off guard, pissed or amazed at my frankness, but he chuckled as I handed him my driver's license and registration.

"This is perfect." I said to myself as I checked the time and saw I had five minutes to make it to the house in time.

Dialing Cecil's cell, I didn't get an answer and I started panicking. Cecil wouldn't throw me under the bus, would he? After all, I'd been the one who had seen his potential and had given him a job when even *McDonald's* wouldn't.

When the officer returned I sat straight up in my seat and extended my hand out of the window, to grab my license.

"Whoa, wait a minute." Officer Brown Sugar said as he snatched the license and registration backwards. "We ran this and it seems like this car has been reported stolen."

If I could've laughed, I would've. My head was still pounding, my stomach felt queasy and my body was just useless.

Blitz

"What do you mean, stolen? I purchased this truck two years ago." I said looking up at him with a dumbfounded look on my face.

"Are you sure this is your car? This isn't an ex-boyfriends' car and maybe he wants it back?"

I was insulted and shocked that, in this day and age, men still believed women couldn't own and purchase their own things with their own money.

"For your information, this is *my* car. You see the registration says my name on it and you see the license matches up. I don't need a man to buy me anything and for you to insinuate that I do is just preposterous and rude." I said not slowing down with my words or the quickness of my hands as I talked.

"I'm just kidding, ma'am." Officer Brown Sugar said as he put his hand on his flat stomach and laughed hysterically.

I stopped mid-rant and scrunched my eyebrows down as I watched the young, extremely handsome officer laugh at me. I felt stupid and I felt ridiculous; most of all I hated the young cop. Who did he think he was?

"Can I go now or would you like to laugh at me some more?" I asked folding my arms.

"I'm sorry." The cop said in between gasps for air "That was wrong of me."

"You think?" I said sarcastically "I really do have somewhere to be, though so can I please have my ticket and be on my way."

"Where are you in such a rush to?"

"Not that it's any of your business, but I'm a real estate agent and I have a showing that's starting right now and I'm late." I said eyeing the clock.

"So I'm holding you up, then?" He asked leaning on my door.

I wanted to say, *"Yes, you are asshole; please let me go!"* but as I looked over and got a good look at brown sugar, I was taken aback by his gorgeousness.

There was no reason for a man to be *that* beautiful, I thought to myself as I looked into his dark hazel eyes and studied them intimately. I bit my bottom lip and caught myself not breathing as I moved my stare up to his smooth brown sugar colored skin and delicious smile. His muscles, which bulged

Ebonee Monique

from his short sleeved uniform, made me lick my lips. You know that moment in *Waiting to Exhale* when the women met *that* man and he made them blow all their past experiences, pain and hurt out with an exhale? Yeah, that's what Officer Brown sugar was doing to me right then and there.

"Huh?" I said knowing I'd been gawking. "Yeah, I mean, you're not holding me up, but I do need to be leaving."

"I'm going to let you go with a warning but make sure you stay within the speed limits, okay?" He said as he handed me my information back.

"Right." I said tossing my license and registration into my passenger seat.

"Well, you have a great day, gorgeous." He said as he slightly tapped the top of my truck.

I watched him, as he walked back to his cruiser, and shook my head.

"I'd be in jail messing with a baby like him." I thought as I sped off towards the showing.
****
When I arrived at the house, which was beyond stunning, I was greeted with about six or seven cars in the circular driveway. I parked mine behind Cecil's and walked into the house confidently, with information on the house and area in my briefcase.

"Hello everyone!" I said as I smiled at a few couples and singles that were going from room to room looking at the house.

"Hey." Cecil said walking towards me with his hands in his khaki pants pockets. Cecil looked presentable; more so than I'd ever seen him before. His crisp white button down shirt and red tie fit the occasion perfectly.

"Where's Lee?" I said not acknowledging Cecil's greeting.

"He decided to leave until the showing was over." Cecil said in a low voice as a couple passed us and headed into the kitchen.

"Can we talk outside?" I said raising an eyebrow.

Cecil nodded his head and walked toward the side door of the house where the garage and trash compactors were held.

"I'm extremely disappointed in you Cecil. I appreciate you picking up the platters and handling Mr. Donaldson but…"

Blitz

"But what?" Cecil interjected sounding a little more peeved than I thought he should've been. "I picked up your slack today. This was *your* showing; not mine." He said in a heated manner.

"Like I said, I appreciate you doing all those things for me; but you overstepped your boundaries."

"You know what Ms. Robinson? No disrespect, at all, but you're completely in the wrong and you're looking for someone to blame, but I'm not the one." He said as he paced.

"I've busted my ass working for you and the one time I go all out, to show you that I'm not the guy you think I am, you tell me I overstepped my boundaries? I don't know what I did to you, or what you think I did to you, but if you don't think this is a good fit then maybe…" He said trailing off.

I was shocked by Cecil. This was the most I'd ever heard him speak out, let alone yell, to me; I wasn't sure what to think of it. I knew I was reaching for someone to blame for my absence at the showing, but I wasn't ready to concede easily.

"Cecil, this isn't about any personal reasons that I might not like you. This is about business."

"Of course; isn't it always?" He chuckled with his back turned to me.

"I don't have time for this, there's a showing going on and I need to make sure that all questions are answered." I said as I turned to leave the garage and head back into the house.

"Why don't you be honest with me? You tell me all about what it takes to make it in the business world, but let me tell you what it takes to make it in the real world okay? Be honest. Tell me what your issue is with me." He said, stopping me in my tracks. I stood frozen as he continued talking.

"You think I didn't notice the looks you were giving me at Brandi's party or the way you ignore me when I'm talking to you in the office? I do. I notice it all. So just tell me what I did wrong to cause you to treat me like you do."

I spun around and faced Cecil and raised both of my eyebrows. I knew he knew why I didn't want to have too much to do with him. With the possibility of him and my daughter having been intimate, my entire perception of Cecil had changed.

"You *know* what my issue is with you." I said forcefully as I walked slowly towards him.

Ebonee Monique

"You don't like Brandi and I being friends; I get that. But what does that have to do with our working relationship?"

"You know that's my only child, right? I'll do anything to protect her and if I see something going on that I know isn't leading her on the right path, I'll do my best to steer her in the right way. But when I have people around me, people whom I've put my trust in, who are sniffing around my child and leading her to do things I know she doesn't want to do, then I get upset." I said.

"What does that have to do with me?"

"Let's not play dumb. I know that you're the father of Brandi's baby." I said staring him up and down. I decided to play a little reverse psychology. No, I didn't know for sure that he was the father, but he didn't know what I knew.

Cecil's eyes widened as he looked over my shoulder in a daze, almost like I'd said something wrong to him.

"Say something; don't you think you owe me that?"

"You know what? I don't even want to entertain this." He said brushing past me as he headed towards the door.

"So it's true?" I yelled.

Cecil stopped and looked at me before turning around. He looked down at the ground and shook his head and finally looked into my eyes.

"Yeah." He said hesitantly "And I'm going to be a great father."

I couldn't believe what I was hearing. Yeah, I'd heard what Andrew had been saying about Cecil possibly being the father, but I hadn't actually prepared myself for the outcome if it had been true.

"How could you....how..." I stammered as heat rose on my face. I'd trusted this kid and I'd allowed him to be close to my daughter; now I didn't have anyone to blame but myself.

"Go home, Cecil." I said as I dropped my head into my hands and pointed towards the door.

A few moments passed before I heard the door open and close and I finally lifted my head out of my hands. My stress level was through the roof, causing my head to pound excessively. As I began to massage my temples, I heard the door open and I stared at a couple who smiled eagerly back at me.

Blitz

In seconds, my personal problems were pushed to the side and I was back to business.

"Let me show you this fabulous three car garage." I said plastering a fake smile on my face.

****

I crossed my legs at the dining room table and slid Lee a number of properties that I'd researched, which he might like to consider purchasing.

"These are nice, Mia." He smiled weakly as he flipped through the pages of the binder.

"Look at the one in downtown Ybor. It's a condo, but you did say you were looking for something with a little less maintenance." I said pointing to a page as Lee stopped and looked up at me.

"What?" I said as his stare became uncomfortable.

"I heard." He said closing the book. "About your daughter. I heard."

"Oh." I replied looking at my shoes.

"It's so sad. I just don't know what's happening with our youth today." He said shaking his head as I felt more and more helpless about my situation.

"Umm Hmm." I responded, not making eye contact with him.

"As much as I want to blame the children, it's our parents that have to take a stand and accept the blame." He said stopping. "But, I'm not blaming you, of course; it's those *other* parents."

I knew good and darn well, that he was talking directly to me. When he looked at me, with sympathy all in his eyes, I knew he was thinking "*She should've done this*" or "*She could've done that*"; but the reality was I'd done everything I knew how to do as a parent and I was done being ashamed of myself. I knew that Lee, along with every other parent and adult in my city, shook their heads when they saw me approaching. It bothered me because I knew there was no way I could possibly change everyone's mind; it just wasn't feasible. My fifteen-year-old daughter was expecting a baby and nothing any of them could say would reverse that.

"Well, let's discuss some of the offers we received today." I said as I changed the subject and flipped open a folder with a couple of written offers from other agents.

Ebonee Monique

"Oh, okay." He said picking up his glasses and placing them on his face.

"I didn't offend you did I? I didn't mean to." He said glancing up at me.

"There's little that can shock or offend me anymore." I said forcing a smile on my face.

With everything going on, the bomb Cecil had dropped, my situation with Charles and my relationship with my daughter, I didn't know what was up or down. To the common outsider, I might have looked put together but inside I was screaming for some sort of clarity.

"Now, with this offer the buyer has..." I started as I pointed to a sheet of paper, just as the front door opened.

"Hello?" I heard the deep voice say from the foyer. Lee and I both stood up and headed towards the voice and I dropped my jaw as soon as I saw the face. It was Officer Brown Sugar.

"Can I help you?" Lee said as I kept quiet.

"Am I too late for the open house?" He asked smirking as he smoothed his shirt and tie out.

He'd changed his clothes and brother man looked scrumptious. He was wearing a grey and black pinstriped suit with a grey tie and black shoes. I was impressed. I didn't think a cop, let alone a young cop, could clean up as well as he did.

"Shoot, no! Come on in." Lee said waving him in.

"This is my realtor Mia Robinson and you are..." He said patting Officer Brown Sugar on the back.

"Sean Nilson." He said respectfully.

"Nilson...why does that name sound familiar?" Lee asked as he tapped his chin and thought about it.

"My father was Police Chief for about fifteen years, Grant Nilson."

"Grant Nilson? Get out of here! We played at the same country club." Lee smiled as he turned to look back at me.

I couldn't take my eyes off of Sean. Even as he talked, I was enthralled. I wanted to know more about him.

"Well, I'll move out of the way and let Mia do her thing and show you around."

"Alright." He said facing me.

"We can start in the upstairs bedrooms, if you'd like." I smiled thinking of the awkwardness of my choice of places to start as we headed up the stairs.

Blitz

"This is the master suite and it's equipped with its own walk in closet and…"

Sean grabbed me by my waist and pulled me into his chest, allowing me to feel all of him, and bent down and placed his lips upon mine. Normally I would've pushed him back; I didn't know where his lips had been and I didn't know anything about him. But in the heat of the moment, all I could do was melt into his arms as he held my back gently and began sucking on my bottom lip. His juicy lips had nothing on Charles' but as he wrapped his around mine, they almost felt like the real thing. I wanted more and as he inserted his tongue in my mouth, I realized how irrational the whole moment was. I mean, I was kissing a stranger.

"Wait." I said pulling back and wiping my mouth "What are you doing?"

"It's called kissing." He said sarcastically as he walked closer to me.

"I know what it's called; why'd you do it to me?"

"You did it to me too." He said grinning.

He had me there. I hadn't fought or protested his kisses and, in fact, I wanted more; I just didn't want him to know I wanted more.

"Why are you here?" I asked stepping back "Do you really want to buy this house?"

"I don't know; maybe." He shrugged as he looked around the room.

"Can you afford this? The house has an asking price of three million." I said reminding him of the seriousness of my job.

"I know."

"How'd you find me…I mean, this open house anyway?"

"Well, to be honest with you, I've seen you around Tampa before and I've always wanted to have a reason to talk to you; today, when I pulled you over, I got my chance. I mean, really, what are the chances I'd pull over the woman I'd been dying to meet? I don't believe in coincidences so I remembered your name, looked up your business and found out about your open house on your website. When I want something, I go after it."

My heart fluttered. This fine, young thing wanted *me*?

Ebonee Monique

"Boy please. I'm at least ten years older than you." I said rolling my eyes. "How old are you?" I challenged

"I'm twenty-two."

"Oh man, you're a baby. I can't do anything with you. Now do you still want to see the house or..." Sean walked towards me, placed his hands on the small of my back and kissed me again until I couldn't see straight. It was something about the flicker of his tongue, while inside my mouth, that made me quiver. It was like he knew the perfect way to kiss me, like no one else had ever conquered, and I loved it. His hands traveled through my hair and they roamed all over my body; my thighs, my arms, my face, my hair and my butt. I couldn't stop myself as my hands went up and down his perfectly proportioned body.

"I can do plenty with you." He said as our lips separated. "Let me take you out; one time and if you don't like it, we can stop."

I don't know what I did while he was talking, but all I could feel was my head bobbing up and down, as I said yes, and a smile quickly appeared on my face.

Was this me? I didn't date strangers, let alone make out with them in houses I was trying to sell; I had a six-week rule, but with Sean I could see myself breaking that.

As we made our way back down the stairs, I felt Sean's hand grab my butt and I giggled. I felt carefree while I was with him and he made me smile, despite all my issues and problems.

Something in me was being renewed but I couldn't have predicted the way things would turn out.

Chapter 11

It had been four weeks since I'd met Sean and, already, life seemed to be looking up.

"I can't believe you just did that!" I squealed as I ducked down in the passenger side of his Mustang Convertible.

Sean was laughing, as usual, as we sped up and down my street. I wasn't looking at the speedometer, but I knew he was pushing at least 70 mph.

"Open your eyes!" He said trying to pull my hands off of my eyes.

"Keep your hands on the steering wheel, Sean!" I yelled as I smacked his hands.

I wasn't much of a racer. I hated the possibility of losing control of a car and, yet, I'd taken up with a man whose passion was race car driving.

I looked over at him as he grinned widely with his arm cocked up on the wheel, his designer shades covering his eyes as he did what he loved.

Normally I would've objected to him driving like that in my neighborhood, but I knew it was late and very few, if any, people would be awake, let alone, on the street.

I don't know how Sean fell into the mix of things but, amazingly, he calmed my world down. I had spoken to Brandi, but not as much as I would have liked. She called and called but I decided to only speak to her once week; this way she could think about her decision to move in with Branson. Charles and I were still in limbo as we both struggled to gain control of what was. I wanted Charles to accept me for what I wanted and he wanted me to live up to what I'd promised. But, the more I was with Sean the more I realized I didn't want to have more children. I mean, I *was* about to be a grandmother. Did I really want my child calling my grandchild-who would be older than them-niece or nephew? The thought of that was weird to me and something I didn't think I wanted to experience. Sean had done a phenomenal job of keeping my mind off of things and he didn't even know it. I rarely mentioned Brandi and he didn't even know who Charles was; it felt perfect.

He was happy-go-lucky, he didn't stress over little things and he didn't want children either. But Sean and I weren't committed to each other at all; he was a good time, and that was all right with me. He took my mind off of the things that I didn't want to deal with or think about and I, in turn, made sure he was satisfied.

As he slowed the car down and we approached my driveway, I felt my purse buzzing.

"It's ten o'clock, who's calling you this time of night?" Sean suspiciously joked as he pulled his Mustang into my driveway.

"It's my daughter. Hold on." I said, holding one finger up in his direction. Brandi never called late at night, so I prayed nothing was wrong.

"Hello?"

"Mia, this is Branson."

Immediately, I thought the worse. Why was Branson calling me from Brandi's cell phone? Was she okay? Was the baby okay?

"What's wrong? Is Brandi okay?" I said clutching my chest, in preparation for the worst.

"Where are you?"

"I'm at home, why?"

"Do you remember what was supposed to happen tonight?" He said quietly into the phone.

"What are you talking about, Branson?"

Branson sighed loudly and brought the phone closer to his mouth.

"You asked Brandi to plan a dinner and invite Cecil over and you and I were going to sit down and talk with them."

I slapped my forehead and looked over at Sean who was checking himself out in the mirror.

"Dammit! Was that tonight? I totally forgot." I said.

"Brandi called you yesterday to remind you, but she never heard back from you." He said with very little sympathy. "You also missed her doctor's appointment and now you don't even show up for a dinner that you made her plan."

"I just told you I forgot." I said defensively.

"I heard what you said, but you've got a six-month pregnant daughter and her supposed baby's father sitting here waiting on you. They've been waiting patiently for over two hours, Mia. You need to get your ass over here now!" He said angrily before he hung up.

I looked at my phone and sucked my teeth as I stuffed it back into my purse.

"Everything okay, babe?" Sean asked returning his glance to me.

I exhaled and rolled my eyes as I threw my head back on the headrest. I looked down at my clothes and shook my head. I wasn't anywhere near being presentable for a dinner with Brandi, Cecil and Branson.

I sat in the passenger side of Sean's car, in a pair of tight leggings, an off-the-shoulder top and a pair of jeweled flip flops. If anything, I looked like one of Brandi's friends rather than her mother. Mentally disregarding how I looked, I knew I needed to get to Brandi quickly before I damaged our relationship any further.

"Can you take me to my ex-husband's apartment? I had a dinner date with my daughter and...I'm late." I said smiling.

I knew with Sean being a police officer, we could speed without worry and still get where we needed to be in one piece.

"Anything for you." He said leaning over to peck my lips.

During the ride to Branson's, I thought about how I was going to introduce Sean. Brandi was too old to fall for the "Uncle Sean" trick. I knew that once she saw Sean and I walk in together, she would piece together what was going on. My only concern was in any of it being relayed back to Charles.

I couldn't ask Sean to sit in the car during the dinner; or could I? Maybe I could make the event an in and out dinner and just have Sean pick me up when I was finished.

I ran a couple different scenarios in my head and picked the best one fitted for the situation as we pulled into the apartment complex. I had only been over to Branson's place once since Brandi moved in a month and a half earlier. Sitting outside his apartment in the middle of the night, somehow made it look a little better, but not much. Why my baby girl chose to live like this as opposed to what I could provide was beyond me.

The neighborhood used to have a lot of gang activity in it and so the graffiti was very noticeable. The three-story, motel like, apartment building had grey rails around the outside and a wooden exterior that looked like it had seen better days. There were wall air conditioners, shiftless people sitting out front and chipped paint everywhere. I wasn't, in the least bit, impressed by where Branson had our daughter, or himself for that matter, living.

As I surveyed our surroundings, Sean turned the car off and turned to face me.

"What are we doing?"

"Do you want to come in? I mean, you don't have to."

"I'm not leaving you here, Mia." He said stretching his arm out over my shoulder. The cop in him was shining through, seems he's always protecting and serving, even when I didn't want him to.

I smiled as I kissed his hand.

"You can come in if you want."

"Let's do it, then." He said opening the car door widely, with no clue that I preferred him to stay in the car.

I took a deep breath and prepared myself for the disaster I knew was coming.

"Hey, there." I said pulling the off-the-shoulder shirt down a little bit, trying to look more presentable as Branson opened the door. He looked pissed off, to say the least.

"Mia." He said nodding his head as Sean appeared behind the wall.

"Hey man." Sean said breaking the awkward silence as he extended his hand. "I'm Sean. Sean Nilson."

Branson looked at his hand for a second before shaking it and introducing himself before letting us both in.

Brandi and Cecil were seated comfortably on the couch flipping through cable channels, before they turned and saw me and my guest walk in.

"Ma, where have you been?" Brandi asked standing up and walking towards me.

Branson's apartment was cute-quaint-but cute. He had it decorated very traditional. A glass coffee table, pretty

African-American art, interesting rugs and neutral cream paint on the walls.

"I'm sorry, baby. I just lost track of time." I said reaching out to hug her.

Brandi fell into my arms and hugged me tightly and pressed her hard belly against mine.

"Every time I see you, you're bigger!" I said stroking her stomach gently as I stared into her eyes, which were staring at Sean.

"Who's that?" She whispered rudely.

"Brandi, this is my friend Sean. Sean, this is my daughter Brandi."

"Wow, you look like you're about to pop any minute!" Sean joked as he touched Brandi's stomach.

"I'm only six months along." She responded with irritation in her words as she rolled her eyes at Sean and walked back to the couch.

"Is dinner still ready or did we completely miss that?" I asked standing in the middle of the apartment staring at Branson and wishing the awkwardness would leave the air.

Brandi laughed as she looked at Cecil, who was stroking her stomach lovingly. "Ma, you know I couldn't go without eating for too long."

"Right." I laughed as I took a seat in a stray chair. Sean stood by my side.

"What are you wearing?" Brandi asked raising an eyebrow.

I shrugged my shoulders, knowing I looked more like a hoe than a housewife. "Just something new." I smiled weakly.

"Mia, can I talk to you in the kitchen?" Branson said walking toward his small kitchen.

I nodded my head towards Cecil, to say 'hello' and he did the same.

"I'll be right back." I said patting Sean's hand.

"It smells great in here." I said trying to smile and be cordial, even though I knew Branson was getting ready to give me an ear full.

"I can't believe you." Branson's words were few, but his anger was extensive.

"What are you talking about now Branson?" I walked to the other side of the kitchen exhaling at what I knew was to come.

"I'm talking about you missing out on all of your obligations, as Brandi's mother, and then you walk in here looking like a street walker with a new young boy toy!" He said angrily, but in a hushed tone.

"Whatever, Branson. I'm here now." I tried to down play his anger and my actions.

"Is he the reason you've been M.I.A. the past couple of weeks?"

"No. You don't even know the half of how busy it has been at work. Don't go assuming things, now." I retorted.

"Your work has never been too busy for Brandi, but now all of a sudden it is? Don't forget you're her mother first and a single woman second. Don't get it twisted Mia."

"This is all coming from the man who missed…"

"Eleven years of my daughters' life. How old is that going to get? You can keep hanging that over my head if you want, but the question still remains, who's here now? She needs you!" Branson looked me up and down in disgust.

For once, I couldn't say anything. I was speechless and agitated by Branson's audacity. He'd had Brandi for a little over a month and all of a sudden he was the self-righteous parent? I was appalled by every syllable that came out his mouth chastising me.

"Branson, I raised Brandi by myself for eleven years; you have her for five weeks and, all of a sudden, you're the hero? I don't think so." I said shoving him a little bit.

"I'm still her mother. Don't you ever forget that!" Anger spoke before I had the courage to do so.

"Then act like it, damn it!" He didn't back down.

I stared at Branson, with his scruffy beard and uncombed hair, and rolled my eyes before brushing past him.

"Hey, why don't we sit and have a talk?" I said, trying to calm the situation down before it became more volatile. I pulled out a chair from the dining room table and motioned for Brandi and Cecil to follow me.

Sean sat on the couch, still watching television as the four of us took seats at the raggedy table.

Blitz

"I still don't understand why we're calling this meeting with the four of us." Brandi said as Cecil helped her sit down. I still couldn't believe my eyes at seeing my child with a belly that altered her abilities at even the simplest of things.

Maybe he would make a great father, I thought as I stared at them interacting together.

"Because we need to talk about this baby, and what's going to happen once he comes." Branson said clasping his hands together.

"You can stay here as long as you need to Brandi, but that one room isn't going to be big enough for the three of you." Branson said looking at me, beckoning for me to jump in.

"Cecil has his own apartment and, if the two of you and the baby decide to live there, your father and I will support your decision. We just want to make sure you get back in school, finish and graduate with your class as originally planned." I said leaning forward as Brandi started to say something. Before she could speak, though, Branson jumped in and responded.

"And since I know how much you like home schooling, your mother and I would be okay with you completing school that way also. We just want the best for you and the baby." Branson stared at Brandi who looked over at Cecil confused.

"I don't understand. You want *Cecil* and me to raise this baby?" She said gawking. "What about Andrew?"

"What about him, honey? He's not the father." I said chuckling "He's out of the picture by choice and by birth-right."

"And it's a good thing, too. That boy couldn't raise a potted plant." Branson joked as he stared at a straight face Brandi.

"I don't know how many ways or times I have to tell y'all; Andrew *is* the father of my child." She said burrowing her eyebrows into her forehead.

I shot a confused stare over at Cecil, who had his head dropped. I cleared my throat.

"You want to explain yourself, Cecil?" The irritation in my words was apparent as I stared at him.

"What are you talking about, ma?" Brandi asked looking at me, as I gazed at Cecil. "Cecil? What's she talking about?" She turned to face her friend.

"Son, you might want to clear everything up for us. You told Mia that you were the father of Brandi's baby." Branson interjected as he slowly blinked his eyes.

"You did what?!" Brandi said angrily as she slid her chair back away from Cecil.

"Brandi, I can explain…" Cecil started to speak, but Brandi interrupted him.

"Why would you lie to them like that? We've never even…you know." She couldn't say the words and let her eyes speak instead.

"I know. I just…I…" He stammered as he rubbed the top of his head with his hands. Confusion dripped from his pores.

"You told me that, knowing it was a lie Cecil? Why would you do that to our family?" I questioned him as his eyes finally met up with mine.

"Cecil…." Brandi whined as she looked at him for an explanation.

"Is this why y'all asked him to be here today?" She asked "Because y'all thought this was my baby's father? Y'all thought I lied to you about Andrew? I know who I've been with and who I haven't." Brandi jerked her head to the side as she looked from Branson to me and back again.

"It's not that we didn't believe you honey, but when Cecil came and told your mother he *was* the father of your child and…"

"But I'm your daughter and I told you the truth, and yet you still questioned what I had to say? Why would I lie to you about Andrew Whittaker, the boy who's dragged my name and reputation through the mud, started dating my best friend and has denied my child? Why would I put myself through all of this if it were not true? If I had to choose a father, don't you think I'd choose someone else?" Brandi shook her head in disgust.

"Honey, calm down." I said softly as I stood up and walked towards her.

"I'm sorry Brandi." Cecil said rising up as he picked his jacket up off the chair. He draped it over his arm and headed towards the front door.

"I'm so sorry." He said reaching for the door knob.

"Cecil, why did you lie?" Brandi asked rushing towards him.

For a second, I thought Cecil was going to push Brandi aside and head to his car and never look back.

But as he picked his head up, he looked her right in the eye, picked her hand up and proceeded to tell the truth.

"I saw the way he was treating you at that party and I heard the way he was dogging your name around town and I knew he'd never be the father you were dying for him to be. He's just a little boy in a young man's body." Cecil said as he looked at me and Branson and then back at Brandi.

"Me, on the other hand? Well, I knew I could be a good father to your son and I would love him with everything I had. I would love him the way you and he deserve to be loved."

"But this isn't your obligation, Cecil." I said kindly.

"Brandi deserves a decent father for that baby; regardless if he was mine, biologically or not, I was going to stand up and be that man for her and for the baby." He said pointing to Brandi's stomach.

"Oh Cecil…" Brandi said as tears began to form in her eyes.

"So the two of you never…" I said not believing my ears.

"Ma, he's like an older brother to me. That's all. That's all it's ever been." She said turning her nose up in the air. "Cecil's just always tried to show me right from wrong with guys. That's all."

"You were going to raise another man's baby?" Sean asked scrunching his face up as he eavesdropped in on our moment in the kitchen. "That sounds a little twisted to me." He laughed.

Brandi looked over to Sean and sucked her teeth.

"I think that's sweet, Cecil. Thank you." She said leaning in to hug him.

I slapped Sean's shoulder, as I walked closer to Cecil and took a deep breath.

"I owe you an apology." I said dropping my head, "I'm sorry I assumed the worst about you and Brandi. But when Andrew dropped your name as a possible father, I allowed my mind to wonder and I started remembering all the times you and Brandi would be giggling all close up and personal, and it turns out, I...I was wrong." I said hugging Cecil tightly. "I'm sorry, honey."

I wondered why Cecil *couldn't* have been Brandi's baby's father instead of Andrew. He had it together; a job, a car, money in the bank and, most of all, he wanted to do the right thing and be the baby's father. Andrew, on the other hand, was making things as difficult as possible.

"How did Andrew even know to drop your name?" I asked looking at Brandi and Cecil.

"I found out that Katrina had been telling him information that I'd told her, in secrecy. She told him that, at one point, I'd had a crush on Cecil. Andrew's trying to do anything to make me look stupid." Brandi replied, answering the questions that were floating in the air.

"So I guess we need to reschedule the dinner with the Whittaker's, huh?" Branson said as he chuckled and crossed his arms across his chest.

I shrugged my shoulders and shook my head, knowing the Whittaker's would be unlikely to welcome us back into their house.

I plopped onto the couch as Brandi walked Cecil out, and then stared at the television as Sean watched it closely. I watched the screen and thought about how I could turn the whole ugly situation around. Brandi had already lost most of her friends, her reputation was in limbo and I could see the stress on her face.

As her mother, I longed to erase it all.

When she returned, I sat her down at the dining room table and we continued to discuss options. The baby would was due in three months and besides a crib and a stroller, we didn't have anything prepared for the arrival.

"I want to plan you a baby shower." I said smiling as Brandi looked at me with no emotion.

"Who are you going to invite ma? Bree and Cecil? Because even you know, those are my only friends." She said laying her hands on top of her protruding stomach.

"Brandi you have other friends."

"I don't want a baby shower, ma." She said firmly.

Branson excused himself from the table, as he sensed the discussion getting tense.

"I just think we need to welcome this baby as much as we can." I said trying to ease the moment.

"Ma, the baby's coming regardless of preparation and besides, none of my friend's parents will let them within fifty feet of me. In case you hadn't heard, being in proximity of a fifteen-year-old pregnant girl is as deadly as flirting with the plague. Bree said her mom was at the PTA meeting and they talked about what to do if I decided to return to school before I had the baby. I can't believe my situation is of enough concern to be an agenda item at the PTA." She said rolling her eyes. "It's like they think I'm sick or something. Being pregnant isn't contagious." Even she had to chuckle at the simple and neurotic concerns of those on the outside of our reality.

I could've cursed right there. All those old hags on the PTA who had always praised Brandi for being a stellar student and beautiful child, were now thinking of ways of keeping her secluded?

"Forget them, Brandi. You're living for him now." I said patting her stomach, hoping my grandchild felt my love. "Have you thought about a name?"

Brandi smiled proudly as she caressed her belly the way seasoned mothers do.

"I was thinking Alexander Jalen or maybe Jalen Alexander."

I beamed, Brandi was getting to that point where she couldn't wait to see and be around her child.

"I love Jalen Alexander." I smiled as Branson entered the room with a letter in his hand.

"This was jumbled up in my mail. It looks important." He said placing the white envelope in front of Brandi as she eyed it suspiciously.

"It says it's from the Alpha Beta Sigma headquarters. Maybe they want to gravel to get my baby back." I smiled as Brandi shook her head.

"I doubt it. I wrote them a really nasty letter, a couple of weeks ago, telling them how stupid their rules were about my situation and I told them when I finally get to college I would be sure to become a member of a different sorority than theirs, all the while, making it my mission to make a big difference in the world. I bet they read it and wished they hadn't treated me the way that they did. Brandi said as she snickered.

"Open it then; see what they have to say." Branson said over her shoulder.

Brandi carefully tore open the letter and unfolded the perfectly creased letter and read it to herself. I could see the expressions on her face as she read the words and I wondered what everything was about. Her eyes grew wide, then she'd squint like she was confused and all of that was followed by a smile before she burrowed deeper into what she was reading. I couldn't take it anymore.

"What does it say?" I asked loudly.

"Oh my gosh!" She squealed as she stood up.

Brandi handed the letter to Branson, and quickly stood up and raced to my side of the table while giggling hysterically.

"Their national board wants to meet with me and the local chapter. Their giving the situation a full review and making a final decision on what to do!" Brandi said jumping up and down.

I couldn't believe it. Where had this new and improved Brandi been when she was living under my roof? The Brandi I knew never would have written a letter complaining about treatment she'd received. The Brandi I knew, would have grunted and moaned about it but, ultimately, let it go.

I grabbed her shoulders and pulled her to me tightly.

"I'm so proud of you." I patted her head and Brandi looked up at me and smiled.

"This is for my baby, ma."

After we rejoiced in the living room, about the upcoming hearing, I made a mental note to remember the date, which was more than four months away and during Brandi's summer vacation. I beamed ecstatically as Brandi dialed Bree and with self-pride dripping from each word, told her the story.

Even if we couldn't guarantee that the local chapter would have their decision overturned, it still made me proud that someone else-the national chapter in this case-understood that their treatment had been *unfair*.

Branson walked Sean and I down to the car and I lingered outside the passenger side as Sean hopped in; giving me and Branson and some privacy.

"How's she really doing?" I asked curiously.

"Some days are up and some are down. She took the Katrina and Andrew thing the hardest, I think."

"I thought she would."

"Do you know they've called here taunting her? Calling her all kinds of names and I just had to call Katrina's mother and tell her if she or Andrew contacted or came near Brandi anymore, I would have a restraining order put out on them." Branson said sounding serious.

I was impressed with him and his attentiveness to our daughter.

"How about school? Is she still getting along with the teacher?

"She loves that teacher. I think, for the first time, she's been able to concentrate on school instead of socializing and it's been good for her."

"I bet it has."

"I started a new job and I work that in the early mornings and take a break, for Brandi's school in the afternoon, and then I go work at Adams in the evening."

"Why'd you pick up another job?"

"This girl is eating me out of house and home." Branson laughed loudly.

"Where's it at?"

"At Brandi's old high school; I saw it as a sign, you know? Maybe I can talk to Andrew or something."

"I doubt a talk is all he needs." I said rolling my eyes. "Someone needs to slap that kid across the face."

"Yeah, I know." Branson laughed shortly. "Mia…"

"What's wrong?" I said, sensing his mood change.

"I need to ask you something and I don't want you to think I don't want Brandi here; because I do." He said slowing down. "Do you think it's time for Brandi to move back in with you?"

I snickered, as I covered my mouth, at Branson's question; only because Brandi proposed the same thing to me. She wanted to come home. But just as I'd done with Brandi her entire life, I had to make her realize that she had made a decision and she was going to have to stick it out.

"Maybe when the baby's born." I said. "But this is what the two of you wanted; you wanted to be closer, you wanted to learn more about each other and you wanted to live together. So now, the two of you have to make it work."

Branson nodded his head as he agreed.

"I mean, don't get me wrong, I love my daughter but this has just been a lot for me."

"Welcome to the club." I said patting his shoulder and reaching for the car door.

"Oh and Mia…I don't know if Brandi told you or not but you need to talk to her about Charles."

"What about Charles?"

He looked like he didn't want to say anything else, but as I shut the car door and walked closer to him; he knew he was going to have to tell me *something*.

"I overheard her tell Bree that he's having a baby; he didn't want you to know, though."

I fell against the car, slightly, and tried to catch my breath as the news settled in my ears. This had to be a big mistake. *My* Charles, the man I figured would be my dream guy, was having a baby?

"Are you sure she said Charles and not one of her friends at school or something?"

"She said Charles, but I know who she was talking about. She said his baby is due a few months after hers."

I was seeing circles and my hands were shaking uncontrollably. Sure, I was Branson's house with another man and I was definitely exploring every part of his young body, but knowing that Charles had ultimately moved on and was starting a family impaired me completely. I hadn't spoken to him in two weeks but he'd never even mentioned anything about a baby to me. How could he do betray me like that and how could he tell Brandi before telling me?

I felt betrayed and, most of all, I felt embarrassed that my ex-husband was the one telling me about my ex-boyfriends' new life; the one that didn't include me. Wasn't I supposed to be one of the first one to know; not my fifteen-year-old daughter? After a few silent moments, I tightened my lips, reached for the door and turned to Branson.

Blitz

"Thanks for telling me." My words were curt as I plopped down into the leather seats of my car.

"Tell Brandi to call me." I said as I hit the side of Sean's car, letting him know to drive off.

"That was deep." Sean said as I sunk further into the seat and thought about Charles and his new family. How could he not tell me something like that? I knew I wasn't in a position, especially with Sean by my side, to judge anyone, but he was starting a *family*. How could he not share that?

"Huh?" I asked snapping out of my daydream.

"I said that was deep; I didn't know your daughter was pregnant."

"Yeah." I said staring out of the window.

"How'd you feel when she told you she was pregnant? I bet you beat her ass, huh?" He began to pick up speed as we left Branson's block.

"She didn't know she was pregnant when we found out, and no, I didn't beat her ass. I wanted to, yes; but I didn't. It wouldn't have changed anything if I did." I said shrugging my shoulders.

"Yeah, but still…she's just a baby."

"She's a young woman, now."

"I heard y'all say something about the Alpha Beta Sigma sorority; you know my mom is in that sorority, right?"

I turned my head and faced him, "No, I didn't know that."

"What was that all about? What did they do to Brandi?"

I explained the entire situation to him, including Katrina getting the crown, Andrew denying the baby and Brandi desperately wanting the crown, title and scholarship that she'd been awarded.

I could see Sean thinking as we turned onto the interstate and drove in silence.

"What?" I asked looking over at him as he clinched his jaw tightly.

"You think they were wrong?"

"Hell yeah, I think they were wrong. No teen is perfect."

"But this is teen pregnancy, baby. Your daughter will be a teen mother and she would be representing that sorority." He said gripping the steering wheel with one hand.

"And…"

"And that doesn't look right. It doesn't send the right message. I think you all are doing the right thing by home schooling her." His words were delivered matter-of-factly.

"Sean, Brandi chose to be home schooled herself after it got unbearable with the rumors and stares in school. And about the sorority, tell me something…do you agree with them?" I already knew his answer but I wanted to hear him say it.

Without hesitation, Sean looked over to me for a second and blew out some air.

"I do agree with them." He said. "But let me explain."

I'd heard all I needed to hear as I stared out of the window.

"I think Brandi is a witty little girl, but I also don't think she needs to represent the sorority, either. Teenage pregnancy isn't something we need to glorify."

"I agree. Teenage pregnancy isn't something we need to glorify but, in the same breath, let me explain that the scholarship and the title she won had *nothing* to do with their precious image. For years they've allowed party girls or boys, who had horrible reputations, to win the title without any kind of uproar about the image they were presenting. Now all of sudden that matters? My daughter will be going to college, she will not be a statistic and she is an excellent role model. Any pregnant teenager, who realizes they need to finish school and actually puts forth the effort to make that their number one priority, should be commended. She shouldn't be penalized because of some personal issues or rigid ideals. That's not fair." I took a long, deep breath. "There are thousands of teenagers who get pregnant every year and Brandi could serve as a role model for them. She's going to graduate; she'll go to college and become anything she wants to be." The need to redeem my daughter could be heard in my voice as I turned away from Sean and eyed the entrance to my house.

"I knew I shouldn't have said anything."

I ignored his comment and rolled my eyes as he pulled into my driveway.

Blitz

Without pausing, I jumped out of the car and walked towards my house, without looking back. The last thing I needed was to listen to someone who thought my daughter was beneath them because of a mistake she'd made and was trying to live through.

Struggling with my keys, I gave them a shake to position them to put in them into the door before I felt Sean's hand on my back.

"Mia, I'm sorry, babe." He leaned down and kissed my neck.

"I was wrong. I should have realized this was a touchy subject. I don't want you to think I'm judging you or Brandi." He wrapped his arms around my waist tightly.

"Sean, I think you should just go home tonight. Suddenly, I'm not in the mood for company." I said as I finally got the door open and broke from his grasp.

Sean's shoulders were slumped over as I started to close the door.

"I love you." He said softly while placing his hands on the door frame to stop me from closing the door. "I would never intentionally try and hurt you."

I wrinkled my brow at what Sean said.

"What did you say?" I took a step closer to him to ensure I heard what I thought I heard.

"I said, I love you and I would never hurt you. It's just, sometimes; I don't know how to communicate the way I want to. I don't think before I speak."

"You don't love me." I said wanting him to explain more.

"You make me feel happy and I don't want you to close the door on us." He said placing his hands on the front door as he pushed it open a little bit more.

I stared into Sean's eyes and forgot all about what he'd said about Brandi and her pregnancy; I just wanted him to hold me. I wanted him to comfort my body the way Charles used to and I wanted to feel loved.

Before I could make a decision, Sean stepped into my house and delicately kissed my lips as I inhaled his very presence. He picked me up in his arms and carried me up towards the bedroom, with no fight from me.

Ebonee Monique

I wanted him. I needed him. And most of all I craved him.

Chapter 12

I was floating on cloud nine as I strutted into my office. It had nothing to do with the amazing sex I'd had with my young lover, the ease I felt concerning my relationship with Brandi or the fact that I'd burned everything of Charles' that meant anything to him or me; my joy came solely from the fact that I'd just closed on Lee Donaldson's house. With his home selling for three million dollars, I had just walked away with close to two hundred thousand dollars.

"Good morning!" My voice was perky as I walked past Cecil, who was on the phone.

"Ms. Robinson..." Cecil said loudly as I walked into my office.

"Why are you shout...?" I said as I stopped in my path and saw Charles sitting patiently at my desk.

"That's what I was trying to tell you." Cecil said walking up behind me.

I smirked, over my shoulder, and flung my hair backwards before walking to my desk and exhaling.

"Charles." I said as I took a seat and proceeded to fiddle with the mouse on my computer, trying to look unfazed by his presence.

"Good morning." He said smiling a stupid little grin. I wanted to reach across the table and rip his heart out through his throat, but that would've been un-lady like.

"Morning." I made it a point not to make eye contact with him.

"I was wondering if you wanted to go get a cup of coffee or something." He leaned forward in his chair.

Was he kidding? Why on earth would I get a drink with him? Maybe he expected me to tell him tricks on how to soothe a teething baby or maybe, just maybe, he wanted to discuss formula options.

"As you can see, I'm working and I have a full day ahead of me." I snapped as I crossed my legs and defiantly stared at him.

"Okay. I understand. I was just hoping I could talk to you today." He said softly as he looked around.

I'd had about enough of Charles portraying himself as the good guy when, in actuality, he had this deep, dark side that even I hadn't seen.

"What do you want to talk about? The fact that you're about to be a father and didn't have the decency to tell me yourself?"

Charles looked astonished that I already knew the news he'd tried, his hardest, to keep from me. His wide eyes and open mouth were clear indications that what Branson had told me was true.

"How'd you...I meant to...I mean..." He stammered as he stood up and walked closer to where I was sitting.

"I was going to tell you, I swear."

I chuckled to myself at the sight of the pathetic excuse of a man what was kneeling beside me; I waved both him and his sorry excuse off.

"When Charles? When were you going to tell me? When the baby came? Or maybe you were planning on having Brandi's christening on the same day as your child's." I said viciously.

"No." He said getting up from the ground as he paced the room.

"You know, at first I was baffled about how you could do something like this to me...to us...then I realized that you never really gave a damn about me. All you wanted was your own family and for someone to help you fill that void in your life. You didn't care if I was fat, skinny, pretty, ugly, white or black. All you wanted was a woman to bear your child, right?" I said straightening out some papers as Charles stopped pacing.

"Mia, you've got it all wrong I..."

"I hope you're happy with your decision and I hope you're happy with yourself." I started getting a little emotional.

As much as I'd prepared myself for facing Charles, I wasn't ready to end it quite so soon; but I had to.

"You've got your woman and your child and now you can just leave me alone." I wiped tears from my eyes as I stood up and walked to a filing cabinet, with my back facing him.

"What are you talking about? I still want to be with you. The baby was…irrational and….we can work through this."

"Are you crazy? What would make you think I would ever want to be with a liar like yourself? I gave you everything I had and as soon as you didn't give you one thing you wanted, it negated all the other things I was to you and did for you." I said, spinning around to face Charles who looked pale in the face.

"I love you, Mia; you know that."

"I don't know anything right now. The man I thought I loved isn't the man standing in front of me today. The man I thought I loved would've never done anything like this."

"What about you? I heard about your little boyfriend that you brought to Branson's apartment." Charles shot back as the veins in his forehead began bulging out.

"I'm not having a baby with him, though; that's the difference. He's just a friend; not my baby's father!" I screamed loudly.

He had some nerve to challenge who I befriended and who I didn't. I was a grown woman with a man who couldn't accept that maybe I wasn't the woman who could give him everything he wanted.

Charles blew out some air as he stuffed his hands in his pockets and continued pacing the room. I took a second to compose myself as I took a seat and stared at my computer. I just wanted the moment to be over.

"So now what?" Charles asked standing in front of my desk.

"You told Andrew to be man enough to stand up and raise his child, so you should be man enough to tell me-out of your own mouth-that you're expecting a child."

I could see the pained expression on Charles' face and I knew all that I needed to know; but I still wanted to hear it from him. I wanted him to hear, with his own ears, what he'd done to diminish our relationship. It was one thing for him to get another woman pregnant, but I figured his saying it out loud would solidify things in both of our minds.

Ebonee Monique

"I'm expecting a…a baby." He said pausing. "But it's more complicated than that because…" He said as I cut him off.

"Forget about me. Forget about us and forget about anything we could have ever been, okay?" I said walking to my door and excusing Charles without as much as a goodbye.

"Mia…"

"Leave on your own or I'll call the police." I said sternly.

Charles stood frozen, staring at me and I could see his eyes filling up with tears as he watched a cold version of the woman he loved, dismissing him.

"Six years and all you say is forget about you?"

"You obviously didn't have a problem doing that when your baby was being conceived." I said locking eyes with Charles as he slowly moved towards the door.

"If you let me explain I could…"

"Please leave, Charles." I started to choke up. I turned my head and tried to block out the thoughts of Charles and I planning our entire lives together that were bombarding my mind. Those were the flashes I didn't want swimming around in my head.

Charles breezed past me and out of the office and I shut my door, tightly, leaned up against it for emotional support, and sobbed silently into my hands.

How could it all be over? How could either of us just walk away from all that we had; all that we shared? I was having fun with Sean, but what I felt for him didn't hold a candle to my emotions and feelings for Charles. Charles made my life feel like an overflowing glass of love and he helped me grow. How could *this* be the ending chapter in our story?

My head swirled as I headed back to my desk and lay my head on it. I needed a break; not just from the moment at hand, but from life in general.

Nothing could make my day any better or worse, I thought. Like usual, though, I was wrong.

****

"Do you have the balloons at your house?" I whispered on the phone to Bree as we discussed Brandi's surprise barbeque and baby shower. It turns out; Brandi had more support than she knew. A number of her friends still loved her and wanted to wish her well with the pregnancy; there were only a handful of them that were on the Andrew and Katrina bandwagon. Those folks, I assumed, weren't welcome in my house anyway.

"I got them! How are we going to get her to your house without her knowing the truth?" Bree asked.

"I'm going to take her shopping for the baby and that will take a couple of hours, then I'll check in with you and see where we are with the decorations and depending on that, we'll either come home for the surprise or get a bite to eat." I said as I clapped my hands together.

Planning a baby shower for Brandi had proven to be just the vehicle I needed to take my mind off of Charles. I had jumped on the idea after hearing from Branson that Brandi was moping around the house complaining that she didn't have any friends, couldn't do anything right and wasn't happy. I knew a party would lift her spirits and let her see that not everyone thought the same. The whole world wasn't against her.

Cecil stuck his head in my office and I held up one finger.

"Okay, Bree go ahead and let everyone in Brandi's corner know about the party. Let them know I will be ejecting people from the party if they decide to act up." I said smiling. "Thanks honey!"

I hung up the phone and motioned for Cecil to come inside.

"I just went ahead and called the butcher and got enough meat to feed us for days." Cecil smiled as he pointed to his piece of paper. "Because you know we like meat!"

"Cecil, I want to thank you so much for helping out with this at the last minute." I said gratefully. I knew, by the way I'd been treating him the past couple of weeks, that Cecil could've easily said, no, when I asked him to help.

"It's no problem, Ms. Robinson."

"I've got the decorations, the food, the balloons, the games and I've even got a couple of Brandi's baby pictures I'm going to blow up and place around the pool." I said as I checked off my list and glanced up at Cecil, just as the front door to the office opened.

"I'll get that." Cecil said as he jumped up.

Before I knew it, Sean was sticking his head in and smirking widely.

Ebonee Monique

"What are you doing here?" I giggled as I stood up from the desk and went to embrace Sean.

"I just dropped by to see you; I wanted to see if you were up for a little trip." He said as he took a seat across from my desk.

"Where to?"

"I was thinking Miami."

"That sounds perfect! What date did you have in mind?"

"How about this weekend? I just purchased my ticket and put the deposit on the hotel room. It'll be so cool." He said, smacking his hands together.

"Oooh." I said slowly bringing my head up. "I can't go this weekend I'm planning a surprise baby shower for Brandi."

I could tell, by the look on Sean's face, that he was shocked I'd rather spend a weekend with my pregnant teenage daughter and her friends than with him.

"Come on babe. They can do it without you, can't they?" He walked in closer to me and began rubbing my shoulders as he stared at me intensely.

I wasn't sure if Sean was joking or not, or maybe he'd bumped his head on the way into my office, but he couldn't possibly be asking me to miss my daughter's baby shower; that was a definite no.

"Sean...this is Brandi's baby shower. I can't miss that." My face contorted as I tried to get him to understand the importance of what I was saying.

"We can slip out of town and you can tell them that you had a business trip or something. My friends and their girls are all headed down too." He continued to try and convince me as he licked his lips seductively.

"No. Maybe you didn't understand me when I said it earlier, but I can't and won't miss my daughter's baby shower."

He sat back in the chair and sucked his teeth and pouted his lips like a child as I challenged him with a crazy look. I know he wasn't seriously upset about me not skipping out on my daughter's baby shower, which I was planning. He had to be kidding me.

"Sean, maybe some other time?"

"There won't be another time." He snapped back as he shifted in his seat.

Blitz

"Why not? You mean to tell me, this is the only weekend we can travel to Miami?"

"Whatever. I'll just talk to you later I guess." He said as he stood up and made his way to the door with a look on his face that suggested he was having a slight temper tantrum.

I dashed after him, although I'm not sure why I did, and I caught him just as he stepped out of the building.

"What's wrong with you?" I asked placing my hands on my hips demanding an explanation.

"I just don't understand why you can't come with me to Miami. What happened to the woman who said she wanted spontaneity and spice in her life?" Sean asked me.

"Sean, this is something important to me and to my daughter. It's her baby shower for God's sake, I can't miss that! Why don't you see that?" I replied, getting agitated by his selfishness.

"I understand that you're trying to make yourself feel better about all of this."

"All of what?" I asked cocking my head to the side.

"Nothing." He said pulling out his car keys and walking around me.

"No, speak your mind. What am I trying to make myself feel better about Sean?"

"Look, Mia, I'll talk to you later."

"Sean, just say what you need to say because, honestly, you're looking like a spoiled brat right now."

"Is that right? You didn't mind this spoiled brat when I was breaking your back or making your legs shake did you?" He replied.

"I'm talking about right here and right now." I said trying not to think about the nights Sean had filled the craving I had for a body to stick to mine underneath the sheets.

Sean huffed and pouted as he turned his head and ignored my comment.

"Sean, I don't have time to run down to Miami with you and your friends. I am a mother and I have a business to run. I can't just up and runaway with you on a whim like that." I said crossing my arms.

"Since when?" He retorted. "For a month you'd been running the streets with me, going to clubs, hanging out with me and my friends and doing any and everything on a whim. I

Ebonee Monique

didn't even know your daughter was pregnant; that doesn't strike you as being weird?"

He had a point, but I wasn't ready to let him get away that easily with his back handed comment.

"My daughter. My business." I shot back. "And don't you ever try to question my parenting. I've been doing this longer than you think."

"Whatever. I'm leaving." He said as he jumped in his car.

Honestly, I didn't care if Sean left. He'd pissed me off beyond words and I had plenty other things to do with my time other than spend it arguing over something so trivial.

I watched as he put his car in reverse, backed up and onto the street.

"Fine." I said as I kicked a small rock and walked back into the office.

Before I had a chance to sit down at my desk, my phone was ringing and Cecil was telling me Sean was on the phone.

"What?" I barked into the phone as I sat back in my chair.

I knew it would be no time before he would come crawling back. I didn't think I really wanted him, but I wanted him to want me.

"I'll be by your house later." He said as the wind whipped inside the phone causing his words to sound as if he was in a tunnel.

"For what?"

"You still owe me twenty dollars for gas that I put in your car."

I stared at the phone for almost a minute, in disgust and shock, before I replied to Sean. I remembered the one time when I'd left my wallet at home and Sean offered to put twenty dollars in my tank and I'd pay him back. Of course, I'd completely forgotten to pay him back and now he was doing the one thing I despised: when people throw favors back in your face. I couldn't believe he was being so petty.

The money wasn't the issue, because I didn't have a problem paying him back, it was the principle. What kind of man...or boy...had I gotten myself involved with? The gas

Blitz

incident had happened weeks and weeks ago and, yet, he felt the need to bring it up at the end of an argument?

"I'll put it in the mail to you; don't come to my house."

"That'll take too long. I'll just call when I'm on my way." Sean said as he cleared his throat.

"Sean, its twenty dollars. Is it really that serious to you? Why are you doing tripping over something so simple?"

"You promised to pay me back and I just want my money; that's all."

"You think I won't pay you back? You think I'm trying to keep your money?" As the words dripped from my lips, I realized how childish the entire spectacle was.

"I don't know." He snickered evilly.

"You can pick the money up from my assistant, Cecil; he'll be here until five o'clock. Do not come to my house!" I hung the phone up in his face, swearing I could feel steam coming from my head.

Running my fingers through my hair and snapping my head side to side to release tension, I stared at the phone and thought about the image of a man that I'd created in my mind of Sean. That image was nothing like what he really was. There was no future between us, and I knew that. My only grasp of getting involved with him in the first place was because he was willing and available. I was starving when I met him; I didn't want him to talk, I didn't want him to think; I just wanted him to hold me and make me feel sexy, loved, and care-free. I wanted to be like him. I didn't want to worry about things and I wanted to run away from serious decisions; but I couldn't. I had my child, my business and my life to tend to here. Sean had served his purpose in my life at the time he was there, but I was officially through with him.

"Everything okay?" Cecil asked as he stuck his head in.

"Perfect." I smirked uncomfortably. "Get twenty dollars from petty cash and keep it handy in case Sean comes by and asks for it. If he doesn't come by tomorrow, mail it to this address." I said, jotting Sean's address down on a sticky note.

"Okay." Cecil said taking the piece of paper from me and heading toward his desk.

Ebonee Monique

"I think I'm going to go home early, Cecil. If you need me, I have my Blackberry." I smiled as I picked up my bags and searched for my keys.

As I drove down the interstate towards my house, I thought about how naive I'd been when starting a relationship with Sean. I knew I loved Charles and I knew what I really was doing, at the time, was trying to escape my responsibility to try and work things out with Charles. When I was with Sean I felt young again, I felt needed and most of all he made me forget about all the problems I was struggling with.

But I was beginning to realize that feeling was only temporary. As I stared at him in the parking lot earlier, it was as if all my problems and then some came crashing back into my life. There was no escaping them and no man, no alcohol and no money could make them disappear. I had to deal with them and running away to Miami wouldn't make them go away. Sean's magical appeal had diminished.

With Sean out of my life and no diversions or distractions around to take my mind off of things, I had to woman up and handle the business I'd neglected and let stack up like trash.

Step number one: Accepting the fact that I was going to be a grandmother.

****

"Ma, where are we going?" Brandi whined as she reached down to rub her ankles. "My feet are killing me."

"Your mother is treating you to a shopping spree for your son and you're acting like you don't want it." I said smiling as I looked over at Brandi.

Her stomach was the largest than I had ever seen it, and it looked like junior wasn't slowing down his growth spurt anytime soon.

I was more and more amazed at Brandi's body each time I saw her. As I looked into her eyes, I saw her happiness peeking out. She had becoming increasingly aware that she was going to have to go through birth without Andrew by her side and she was at ease with that. Her cute button nose had spread like butter and her hips were wider than ever as well. Still, though, she was a cutie pie.

Blitz

With her hair parted down the middle and flat ironed straight, she flung her hair to one side and looked over at me with a sly grin.

"You know I want to shop; I just want to know where we're going next."

"Do you have somewhere to be?" I asked, knowing she didn't.

I'd cleared everything with Branson, who was pretending to be at work while he helped Cecil and Bree decorate my house for the shower, and Brandi didn't have anything planned.

"You know I don't." She laughed playfully as she stared out the window.

We had bags and bags of clothes, shoes and toys for the baby, which were literally spilling out of the trunk.

"You hungry?" I asked turning onto Dale Mabry and scouting out the restaurants along the way.

"I can always eat." Brandi grinned as she looked down at her stomach and then back up at me.

I reached over and stroked her stomach and kept my hand on top of hers.

"You know I love you, right?"

"I know, ma." Brandi said smirking.

After going back and forth, we finally pulled into a Village Inn; quickly found a booth and got settled and then I excused myself so I could call Bree and check in on the status of the party.

"How's everything going?" I asked smiling. I was eager for Brandi to see the effort that we'd put into her baby shower and I couldn't wait for her to see my special gift.

"Everything is on schedule. There are a few people here already and everyone's just chilling by the pool." Bree said in a polite tone.

"We should be there in about thirty minutes." I said as Bree greeted someone at the door. "I'll call you when we're on our way."

"Okay, Ms. Robinson. I'll see you then!"

Brandi and I mulled the menu and finally made our decisions.

"I'll have the bacon cheeseburger." Brandi said handing her menu over and looking up at the waitress. "Do you think you can add extra onions?"

"You got it." The waitress said jotting down the order on her pad.

"And I'll just have the cob salad with ranch dressing."

"I remember when I used to eat light like that." Brandi giggled as she sat back in her seat and exhaled rubbing her belly in circular motions.

"Honey, you're eating for two now. You can't afford to eat light." I laughed.

"Yeah, I guess you're right."

"So, what's new with you? We haven't really had a chance to sit down and talk in a while." I asked as I took a sip from my iced tea.

Brandi shrugged her shoulders and followed my action by taking a sip of her fruit punch.

"Nothing really. Branson…I mean, dad…we're getting along better. I think it was just really new for the both of us." She said not taking her eyes off of the juice. "For the first two weeks, I cried every night for him to take me home."

"I'm glad you stuck it out with him; he's an okay guy."

"Can I ask you a question, mommy?" Brandi asked raising one eyebrow.

I shook my head and watched her closely as she formulated her question.

"Why'd you keep me from Branson? You didn't know about him being locked up or being in rehab so…why'd you keep us apart?" She asked calmly.

I didn't know how to respond to her question. Of course, I knew the truth; but I also knew the truth would hurt Brandi beyond words. She'd grown to love, respect and cherish her long-lost father and, remarkably, so had I. I didn't want to change the way she saw him through her eyes. My forgiving spirit, when it came to Branson, didn't take away my memories of abuse that lingered in my head; but, for the sake of my daughter, I had been able to put it behind me. I saw Branson trying to do better and if I continued knocking him, I knew he'd be out of Brandi's life sooner than later.

"Brandi it's a long story and…"

Blitz

"I just want to know. I asked him and he won't tell me. He said you had to be the one to tell me…if you decided to." She said slowing down.

"We can talk about this another time." I said, caressing her hand softly as she continued staring at me.

"Mommy, I'm not a kid anymore. I can take whatever it is that you're not telling me. I don't need you to protect me anymore. I just want the truth."

Could she handle the truth? I hesitated, weighing my options, and then I dropped my head, clasped my hands together and began telling Brandi the story of her father and me even from the beginning.

"I loved your father more than I could ever begin to explain. I would have done anything for him."

"Kind of like me and Andrew, huh?"

"Exactly." I said shaking my head. "Except, well, your father had a really bad temper and sometimes he…he hit me."

I could see the information registering in Brandi's brain as her expression went from shock to disbelief. I couldn't tell if she had tears of sadness or anger in her eyes; but I continued nonetheless.

"It went from one beating a day to one beating an hour and, as you got older, I realized he wasn't the person I wanted you to end up with. I didn't want you looking at your father, doing the things he did to me, and think that was a normal relationship." I said dropping my head.

"Was it…I mean, I know it was bad but… was it *really* bad?" She asked squinting her eyes.

I nodded my head and kept my eyes on the table. "It was really bad, baby."

"Oh my gosh." She said covering her mouth with her hands as she gasped.

"It was so bad, the people in the emergency room knew me by name." I said trying to crack a joke. Obviously, though, it didn't go over with Brandi who had tears streaming down her cheeks.

"Mommy…I'm sorry I forced you to…I didn't know." She said as she attempted to reach out to me. I grabbed her hand and softly caressed it.

"I know you didn't know and regardless of what your father did to me, I shouldn't have kept you from him and not given you that option of knowing him for yourself or not. So, for that, I'm sorry." I reached across the table and wiped one of her tears away.

"If it was me, I would've done the same thing. I'd never let my baby grow up seeing that." She said as she slightly hugged her stomach.

"I didn't want to tell you about it because I thought you'd think I was weak."

"Weak? Why would I think you were weak?"

"For staying with your father after he beat me so badly. I thought you'd be ashamed to have a mother who hadn't been strong enough to leave as soon as it started."

"Mommy, you're the strongest woman I know and nothing you could have done would have made me think differently."

I smiled widely at my daughter, the one I'd raised, and wondered where the time had gone. It seemed like yesterday she was learning how to walk and talk and here she was giving me inspirational talks.

"And when you and your father started getting close, I didn't want you to look at him differently because he *was* trying to change. I didn't want *our* history to dictate the future between you two. "

"I love him, ma; but he'll never be my father. Charles has been the only father I know and Branson…is only a man who I call *dad* from time to time."

"I know and we're not pressing you to call him anything you're not comfortable with."

"I know. I'm just saying." Brandi said as she watched the waitress place her bacon cheeseburger in front of her and my cob salad in front of me.

Brandi immediately plunged into the mountain of French fries and stuffed her mouth excitedly with them as if she hadn't eaten in days. I had forgotten the love affair pregnant women have with food.

"Dad told me he told you about Charles' baby." She didn't take her eyes off her food as she continued shoveling fries into her mouth.

I placed a forkful of my salad in my mouth and tried to think of what I was going to say to her about her fathers' love child.

Blitz

"We talked, very briefly about it." I said taking a sip of my drink as I returned my stare to the salad.

"Ma, he said it's not what it seems and he really wants to talk to you." Brandi wiped her mouth with her napkin as she stared at me with puppy dog eyes.

"Honey, honestly, this isn't up for discussion right now. I don't want to talk about Charles because he and I are done." I said raising both of my eyebrows to show her I was serious. I knew the moment I started talking about Charles, or thinking about his child, I would wind up in the same ball of confusion I'd been in earlier in the week and I was tired of visiting that place.

"I just think you should hear him out. How do you throw away six years without…?"

"Brandi." I said, knowing Charles had gotten to her and unloaded his list of excuses about his child. I didn't want to hear it though. I just wanted to spend quality time with my daughter before our lives became much more hectic with baby making three.

"Okay." She said laughing as she held her hands up in the air. "I get it."

"What about names? Have you chosen your favorites?" I asked crossing my legs.

"You know? I just want his name to mean something to me so…" She said grinning at me "I was thinking Brian Charles Robinson."

Instantaneously, I loved the name. It included her father and her name all in one; it was so beautiful.

"I love it!" I said clapping my hands together.

After we finished our food I grabbed her hand as we walked to the car. I knew how touchy teenagers were about holding their parents hands in public, but I didn't care. This was my child and she was having a child and yet I didn't care what anyone thought as they saw us walk hand in hand.
****

When we pulled up to the house, Brandi was clamping her legs together as I fidgeted with the keys. I'd planned it so that everyone would park out of sight and Brandi wouldn't immediately notice anything when she walked in the house. All of the decorations, people, music and gifts were in the back, by the pool.

Ebonee Monique

"I've gotta pee." Brandi shot past me towards the guest bathroom. Pregnant women can't hold their water and Brandi was reminding me of that fact.

I snuck a peek at the pool and gasped at how many people had shown up. There had to be, at least, seventy five people standing beside the pool with friendly smiles and excitement, staring back at me. I could've cried because I already knew how excited Brandi would be about the party. It touched me that so many people cared and loved my daughter enough to come out for her baby shower.

As I heard Brandi's flip-flops approaching, I closed the blinds, which restricted the view of the pool and people, and led her back towards the staircase.

"I've got something for you." I said winking my eye

"Ma, you've given me enough." Brandi laughed as she pointed toward the car full of goodies.

"Come on." I said pulling her arm towards her bedroom.

Brandi walked in silence as we went past her room, my room, my home gym and past my home office. We slowed down as we stood outside of one of the guest bedrooms.

"Go ahead." I said nodding towards the door. "Go inside."

Brandi looked skeptically at me but finally reached for the door knob and twisted it.

As soon as she stepped inside, her eyes were filled with so many tears she had to wipe her eyes continually in order to see clearly.

"It's beautiful." She said while she gasped for air.

She strolled her hand over the crib, the changing station and finally she stopped and took a seat in the wooden rocking chair which sat by the window.

"This is the baby's room I'd dreamed of." She said looking around at the baby blue and brown painted room.

I'd slaved for hours painting and decorating the room perfectly. I didn't know the future of where Brandi and the baby would be living, but I wanted her to know she *and* her baby were always welcome in my home. I was ready for the change and the new life.

As I watched Brandi take it all in, I leaned against the wall and sighed. As long as I didn't shop for the baby, in my mind, he didn't exist; he wasn't real. The moment I hung the beautiful pictures of black babies around the room, my heart felt proud and everything was cemented in my heart. I was about to be a grandmother and I was excited. Sean had made my body feel wonderful, but he'd also allowed me to forget about my priorities; I didn't need a man who made me do that. I needed to check myself and my priorities and I needed to be reminded when I was slipping.

"I love you." Brandi said rushing towards me with her arms extended.

She buried her head into my bosom and clung to me closely. "I love you so much."

"I love you more." I said kissing her forehead.

I knew the moment we were having was not the norm. Most teenage parents had to completely fend for themselves, find a job, and drop out of school while, basically, struggling to make it. Since I had the financial means to assist Brandi, I wasn't going to turn my back on her. I wanted her to succeed and prove the naysayers wrong.

"I have one more surprise for you." I said pushing her back, slightly, and staring into her red, tear-filled eyes.

"I don't think I can take much more." She said wiping her eyes as she smoothed out her baby doll dress and stared at me.

"Come on." I said as I pulled her from the room and back down the stairs towards the pool.

We stood in the kitchen and I took a deep breath as I slowly pulled the curtains back to reveal the group of people who were remaining silent until they saw Brandi's face.

"Surprise!" They all yelled as they threw their hands in the air and jumped up and down as Brandi fell backwards into me.

"Oh my goodness!" She yelled as she scanned the crowd and smiled at all of the people who were all slowly walking towards her with smiles on their faces.

That feeling, in my stomach, that I normally got when something was about to go wrong, was nowhere to be found. A feeling of joyful butterflies was there instead.

"What is…what's this?" Brandi said turning to face me and then looking over at Bree who was grinning as well.

Ebonee Monique

"It's your baby shower, honey." I smiled as I pushed her towards the group of her friends.

"All of these people came out for *my* baby shower?" She asked in disbelief.

"Yep." Bree smirked as she hugged Brandi. "We all love you."

"I don't believe this." She said looking over the crowd. "How'd you guys pull this over me?" She said loudly as she stroked her stomach in circles once again. Apparently, the baby was excited about the shower as well.

Once Brandi had hugged everyone and had taken her seat beside the Deejay booth, I took a breather and went into the kitchen in search of some paper plates.

"She's really happy out there." Charles said walking in behind me.

I'd seen, and ignored him, out by the pool as he continuously stared me down.

"She is, isn't she?" I replied as I opened up drawer after drawer in search of the paper plates that Rose had, obviously, hidden from me.

"Can we talk?" Charles asked. "It'll just take a minute for me to explain."

I looked up at him and sighed heavily.

"Charles, I'm just tired. I'm tired of us going back and forth and I'm just worn out. This is all so old for me. It is what it is, so, no. I don't want to talk about this."

"Please." He said walking closer to me. "I'm begging you."

I inhaled his scent before he even got close to me. It was familiar. It soothed me even though I didn't want it to. I knew I needed to make a decision quickly. The closer he got, the more likely I would be to give in to anything he was saying.

"Charles, let me ask you one question. Do you have a child on the way?"

Charles dropped his head and exhaled noisily.

"Yes, I do."

"Then, no, we don't have anything to talk about." I said as I walked out of the kitchen and right into the path of the last person on earth I expected to see.

"Andrew what are you doing here?" I shouted as I prepared myself for the fight of the century.

Blitz

"I need to talk to Brandi." He said as his parents appeared behind him.

Something told me this visit wasn't about to be like anything I could have ever anticipated or planned for.

Chapter 13

"**B**randi's water just broke!" I screamed into the phone as I picked up her bags and tried to shuffle her into the car at the same time.

"Mommy!" Brandi whined as she clutched her wide stomach tightly "It hurts! It hurts bad!" Her body was shifting from side to side as she tried to relieve some of the pain.

"I know baby." I said as I started the car and dashed back into the house to gather my purse.

"We're on our way to the hospital." I screamed to Branson before I hung up and began dialing Charles' cell phone number.

"Hey, is it time?" He said answering the phone groggily.

"Yeah, we're on our way to Women's Hospital now." I said shortly as I locked the front door and headed to the car.

Brandi was laid out, with her seat reclined, in the passenger seat squirming side to side in between taking deep breaths.

"You okay, honey?" I asked stroking her head as I threw the car in reverse.

"I'm okay now, yeah." She said looking over at me and then down at her stomach.

It had been a world-wind three months since Brandi's baby shower and even *Ms. Cleo* couldn't have forecasted the turn of events that took place. After Andrew and his family showed up at Brandi's baby shower, I was ready to throw them out with a quickness. These were the same people who had tried to get my daughter booted out from school, called her a liar and basically said she'd slept around; there was no way I wanted them anywhere near me or my child. But after Branson explained that he'd invited Andrew and his family, I backed down a little bit. Andrew confessed that he knew he was the father of Brandi's baby and was just scared of growing up quicker than he wanted to. After his parents found out that they'd put us through all that they had unnecessarily, they demanded he step up and apologize while also actively being in his baby's life.

I wasn't convinced that Andrew had gotten rid of all of his old ways. He was, after all, still a seventeen year old boy who was starting his senior year of high school. I had a hard time buying his "changed man" routine.

Apparently, he'd dumped Katrina after finding out that she had been the one who had created the seed of doubt in the first place. She had been the one who'd told him about Cecil and made up the rumors of Brandi sleeping around; once she saw she had a place to slide in, she took her place as Andrew's next girlfriend. When Andrew found out the truth, he kicked her to the curb.

I didn't care about any of that, really. I just wanted to know if Andrew and his family were up to being a part of my grandson's family; because either way my grandson was going to be loved; with or without them. After they assured me that the baby would receive love and support from their side, I was content.

I zoomed in and out of traffic, bypassing red lights, and kept checking on Brandi's progress as we approached the hospital. Regardless of her age, she was having a baby and was about to experience the most painful, yet rewarding, physical labor any human being could experience.

"Her water broke!" I screamed at the nurse as Brandi waddled in hanging onto my arm.

"Let's get you to triage so we can check you out." The friendly white nurse said as she put Brandi in a wheelchair and directed a male nurse where to take us.

I was frantic. I knew about births and I knew about the procedures, but this was *my* baby and everything had to be right. She was already nervous about everything going on around her and the last thing she needed was some insensitive nurse servicing her.

Charles and Branson arrived around the same time as I paced outside of the triage curtain.

"Is she okay?" Charles asked with a proud grin on his face. He'd come to accept the baby, that would be born any minute, which would call him grandpa.

"They're in with her now, seeing how far she's dilated." I said not taking my eyes off of the curtain.

"What happened?" Branson asked eagerly as he wiped his eyes.

"I was working on some paperwork and Brandi was up folding some of the baby's clothes and, out of nowhere, I heard her scream." I said talking with my hands. "I went in there and saw that her water had broken and she was having contractions."

"It's happening so quickly." I said trying to contain my enthusiasm.

"Ms. Robinson, Brandi has dilated quite rapidly." The doctor said as he walked closer to me.

"Really?"

"Yes. She's already five centimeters dilated. The baby will be here shortly." He said with a grin. "We should have a baby, I'd say, within a few hours if we keep moving at this rate."

The three of us jumped up and down and hugged one another and, in that instant, none of the other drama mattered. I didn't care that Branson and I had a past that was less than perfect, I didn't care that Charles was having a baby by another woman and I didn't care that people thought I was a bad mother for raising a girl who would give birth at the age of fifteen. None of that mattered. I didn't care about any of it because my grandson was on his way into this world.

"Bran, how do you feel?" Charles said as he kissed her forehead, just as a contraction ended.

"I'm so tired." She whined as she looked up at him. "And it hurts, dad. It hurts really bad." She tried to be strong, but the youthfulness of her being was showing.

"Brian will be here in a few hours, though, honey." I said as I picked her bags up and followed the nurse as he wheeled her into an actual room.

Brandi's contractions had slowed down and she was finally able to take a short nap.

Branson, Charles and I strayed into the hallway as Brandi rested and contemplated who was going to call Andrew.

"Branson, you have some sort of relationship with them, so I think you should be the one to call." I said, not wanting to deal with it.

"I guess." Branson chuckled as he dialed the number and broke the news to the Whittaker's that their grandson would be born in a few short hours.

"I think you all and Andrew should get here as fast as you possibly can. The baby is not going to wait too long before making his debut." He said before hanging the phone up and rejoining me and Charles.

"What'd they say?" I asked.

"They're on their way." He said staring at the phone. "And they sound very excited."

I had to admit, I was totally shocked that the Whittaker's had actually taken a genuine interest in Brandi and the baby. Andrew and his mother had attended a few of Brandi's final doctor appointments and, despite the obvious tension between Brandi and Andrew; I was pleased with his willing participation.

That, of course, didn't take away from the fact that he'd hurt my daughter, but as long as he did his job as a father, I was able to look past that and not hold it against him or over his head.

The three of us took turns spending time with Brandi in her room as we awaited Brian's arrival, while the others paced the hallways in anticipation.

Andrew and his parents arrived and Brandi allowed them into the room for a few minutes. She'd made it perfectly clear, to all of us, that if Andrew wanted to be in the room he could be, but his parents were to stay in the waiting room, along with Branson and Charles.

The doctor passed by me, Charles and Branson and prepped himself for the final examination, to determine if Brandi would be ready to push her baby out and in to life.

"Ow! Mommy!" Brandi screamed loudly as a powerful contraction caused her to cry.

"I'm here baby." I said brushing past the doctor as I grabbed Brandi's hand tightly.

"Okay, let's take a look." Dr. Valdez said as he stuck his gloved fingers inside of Brandi and turned and twisted them inside her.

It was apparent his actions caused her pain, but Brandi was a champ and she bit down on her lip and handled it all like a woman.

Ebonee Monique

"We're at ten centimeters, ladies and gents! Are we ready for this baby?" He asked as he turned to the nurse and gave her a few instructions. "Go ahead and prep for delivery." The doctor commented coolly to the nurse.

Brandi looked over at Andrew and bit her lip as a contraction came. She grabbed his arm and squeezed it until red marks appeared on his high yellow skin.

I could see the fear in his eyes as he struggled to provide support to the girl giving birth to his off-spring. It was painfully clear that he was not prepared for the moment before him. I just hoped he wouldn't puke.

I wondered, while staring at him, if he wished he could go back and un-do the moment that had conceived his child. Was that orgasm worth what his eyes were witnessing? I prayed that he saw the joy in the moment and took it for what it was; the welcoming of his child into the world.

"Okay, honey, we're going to prop your back up a little bit and whenever you feel the urge, just go ahead and push." The nurse said as she examined Brandi with her eyes.

I watched as Brandi took a deep breath and pushed with everything she had. I could see the little lines and veins that were popping out of her head and I wanted to take it on for her; but I knew I couldn't. This was her journey and struggle and she had to experience it for herself.

She threw her head back on the pillow and exhaled deeply and cupped both my hand and Andrew's as she tried to muster the strength to do it again.

As I stared at her, I couldn't stop the overwhelming feeling of pride that was running throughout my heart. My baby was handling things like a true champ. She was in pain, but she endured it all like a woman, even at the ripe old age of fifteen.

"Oh my gosh! This huuuuurrrrrrts!" Brandi wailed as she pushed again until she couldn't breathe.

Exhausted and breathless, she rolled her eyes towards the ceiling and took small breaths until she automatically began pushing again. She may have been just a child, but her body was in control of adult things.

This time, though, I could see the crown of the baby's head.

"Doctor!" The nurse screamed loudly before Dr. Valdez came

dashing into the room with his paper cover up gown and latex gloves on his hands.

"Brandi, sweetie, a lot of women are going to hate you when you tell them that you had a thirty-minute labor." Dr. Valdez joked as he poked and prodded in Brandi's vagina. His bedside manner was perfect for a girl of her age. I had her hand and I was watching over the sheet of paper that they'd placed on Brandi's abdomen.

"Go down there and watch your son being born." I said to Andrew, who hesitantly dropped Brandi's hand and went to stand behind the doctor.

"I see his head, Brandi!" Andrew said covering his mouth as his eyes teared up. I cracked a crooked smile as I thought that he wasn't as big of a prick as I had thought.

Brandi gripped one part of the rail and grunted as she pushed a couple more times, hoping each push would be the final one.

"Mommy, I'm tired." She exhaled her statement, knowing that none of us could change things even if we tried.

"I'm so proud of you, honey!" I said kissing her forehead as another contraction started. "It's almost over. Soon you will be kissing your baby and all this pain will just be a memory."

Brandi pushed herself forward and screamed loudly as she pushed with everything in her. "Please take him out! Just get him out of me!" She moaned as she continued to push.

"You're almost there! You're a strong girl. You can do this. Your baby would be proud to see how much you love him by doing all you can to get him here." Dr. Valdez said as he helped pull the baby out while Brandi pushed.

"Brandi he's almost out!" Andrew shouted with excitement. "You can do it! Oh My God, I can see him Brandi. Push one more time for our son."

Her eyes lit up just hearing Andrew say the words, "Our son", and with that she gave the hardest push of all.

I peeked over the sheet and before I knew it, I saw pink baby with slimy red blood all over his body, sliding out of my daughter.

I watched as Brandi fell back on the pillow and caught her breath. The exhaustion in her aura was apparent to all, but her job was done. Andrew was watching closely as a few tears fell down his cheeks.

"You did it!" I said in Brandi's ear as I kissed her cheek.

She looked over at me, with her eyes half way opened, and grinned.

"I did it, ma. I really did it!"

After they'd delivered the after birth, I finally broke from Brandi and went to look at my beautiful grandson. By the time I'd reached him, he was already covered up, Eskimo style, in a white and blue blanket, and had a white knitted skully on his head.

"He's gorgeous." I said trying to contain my emotion.

But as I saw the chubby, pinkish brown baby with a full head of hair in front of me for the first time, I couldn't do anything but break down.

"Welcome to the world Brian Charles Robinson-Whittaker." I said as I played with one of his fingers.

"I'm your grandmother."
****

"I have to say that I think he's the most beautiful baby in the entire world." Charles said to Branson as we all sat at the cafeteria table, having coffee. Brandi may have been the one exerting all of the physical effort for Brian's birth; but we all needed a pick me up for our efforts as well.

"I gotta agree, man." Branson said raising his glass in the air.

I couldn't stop grinning; not even if I tried.

"I still can't believe my daughter, you know, pushed that baby out of her." I said shaking my head as a smile crept on my face. I had so much love for that baby and he'd only been in the world a few hours.

The two guys agreed and chuckled at how quickly Brandi had asked for a shower, a typical move by the queen of clean, I thought.

The Whittaker's had quickly rushed into the room, to see their grandson, and were just as emotional as Andrew had been. Even if those people had tried to deny Brian as being Andrew's son, as soon as they laid eyes on him, I knew there would be no more denying that he was at least partially one of them. He looked almost identical to Andrew; almost as if he had spit him out.

"I've got to ask, Branson, how the hell did you get Andrew and the Whittaker's to finally come forward and accept responsibility?"

Branson smiled as he sat back in his chair, in a reflective mood, as he crossed his arms across his chest.

"Since I started working at the school, I started hearing the high school gossip about Brandi and Andrew and about how Katrina was trying to sabotage everything between the two of them. Since no one knew I was Brandi's father…"

"You had the insider information." Charles added raising an eyebrow of undercover acceptance.

"Right." Branson nodded. "So, one day I pulled Andrew to the side and I just gave him a man-to-man talk." Branson said shrugging his shoulders. "It was new to me, but I knew the whole situation was new to him as well and that even though he would never say it out loud, I knew Andrew wanted to talk to *someone* about it all.

"What'd you say?" I interjected. Curious and slightly impressed at the same time.

Branson looked at me closely and without speaking, his eyes surveyed mine. He tilted his head a bit and smirked before speaking. He seemed to sense my thoughts that he had done 'good' even though I did not say it.

"I told him that if he missed out on his child's life he would regret it forever. I knew a little bit about that feeling, so it was easy for me to share it. Personal history told me he was scared, but being scared wasn't an excuse for not manning up and being a father. I told him how scared and alone Brandi had been, but that she did not have the option of running away that he did…instead, she was still pressing forward and being the best mother she could be." He said dropping his head.

"He tried to tell me it wasn't his, but I just stopped him and asked him if he truthfully thought Brandi loved him. He said yes; and I asked him if he thought Brandi loved him, then *why* would *she* lie on him if she had no reason to."

"Branson, you didn't have to." I said feeling impressed by the steps Branson had taken to look out for his daughter.

"I told Andrew that he might not be as lucky as me to have a second chance with his child once he made the decision

Ebonee Monique

to leave her to struggle alone." I tried my best to make Andrew learn, in a short amount of time, the lesson it had taken me over a decade to learn. I didn't want him to have to endure the pain I had to endure. If I could be an example of what not to do, then at least I had helped someone else walk a path of the straight and narrow. I poured my heart out to Andrew and because I came from the standpoint of "been there, done that," he listened.

I smiled at Branson and wondered how, after everything he'd been through; he'd turned out to be the decent guy that stood in front of me. Branson was breaking out of every box I'd ever placed him in and he proved that he did love being a responsible parent to *our* child.

"You realize you single-handedly brought that whole family around?" I asked.

"I don't know if I would say all that; but I just gave him something to think about."

"You're a good man, Branson." I said rubbing his hand as we all sat in silence, reflecting on the remarkable turn of events. I was grateful to Branson and I never, ever, ever thought I'd utter those words while I had the breath of life in me.

"Man, I hate to break out on you guys but I've got to get to the high school and report for duty. It was kind of hard to get this job, so I don't want to mess it up." Branson said, tossing back the rest of his coffee.

"It's okay, Brandi will understand; plus she's sleeping right now, there's no need for three of us to sit and watch her do that." I said as I stood up to hug my ex-husband.

With a new life entering all of our lives, I couldn't contain the joy I felt in my heart. Despite our past, Branson had stepped up and been there for Brandi when she needed him the most.

I hugged him tightly, getting choked up as I gently pecked his cheek. He wasn't the man for me; but he was a father figure that Brandi needed in her life and I was thankful for that.

"Thanks so much for everything you've done for her."

"You don't need to thank me, Mia. I need to thank you for raising such a beautiful daughter." He said as he patted my back and headed towards the exit. "Tell Brandi I'll be back after work."

Blitz

Charles and I sat across from each other and smiled. "We're grandparents." I said before I burst into laughter.

"That sounds so weird." Charles chuckled.

"He's so beautiful." I said closing my eyes and envisioning the beautiful little boy, that was my grandson, in front of me.

"You know, she never would've turned out half as good as she did if it wasn't for you." I said opening my eyes and staring into the soul of the man I loved, but couldn't be with.

"Don't give me that credit." He stared into his coffee.

"Charles, you stepped up and you were a father to a little girl that didn't have your DNA; you loved her and you taught her right from wrong." I smiled proudly. "You can take credit for that."

He shrugged his shoulders and looked up at me before returning his stare towards the ground.

"She had you for a mother, so I know I didn't have to do much to have her turn out as a good kid."

Sitting with Charles, without a care in the world, I started to feel like we were the people we were nine months earlier. I felt like he was my man and I was his woman; together we were unstoppable. But the reality of the situation was that we were two completely different people.

"Charles?" I heard a woman's voice say, from behind me.

I slowly turned around and saw Anita smiling at me. Immediately, my eyes went to her baby bump. She had to be at least five months pregnant. I looked over at Charles and started nodding my head.

"Why would you do this here?" I said as I started to stand up.

"This is the only way I knew to explain things to you." He said as he followed me out of the cafeteria, Anita close on our heels.

"You wanted to rub your happiness in my face?" I said not noticing that I had begun to cry.

I'd closed Charles out of my life and, for three months, I had been able to keep myself busy enough to not need or think about him. I'd convinced myself that I didn't need to be with him and regardless of how much I missed him, I knew that was best.

"I'm not happy, Mia, because I'm not with you!" He screamed, making me stop in my tracks.

I spun around and faced him and Anita together, side by side, as he professed his love for me.

"I can't sleep at night, I can't eat and I can't stop thinking about you. I love you and only you, Mia Robinson. What part of that can't you understand?" Charles was very convincing as I kept my eyes on him and Anita, who was motionless.

"What about Anita?" I asked as I pointed to her obvious pregnant stomach.

"That's what I was trying to tell you…" He said as he grabbed Anita's hand and mine at the same time. "We're not together."

"Anita is my baby's surrogate mother."

"Your what?!" I strained trying to get a better understanding of what Charles had said.

I had to have heard him wrong. I'd heard of surrogate mothers, but they usually were for infertile couples who were desperate for children; not single men who longed for a baby.

"Anita and I were matched up through a program for single individuals looking for surrogate mothers to carry their children and she agreed to carry my child with half of my DNA and half of hers, and when she delivers the baby will be all mine." He said smiling widely.

I snatched my hand from Charles' as I stared at him and Anita.

My mind was full of skepticism. "I don't know what kind of sick game you're playing but I don't have time for it." I said as I punched the elevator button.

"Mia, this isn't a game. You made it perfectly clear that you didn't want to have any more children but I figured if I kept you out of the equation and had a surrogate deliver the baby, we could still be together as a family."

"What made you think I would be okay with that? You've lied to me for months and you've made me feel like shit and now you come and tell me some sob story about Anita being your surrogate." I punched the elevator button again.

Blitz

"It's true, Mia. I offered my services to Charles after I heard how desperate he was for a baby. He wanted this baby to be raised with the two of you as parents. He wanted you all to be one big happy family." Anita chimed in as she rubbed her stomach.

"Well, I appreciate you coming down here and clearing this up but my family is my daughter and my grandson." I said as the elevator finally chimed, letting me know the doors would be opening anytime soon.

"Mia…I did this for us."

"No, you did this for yourself and you lied to me in the meantime." I said over my shoulder.

How could Charles even think I would be okay with raising his child, which he created with a surrogate? What type of drugs was he on?

"So what am I supposed to do now?" There was confusion in his voice.

"Go on and raise your family. That's what you wanted, right?" I said harshly as I got on the elevator.

"Yeah, but I wanted you too. I wanted a baby *and* a wife."

"You've lost me, Charles; this time it's for good. So, do yourself a favor and just be a better father than you were a boyfriend."

I watched, almost in slow motion, as the doors closed and Charles and Anita stood close by each other. I couldn't take my eyes off of his, and yet, I knew this was our final goodbye.

I had a daughter and grandson that needed me; I needed to walk away from Charles so I could be everything for them.

As much as it hurt, I knew my pain would be temporary and I'd get over Charles just as quick as I'd fallen for him.

But had I made the right decision? Only time would tell.

Chapter 14

B randi cuddled Brian tightly to her chest as we entered the same sorority house that had been the source of her crying herself to sleep months earlier. It was unbelievable to me that only a month and a half earlier, we'd brought Brian home from the hospital.

He was the spitting image of his father and had the chubby cheeks and thick hair that Brandi had as a child. In a nutshell, Brian was still the most beautiful baby in the world.

"Hold his head, Bran." I said as I gently repositioned her hands teaching her how to protect her baby.

As we entered the house, all eyes were on us as women, old and young alike, stared at us like we had the plague.

I didn't mind, though. I knew what to expect and I was prepared for their insults, rumors and judgment.

"Good morning," I said as I smiled brightly at all of them.

I knew, coming into the situation, that Brandi would have an uphill battle to fight if she really wanted the Miss Princess title, crown and scholarship. She would have to be ready to face Katrina and the ladies who had, basically, told her she wasn't worthy of their title.

"Good morning." One person said as Brandi and I took a seat across from everyone else at the same exact table.

Brandi looked down at a sleeping Brian and grinned as she grabbed his cheeks.

After she gently sat him down in his car seat, on the floor, she crossed her legs and took a look around the room. There, staring right back at her rebelliously was Katrina.

She looked bad, too. She had red and black weave in her hair; she looked like she was wearing make-up that was too light for her and her clothes looked wrinkled.

In a shocking move, Katrina stood up and made her way over to Brandi-with attitude written all over her face.

"Hey." Brandi said being polite to the girl who had theoretically stabbed her in the back and then wiped the blood on her shirt.

"I just want you to know that Andrew and I will never be through; that's *my* man and nothing you do will ever stop that." She said as she moved her neck from side to side ghetto style.

I sat, with my mouth open, not believing what was happening. Was Katrina, the girl who prided herself on being Brandi's best friend and had, yet, drug her name through the mud, acting like the victim?

"Trina, you can have Andrew. I don't want him and if he wants you, then I think the two of you deserve to be together. My only concern is that he's there for his son." Brandi said rolling her eyes "And despite what you tried to make him think, this *is* his son."

Katrina crossed her arms and looked down at a sleeping Brian and sucked her teeth. "Whatever. Don't act like you didn't tell me you were messing around on him." Katrina said loudly as the women leaned in closer to hear our conversation.

Brandi shook her head and chuckled "If it makes you feel better to lie about me, all so you can try to *be* me, then go right ahead. But people know the truth. All I want to know is why? You were my best friend and I trusted you."

"I don't know why. I didn't trust you. I knew you were talking behind my back about everything you had that I didn't, so I decided to show you how it felt to be talked about. You think you're so great because you're rich? Well, guess what? You're not." Katrina spewed as she leaned closer to Brandi's face.

I thought I would see my sensitive daughter begin to tear up, but instead I saw her ball her fists up and stand face to face with her former best friend.

"I *never* talked bad about you, Trina. You were my best friend. My *best friend*! I loved you like a sister and everything I had, you had; At least in my eyes. But it's sad that you think I would betray you the way you found it so easy to betray me. But I guess it just shows who's real and who's not, right?" Brandi said looking her up and down.

"And if you think I'm better than you because I have money, that's an issue you need to take up with yourself, not me." Brandi took a deep breath before sitting back in her seat.

"Brandi, don't try to act like you're better than me because…" Katrina yelled as her mother came up and pulled on her arm.

"I *am* better than you, Katrina. I am; because I never would've done the things, to you, that you did to me. Never in a million years. But regardless of all that, I don't have time to be mad at you. So, I forgive you." Brandi said staring deeply into Katrina's eyes.

Brandi was a better woman than me, because I would have slapped that disrespectful, ungrateful, rude little girl down the second she walked up on me. But, as I learned, Brandi had begun to forgive all those who had hurt her, including me; I appreciated that.

I looked over at Regina as she struggled to get Katrina to go back to her seat; the look in her eyes was that of embarrassment and apology rolled into one.

Brandi shook her head and laughed as she leaned over and whispered in my ear.

"She looks a hot mess."

"Yeah." I said as I patted Brandi's legs softly.

Just like before, a straight line of women appeared from a back room and took their seats at a table in front of me and Brandi. I was ready for whatever daggers they were going to throw.

Charles and Branson had been unable to attend and I was glad; I wanted Brandi and me to redeem ourselves together, with no outside help.

Everyone stood up and listened closely as the head woman began talking.

"Miss Robinson, my name is Casey Pierce and I'm the National president for Alpha Beta Sigma sorority."

"Hello ma'am." Brandi said politely.

"Please have a seat, everyone." The woman said quickly as she placed her hands on top of the table. "I understand you have a problem with how the local chapter handled your scholarship and crown, is that correct?"

Brandi stood up again and nodded her head.

"Yes ma'am. I think it was extremely unfair that I had my crown taken from me because they didn't think I fit their image of what Miss Princess should be. I made a mistake by having sex at such an early age, but my son…he's not a mistake." Brandi rambled on as she looked down at Brian as he squirmed around in his car seat.

"Okay, thank you Miss Robinson. You may have a seat."

Brandi took her seat and looked over at me and I patted her hand to let her know she'd done great.

"Beulah, you're the president of the local chapter. What say you?"

I watched as the overweight, blue-grey headed woman struggled to stand up and I chuckled to myself.

"Madam President, we decided, as a chapter, that Miss Robinson did not reflect the type of young woman we thought should have the scholarship. We don't think that Alpha Beta Sigma should be glorifying teen pregnancy."

Brandi rolled her eyes and shook her head as she held one finger up, to get the attention of the President.

"Yes, Miss Robinson."

"I'm sorry to interrupt but, ma'am, I've been on the honor roll for as long as I can remember, I've never been in trouble in or out of school, I've always done community service and I was *voted* as Miss Princess by my peers. The only thing they can say about me is that I was a teen mother; I don't want to glorify teen pregnancy, because I know not everyone is as blessed as I am to have a supportive mother, two fathers and a bunch of friends, but I don't think teen mothers should be penalized or be made to feel like outcasts either." Brandi took a breath and continued,

"They made me feel like my entire life was over because I was having a baby. Sure, I might have slowed things down a little bit but I guarantee I'll be in college, I'll graduate and I'll focus on bettering myself for my son. They took my title away because they were embarrassed by me and they were ashamed to admit that girls do have sex and get pregnant in this day and age." Brandi said stepping away from her chair and placing her hands on her hips.

Ebonee Monique

"Instead of trying to shun me, they could have used the opportunity to educate other teens so that they wouldn't make the same mistakes I did." She said facing Beulah and her clan of sorority sisters.

"You are a really cold woman and I don't care what happens today, I just want you to know that you'll be sorry that you ever treated me the way you did; because I'm going to be more successful than you could have ever dreamed. The more you doubt me, the more amazing it will be when God does the unthinkable." Brandi said returning to her seat as she turned and faced the President.

"I'm sorry ma'am."

Casey smiled and turned to look at Beulah, who was red in the face.

"Do you have anything to add, Beulah?"

"Just that we've already replaced Miss Robinson with Katrina Butler, a very well-known and sociable teen who is proving to be a valuable asset to our programs." Beulah said as she pointed to a beaming Katrina.

Brandi shook her head and looked back at Casey who nodded her head.

"I think I've heard enough and, in fact, I had my mind made up before I flew down here. But since we have to follow protocol, this is how we have to do things."

I gripped the side of my seat as I tried to figure out what they were going to say. Would they give Brandi her title back or, maybe, they'd compensate her for her pain and suffering.

"I believe that, without a doubt, Miss Robinson made a mistake at getting pregnant at the age of fourteen." She started as she raised an eyebrow in our direction. I could hear Katrina snickering as her mother tried to shut her up.

"There are probably plenty of things that both Miss Robinson and her mother have discussed that she could have done differently." She said as she spoke in a proper tone.

I could see Beulah and her hens whispering to one another as they kept their eyes on me and Brandi.

"But with that being said, I don't find it to be the place of the sorority to decide, for the school, who should and should not be Miss Princess. Miss Robinson seems to have the academics, the drive and the passion to be Miss Princess. I don't understand the thinking behind booting her out of her position, but please believe that there will be an internal investigation into the dealings of this local chapter." Casey said as she looked in Beulah's wide eyes.

"Miss Robinson, Alpha Beta Sigma sorority owes you a sincere apology. Not only will we be reinstating your scholarship monies, but we will allow you to serve as Miss Princess next school year to make up for not being Miss Princess this year." Casey said smiling.

"Thank you!" Brandi squealed happily as she hugged my neck.

I was in shock. I mean, these types of things didn't happen in real life. Bad guys normally got away with bad stuff, while good guys struggled to do the right thing. Was Casey telling my daughter that she agreed with us?

"And, in all actuality, I'm going to revoke the title from Miss Butler and, instead, give that scholarship money to Miss Robinson for her son's college fund."

"What?" Katrina yelled from the back of the room as she stood up "You can't do that!"

"I can and I just did." Casey said matter-of-factly. "Now sit down!"

"According to the rules, children of sorority sisters are not eligible for the contest. Being that Miss Butler's mother is a sorority sister, she's no longer Miss Princess."

The women in the room were buzzing loudly as they stared at Casey and Brandi and tried to understand what had just happened. All of them had figured they would come in, their Queen Bee would agree with them, and they'd laugh and ridicule my daughter for going over their heads.

But I was proud of her. I was proud that she'd done the right thing and had kept her pride in the meantime.

"I don't agree with this decision madam President." Beulah said as she adjusted her glasses and took deep breaths.

"This is a teenage mother who has influence over other teenage girls. By giving her the okay, we're telling other young girls that it's okay."

The other women shook their heads in agreement, and started talking loudly as Casey stood up and waved her hands.

"Like Miss Robinson said, you can use her influence to educate other teenage boys and girls about safe sex. This

Ebonee Monique

would've been a perfect time to introduce Alpha Beta Sigma to a totally new generation of students. But, instead, you all turned your noses up in the air and thought that you were better than this young woman." Casey said as she removed her glasses.

"I'm sure plenty of you don't know that I had my daughter, Blaire, when I was only sixteen years old. I was scared, alone and confused about what to do. But I got my stuff together, with the help of this very sorority, and I was able to accomplish everything that I have in my life. So, let's keep our judgmental attitudes in check, okay?" Casey smiled as she picked up her folders and walked down towards Brandi and Brian.

"The best thing you can do for your son is to get your education and use your testimony to help others." Casey placed her fingers underneath Brandi's chin.

"I was once right where you are right now. You can do whatever you put your mind to, baby." She said in a sweet tone.

"Thank you, ma'am." Brandi said kindly. "Thank you so much."

I stood up and embraced the woman tightly. She had officially given Brandi back her confidence and ability to see beyond her current state; I was grateful beyond words.

The blitz in our lives had turned into the inspiration for Brandi's dreams.

Epilogue

The fall leaves were hitting Brian's face as he playfully giggled at Brandi's goofy faces.

"Hey mama's baby!" Brandi said as she kissed his cheeks and returned to making more silly faces to entertain her child.

Now six months old, Brian was developing into one of the best things that could've ever happened to me or Brandi.

He was our first concern when we woke up and our last thought when our heads hit the pillow at night.

Brandi had just started school and loved the six hours, or so, of freedom that she got from the baby. I could see the maturity in her face when I saw her handling Brian's chubby body.

No one could have predicted that I would be as proud as I was of my grandson and daughter, but I was.

Brandi had gotten a part-time job at a small boutique in the mall, she was back in school and she even had a cordial relationship with Andrew.

"Pose right there." I said as I snapped away with my digital camera.

Brandi and Brian were looking more and more alike, although his color was still just like his father's. His chubby cheeks and slanted eyes were evidence that Brandi and Andrew had created something beautiful together.

My heart fluttered each time I saw his little gums exposed while he smiled. He was the most handsome man in my life.

Speaking of men in my life, Branson is still very much involved in his daughter's life and watches Brian on Tuesdays and Thursdays for Brandi.

I'm so blessed that their relationship is blossoming.

Charles and I haven't spoken since that day in the hospital. Brandi respected my wishes and kept her visits with him to times when I either wasn't home or was asleep. I couldn't see Charles and face him after what we'd gone through. I'd burned the bridge and I didn't want to go back through our same old drama. I was free, I was happy and I was loved.

My business is still booming, but since Cecil completed his real estate classes, he now handles a number of the high profile clients that I just can't commit the time to.

After Brandi returned to school in the fall, the school administrators asked her to speak to all of the students about safe sex and teenage motherhood; Brandi obliged.

So there she stood, on the second week of school, with her hands shaking and her eyes darting around the room. I stood at the back of the gym, with Branson and Brian, and watched as everyone got quiet as she pulled the microphone to her mouth.

"I'm fifteen years old and I have a son named Brian." Brandi started as she went into her lecture.

After she finished her story and the hundreds of children exited the gymnasium, there were a couple of girls who strayed behind and asked Brandi a bunch of questions about sex and being pregnant.

We found out, right there, that one of the girls was actually two months pregnant. The exact same place Brandi had been one year earlier.

As I watched Brandi try and counsel the nervous mom-to-be, I got an idea that would change our lives.

In two months, we will open the doors to our teen pregnancy outreach center, *Baby's Baby*, and Brandi will act as the teen liaison for all of the schools in Hillsborough County. With help from Bree's brother, who is the Superintendent of the school system, it will become a required presentation for all high schools and even some junior high schools in Tampa starting next year. Just like teachers make sure students know about drinking and driving, SAT's and career options, *Baby's Baby* will educate on safe sex, teen pregnancy and parenthood. Our center will give teenage mothers and fathers a place to go to get tested, counseled, find information, and provide teen mother (or father) mentors for all new pregnant teens, all while they escape the judgments that outsiders sometimes have.

Blitz

Looking at Brian, I hoped he would one day know that through his birth he had helped other parents and babies. He was our little muse.

Brandi knew that things for her, Brian and Andrew would be far from easy, but she also knew that all the sacrifices they were making were totally worth it. They would have to balance school, work, extracurricular activities, sporting events and even part-time jobs and still be parents to their son.

Sure, I would help out when I could, but this was their child; not mine, and I vowed to help them see that their lives weren't over but rather just beginning a new chapter.

Brandi smiled at the camera, as she sat Brian in her lap, and looked over my shoulder at the trees in the background.

"Smile naturally, Brandi." I said through a laugh.

But just as I said that, Brandi's face became frozen.

"Hi Mia." I heard Charles say from behind me. I kept my back turned and tried to give myself every reason not to turn around and lock eyes with the man I had loved.

So, slowly I turned around and stared deeply into the eyes of the man I once had known as my future. He looked handsome as ever and I couldn't remove my eyes from his.

"Hey...hey, Charles." I said allowing the camera, which was around my neck, to dangle.

Being so caught up in my dejavu, I didn't even notice the stroller that Charles was pushing.

"How have you been?" He asked me sweetly as I looked back up at him.

I tried to tell myself that the months that we'd been apart had driven a wedge in our connection; but, with him standing right in front of me, I knew it was a lie. I felt it and I knew the emotions, the feelings and the bond was still there.

"I've been well."

"I heard about the outreach center; I'm so proud of the two of you." He said smiling.

"Thanks, but it's nothing that we're doing for recognition. There are so many teenage parents who go through this type of thing all alone and we just wanted to be there for them." I said smiling.

I wondered if he thought I still looked beautiful; if I still had the spark that had drawn him to me in the first place.

"That's so true." He replied.

Ebonee Monique

I studied Charles' face, his hands and his mannerisms and I knew my heart missed him terribly. By throwing myself into my business, the baby, Brandi and the outreach center; I hadn't allowed myself to think about him completely.

"Waaaah!" I heard the baby in the stroller cry as Charles quickly moved to pull the cover back and check on it.

"It's okay, baby." He said as he reached in the baby bag and pulled out a bottle, picked the baby up and stuck the bottle in its mouth.

"What's her name?" I asked moving my purse from the bench, so Charles could sit down.

"Laila." Charles said as he smiled brightly at the way she sucked down the bottle.

All of the confusion, the anger and the betrayal I'd felt when Charles told me about the surrogate and the baby, washed away the moment I laid eyes on Laila. She had Charles' beautiful skin and eyes and a head full of curly jet black hair, which I had to touch.

"She's beautiful." I said.

"Thank you."

We watched, in silence as Laila sucked on the bottle and watched us back. There were things that needed to be said, long discussions that needed to be had and wounds that would have to be opened in order for us to get past the awkwardness; I wasn't sure if I was ready for all of that.

"Mia…" Charles said looking over at me, as he caught me staring at him.

"Yeah." I replied, trying to keep my mind from wandering.

"I know you don't want anything to do with me or Laila, but I was curious if you would be her god-mother." Charles asked with a small smirk on his face.

I held my hand over my heart and blew out air. I knew what I wanted to do and I knew what I couldn't do. How I would tell Charles, though, was the difficult part of everything.

I loved this man, I craved this man and I'd been hurt by this man; despite the latter, my heart still adored him.

He had taken me from a damaged, frail, bitter woman with a daughter who didn't have a father figure, and turned me into a confident, independent woman who had a daughter with two fathers; I knew my decision was final.

Blitz

"Charles, I can't be Laila's god-mother." I said as I tried to get everything out before I got completely choked up.

"Because, if you'll let me, I want to be her mother." I said as tears fell down from my eyes on to my cheeks and finally down my shirt.

I could tell the shock on Charles' face was genuine and when he laid Laila down in her stroller, he grabbed both of my hands and stared into my eyes.

"What are you saying?" His eyes begged me to repeat myself.

I caught my breath and stared towards the sky as I tried to get it all out.

"When I met you, I didn't know what type of father figure my daughter would have; you accepted her as yours with no questions. We always knew she wasn't yours biologically, but you loved her nonetheless. You accepted us as a package; not a lot of men would've done that." I said as I realized how selfish I'd been to the man who'd given me more than I knew what to do with.

"And I want you, but I want all of you; that includes Laila. I can't go on ignoring how I really feel about you." I said as I forgot where I was and placed my lips on his.

"Are you sure?"

"I'm sure."

Charles wrapped his arms around my body and hugged me tightly as we allowed ourselves to grope and kiss each other passionately. I couldn't remove my hands from him and I couldn't stop crying as I tried to piece together the puzzle that had led us to where we were.

Brandi came over with Brian and smiled as she saw what was happening.

"We *are* in public, you guys!" Brandi said as she held Brian on her hip.

I leaned into Charles chest and exhaled. I was where I wanted to be and I was completely content. Nothing could make the moment more perfect than a picture.

"Brandi, get closer to Charles and hold Brian up higher. Charles, I can't see Laila." I said as I started snapping away.

Ebonee Monique

"Excuse me, ma'am do you want me to take your picture with your family?" A young white kid said, wearing his hat backwards.

I smiled as he said *your family*. "Yeah, that would be wonderful. You just push this button." I said as I pointed to the camera.

I scurried over to the group, including my daughter, my grandson, my boyfriend and my daughter, and I scanned the group of people I loved.

Yeah, this *is* my family.

Bill Cosby might not have scripted my non-traditional, unconventional and almost shocking life story, but this was my life and despite our short-comings and uniqueness, this was *my* family.

I guess there are some things more important than money.

Peace In The Storm Publishing, LLC is the winner of the 2009 & 2010 African American Literary Award for Independent Publisher of the Year.

www.PeaceInTheStormPublishing.com

MEET EBONEE MONIQUE

EBONEE MONIQUE graduated from Florida A&M University
with a Bachelor of Science degree in Public Relations. She was
nominated as Breakout Author of the Year for African
American Literary Award Show in 2009. Prior to becoming a
published author, Ebonee Monique served as Morning Show
Host and Operations Manager for WANM 90.5FM in
Tallahassee, Florida and produced an on-air weekly
entertainment segment on TOUCH 106.1FM in Boston, MA.
She currently lives in the state of Florida.

Follow her on Twitter at www.twitter.com/eboneemonique
Friend her on Facbeook
www.facebook.com/authoresseboneemonique

CPSIA information can be obtained at www.ICGtesting.com
231579LV00001B/48/P